MOMENT OF TRUTH

Nick listened for the rhythmic signal of Karamanov's stressed heart. . . . If he should lose this one, if despite his most skillful effort Karamanov should die, he would lose far more than his patient, Nick realized; it would make all the torment he had suffered meaningless. He would emerge a false hero—if his Russian keepers permitted him to emerge at all.

DON'T MISS THESE BESTSELLERS BY MARSHALL GOLDBERG, M.D.

MARSHALL GOLDBERG, M.D.
THE KARAMANOV EQUATIONS

LEISURE BOOKS ⚭ NEW YORK CITY

ACKNOWLEDGMENTS

Though the events and major characters of this novel are fictitious, the surgical procedure of gas endarterectomy is a real one, developed by Drs. Philip Sawyer, Sol Sobel, and Martin Kaplitt of the Downstate Medical Center, Brooklyn, New York. Dr. Sawyer is a personal friend, and I am indebted to him for his advice throughout the preparation of this manuscript.

THE
KARAMANOV
EQUATIONS

1

Bogdanov woke from the dream of his beloved Armenian mother and his child-self strolling through the fields of their ancestral home in Sevastopol. Reluctantly, he watched the dream images dissolve into grayish haze as he groped about for the telephone. By the third ring, he realized he was not in his Moscow apartment but in a hotel room in Sochi-Matsesta.

"Good morning, General," said the switchboard operator. "I have a call for you from Moscow."

"Yes, yes," Bogdanov muttered. "Put it on." He recognized the voice of his deputy, Colonel Federov, instructing the operator that their conversation was not to be monitored, and waited impatiently for him to proceed.

"A thousand pardons for disturbing your sleep, Comrade General. This is Federov . . . My apologies again, but before I go on, I must ask if you're alone?"

"Yes, Federov," he replied with an exasperated sigh. "Regretfully, I am all alone. No women as yet, just rest. Please get on with it."

"I have been ordered by Marshall Stakhanov to request your immediate return to Moscow."

"Return! Mother of God, what for? Can't that jackal manage by himself for a week? This is the first time off I've had from him in two years. What did he do now —find a tunnel from his wine cellar to the American Embassy? Well, Federov, spare me the suspense, what calamity has befallen us now?"

"It's Comrade Scientist Karamanov. He's ill. He was admitted to the hospital last night."

"Ill! How ill? What's wrong with him?"

"A stroke of some kind. It happened while he was dining with Kapitsa. I'm told he couldn't talk or move his right side for thirty minutes. Now they say he's recovered, though he stumbles over certain words. The doctors in Dubna suspect a brain tumor. They're transferring him to a

Moscow hospital today. The Neurosurgery Institute, I believe."

"And my orders?"

"Marshal Stakhanov is dispatching a plane for you immediately. It will arrive at the Sochi Airport at 0900 hours. You are to meet with the members of the Special Committee at 1400 hours. I myself will pick you up at the airport to take you there."

"Very well. Your instructions are to obtain a detailed medical report on Karamanov's condition. Do whatever is necessary, but have it waiting for me at the airport. Is that understood?"

"Understood, Comrade General."

Once releasing the phone, Bogdanov's reaction to his deputy's report was abrupt and visceral, a muscle-tightening spasm squeezing up stomach juices until they burned in his throat. What a disaster! Should the physicist die, or should he for any reason be unable to continue his work, it would cost the Soviet government thirty billion rubles. And, as one of the original sponsors of Karamanov's project, one of its most persuasive proponents, it would almost certainly cost him his hard-won rank as deputy chief of the KGB.

Since preparations were already underway at Dubna to construct the electromagnetic wave accelerator which constituted the heart of Karamanov's antimissile system, there could be no honorable retreat. Kosygin was too much of a businessman to condone the expenditure of thirty billion rubles on scientific folly. And what Kosygin would never forgive was the decision of the Special Committee to plunge ahead with the project despite the realization that Karamanov's Unified Wave Theory remained unproven; that in actual, unmentioned fact, the genius, the abstract mentality necessary to compute the final equations which would make the weapons system operational, resided exclusively in the brain of one mortal man. Now, should the project fail, there would have to be an archvillain they could denounce—and Lieutenant General Denis Bogdanov didn't doubt that Stakhanov, scavenger that he was, would designate him for the part.

Dressing only in his pajama bottoms to escape the oppressive heat, Bogdanov phoned room service to serve his breakfast on the terrace overlooking the Black Sea. Though he had vowed to give up cigarettes forever during this vacation, the mounting tensions within him weakened his resolve. Hesitanting momentarily, he cursed this breach in his otherwise Spartan self-discipline and reached into his valise for an unopened pack.

As he inhaled his first cigarette in two

days, Bogdanov lay back in bed and comtemplated the incredible series of mishaps the Soviet missile program had suffered in recent years. His childhood friend, Marshal Yuri Nedelin, had been among the first to go, blown up along with three hundred others on the launching pad at Dnepropetrovsk because of Khrushchev's hare-brained scheme to test-fire an atomic-powered missile. Then, Lev Davidovitch Landau, physicist and Nobel Prize winner, shattered his brain in a senseless automobile accident. Next, Sergei Korolev, designer of almost every Soviet satellite put into orbit, died on the operating table, setting back the space program at least two years. And now Nikolai Pavlevitch Karamanov . . .

"Oh, what a whore you've turned out to be!" Bogdanov said, reaching into his valise for the icon of the Armenian saint his mother had given him, the one chosen to be his guardian angel. Raising the cherished icon to his lips, Bogdanov kissed it while praying briefly to his mother. "Damned superstition," he muttered, reviling his own half-certain belief.

2

Once sequestered in the rear compartment of the Aeroflot jet he had boarded for his return to Moscow, Bogdanov removed his tunic and lit a cigarette. He gazed aimlessly out the window at the Caucasus Mountains showing through breaks in the clouds. Karamanov wasn't dead yet, he reminded himself. And though lacking expert knowledge in the field of neurology, Bogdanov had a basic understanding of that subject, gained first as a medical student and later as a psychologist. The German invasion had interrupted his medical training at an early stage; and afterward, imbued with a fascination for war, he had chosen to enter the Military Diplomatic Academy rather than spend the additional years finishing

medical school. Still, his interest in the
nervous system, morbidly begun in the
anatomy laboratory, was not wasted. It
was in the tradition of the KGB to verse
its officers in the psychological art, and
Bogdanov had been granted special leave
over the years to complete his training.
His superiors had even allowed him to
study in Paris briefly, and for a longer
time in Peking.

Karamanov might not have a brain
tumor after all, he mused. Such initial impressions were notoriously inaccurate. Or
even if he did, the tumor might still be
surgically curable. Perhaps he'd merely
suffered a temporary spasm of one of his
cerebral arteries. Stalin suffered these for
years without any noticeable impairment,
as did the American President, Eisenhower, at one time. Whatever it was, as
long as it didn't disrupt Karamanov's
memory circuits, impair his reasoning,
Bogdanov knew he still had a slim chance
of emerging from this setback with his
rank and reputation intact.

Opening his briefcase, he removed the
official transcript of the Karamanov proposal. The conference had taken place in
the maximum security cell of the Kremlin
basement eight months ago. Composing
the Special Committee of the Council of
Ministers were fourteen of the most
powerful men in the Soviet Union, includ-

ing four members of the Politburo. Bogdanov began reading and remembering.

Arriving several minutes early, Bogdanov had joined Marshal Zakharov, Chief
of the General Staff, at the portable bar in
the far corner of the room. Eschewing the
imported cognac in favor of vodka, he'd
toasted Zakharov's recent election to the
Central Committee, then took his assigned
seat at the conference table. He had
watched expectantly as the empty seats
filled and the chairman, Minister of
Defense Andrei Malinivski, banged his
gavel calling the meeting to order.

"Comrades, as you are all aware, this
Special Committee has been assembled to
discuss the merit of a radically new antimissile system proposed by Comrade
Scientist Karamanov. To begin, I would
like to call on our distinguished Minister
of Foreign Affairs, Comrade Gromyko, to
sum up the current thinking of the Politburo on the desirability of perfecting such
a weapons system."

"Thank you, Comrade Chairman,"
Gromyko said, removing his glasses. "I
need not remind you that the creation of a
truly effective missile defense system is
an extraordinarily expensive undertaking.
We recognize this, and so, of course, do the
Americans. Their President has shown
himself most eager to reach a mutual

agreement with us, preventing either of our great nations from embarking on a crash program to develop and deploy such an antimissile network. It would be to our distinct advantage to cooperate with the Americans and abandon our efforts to further extend our present missile defenses beyond Moscow. Indeed, this would be the prudent thing to do, not to placate the Americans, of course, but to protect our economy. Unfortunately, such an option is no longer practical. The American imperialists have been superseded as our principle enemy. That distinction now belongs to our lunatic neighbors in China. Comrade Lermontov, sitting beside me, has estimated that by the early 1970's the Chinese will have an armada of over one hundred intermediate-range, and perhaps a scattering of intercontinental-range, nuclear-armed missiles. Naturally, the preponderance of shorter range missiles represents a much greater threat to ourselves than to the more favorably situated Americans. It is therefore the opinion of our farseeing Politburo that an effective antimissile network is an essential requirement for the defenses of the Soviet Union in the Seventies."

"Thank you, Comrade Gromyko," the chairman said. "I would now like to call on our Civil Defense Chief, Comrade Chuikov, to bring us up to date on the progress our scientists have made in this field."

"Regrettably, Comrade Chairman, my report contains nothing new. What our top scientists, working at maximum capacity, have developed can best be summorized in two short phrases: too experimental and costly, or else too experimental and frightening. For the first, I refer to the conventional antimissile missile employing radar as its tracking mechanism. The precision of that radar itself is continuously being improved, but alas, so are our adversaries' decoy and radar-absorbing devices.

"The second method that has been proposed to defend our cities is not nearly so prosaic. Nor is it for the squeamish, I might add. As shown by our last series of atmospheric tests, a gigantic hydrogen explosion, such as the fifty-megaton blast ordered by former Chairman Khrushchev, is capable of dispersing a sufficient shower of neutrons to temporarily disrupt electronic communications over a wide area. A network of these atomic monsters could be developed in such a manner that, provided adequate warning time is supplied, they could be exploded above the atmosphere, impairing the enemy missile guidance systems or prematurely detonating their warheads. Though theoretically feasible, we have only indirect evidence that such a strategy would be sufficiently effective to warrant the risk to ourselves. And the risk of poisoning our atmosphere, comrades, would be real and prohibitive. We would, in effect, spare our Chinese friends the trouble of killing us.

"This being the present extent of our progress, I am more interested to hear of Comrade Karamanov's departure from such unrewarding alternatives."

"Thank you, Comrade Chuikov. Before asking the distinguished President of the Soviet Academy of Sciences to present Karamanov's proposal, I would first like to call on Lieutenant General Bogdanov, Chief Security Officer of the Dubna Nuclear Research Center and Deputy Chief of the KGB, to provide us with a resume of Comrade Scientist Karamanov's career."

Bogdanov rose with a small notebook in his hand. "Thank you, Comrade Chairman. . . . Nikolai Pavlevitch Karamanov was born in the Black Sea port of Novorossisk in the year 1910. His father, a schoolteacher, died of typhoid fever in 1915, so did not live to take part in our great Revolution. At age twelve, Nikolai Pavlevitch joined the Komsomol and remained active in that organization for six years. At nineteen, he graduated from Moscow University with highest honors. As a reward for his diligence, he was granted permission to study in Berlin for a year with the eminent physicist, Max Planck. Returning home in 1929, he joined the faculty of the Institute for Physical Problems. There, in collaboration with Lev Davidovitch Landau, he did original research in quantum mechanics, but left that field in 1935 to begin his life's work on the interaction of gravitational and electromagnetic waves, hoping to succeed in Einstein's futile quest for a Unified Field Theory. During the war, he was commissioned a colonel and performed invaluable research in the field of radar. Afterward, he played an important role in the development of our first thermonuclear device and was a member of the elite special committee that evaluated the espionage reports of the Third Directorate. This, of course, required top security clearance. He spent the next decade at Moscow University, helping to construct the world's second largest linear accelerator. Upon its completion, he moved his entire staff to Dubna to inaugurate his present studies."

Karamanov had joined the Communist Party in 1929 and played an active role in his district for many years. After the war, he withdrew from active participation and avoided association with any particular cult. Bogdanov concluded from interviews of many of Karamanov's former students

that politics was never mentioned in his
classroom.

Karamanov was married in 1938 to
Elena Lifshitz, a Jewess from Leningrad
whose father was composer in residence at
the Leningrad Conservatory. Elena was a
concert pianist of considerable repute.
Their marriage was blissful but short-
lived, ending in her death in an air raid in
1942. Shortly afterward, Karamanov
suffered a nervous breakdown and had to
be institutionalized for a brief period. His
hospital record revealed he was afflicted
only with severe grief and displayed no
insane tendencies. His recovery thereafter
was swift and complete, judging by the
enormous contribution he made to the war
effort the following year. Driving himself
with incredible vigor, Karamanov was
almost single-handedly responsible for
perfecting the Soviet radar defense
system, improving on the British design.
In recognition of this superlative effort, he
was awarded the Stalin Prize in 1945.

"Karamanov has not remarried nor kept
company with any particular woman since
his wife's death, evidently preferring a
celibate, somewhat cloistered existence,"
Bogdanov continued. "He has one child, a
daughter, Galina, who lives with him from
time to time. She is now in her senior year
of medical studies at the Lenin Institute.
For completeness' sake, I interviewed her

and found her to be a bright, opinionated young lady devoted to her father, her studies, and a rather foppish young poet in that order. She, like her father, is an atheist.

"The one unusual finding unearthed by my investigation, comrades, I will now report in some detail."

The group stirred.

The initial impression Bogdanov gathered from talking with many of Karamanov's co-workers at Dubna was that he was a dedicated, iron-willed perfectionist who had time only for his monumental research and little else. Recently, however, he seemed to have undergone a personality change. A graduate student who had resigned his post in Karamanov's laboratory some six months before told Bogdanov that the man was an automaton, obsessed with his desire to reveal the orderliness of nature. "Hearing this," Bogdanov told the group, "I immediately sought confirmation from his other apprentices. Their opinions were somewhat more charitable. Conceding that Karamanov was a severe taskmaster, they nonetheless admired his self-discipline and were awed by his brilliance. What did emerge from these soundings, however, was that his co-workers, too, were becoming increasingly concerned over his personal behavior."

Beginning shortly after the New Year, Karamanov had grown more irascible, more antisocial, secluding himself in his laboratory until late each evening, sending out for his meals but rarely touching them, subsisting mainly on coffee. Though owner of a late model Zim, he no longer drove it, preferring to requisition a staff car to transport him to and from work. The lectures he customarily gave his graduate students were assigned to subordinates, and the few he did give lacked their usual continuity.

Bogdanov had discussed the situation with two of his closest colleagues, Comrade Artsimovitch and Tamm, who immediately visited him and persuaded him to seek medical attention. Karamanov was irked by this interruption in his schedule, but finally entered the hospital. He was confined for one week and underwent an exhaustive battery of tests, including psychiatric interviews. "Though ethically bound from reporting to you all that Karamanov divulged during these sessions, I can assure you, comrades, that this man's mind is as sharp as the finest surgical blade. Rather than insane or fanatical, he was merely on the verge of physical collapse. Following a week of sleep therapy, including several Amytal interviews by Professor Nesterov and myself which further substantiated our belief in his sanity, Karamanov was ordered to take a fortnight's vacation at a Crimean spa. His daughter Galina accompanied him to insure that his mind was occupied by nothing more taxing than her boyfriend's poetry.

"He returned to Dubna only last week and the change in him, comrades, is truly astonishing. The haggard expression is gone and his hands are now as steady as a watchmaker's. It's Professor Nesterov's opinion he has made a complete recovery and, except for a mild cardiac condition, enjoys excellent health."

Bogdanov closed his notebook. "Are there any questions, comrades?"

"Tell me a little more about Karamanov's extraordinary drive, and what motivates it," said Marshal Zakharov. "What I'm getting at, Bogdanov, is—who does he consider to be the ultimate benefactor of his work? Himself or Mother Russia? Surely you were able to deduce this from your Amytal interviews."

"Much of it, yes," conceded Bogdanov, recognizing that Zakharov's question backed him to the wall: to answer it would be a breach of ethics; to evade it would, in effect, portray Karamanov as an opportunist. "However, you ask a most difficult question, Comrade Zakharov. It sometimes takes years, not weeks, to discover why a given individual does anything."

"I'm well aware of that, Bogdanov. Nonetheless, I am interested in hearing your views. I, for one, would be most reluctant to proceed with such an unorthodox project without knowing more about the man upon whom so much depends."

"As with most scientists, Comrade Zakharov, there is a great deal of egotism in Karamanov's work. His mistress is nature and he is enamored of her secrets. This, of course, is understandable, since she offers the promise of immortality with each successful breach: Planck's Constant, Maxwell's Equations, Newton's Laws, Bernouilli's Principles. . . . In Karamanov's case, there are more praiseworthy motives, however. Just as he set out to do thirty years ago with his discoveries in radar, his most cherished goal now is to protect his countrymen from a scourge far deadlier than the Luftwaffe: atomic disintegration. In psychological terms, it is compensation for his failure to protect his wife from the enemy bombs that killed her. Irrational as it may seem, he has never forgiven himself for not being there to save her. Now, of course, it's his daughter he wants to protect. What compelled Karamanov to drive himself at such a killing pace was not some mystical quest for Godhood, but something far more ordinary. My investigation shows that his personality change really began the day the Chinese exploded their first hydrogen bomb."

"I see," said Zakharov.

"And one more substantial bit of evidence, comrades," Bogdanov said quickly. "Four years ago, Karamanov successfully solved the basic equations to his Unified Wave Theory. Publication at that time would almost certainly have made him the toast of the scientific world, a leading contender for the Nobel Prize. Instead, fully realizing the potential value of his discovery to his country, and the equal value it might afford her enemies, Nikolai Pavlevitch swallowed his pride and permitted his monumental work to go unpublished. As I'm sure Comrade Kapitsa would be the first to avow, such a gesture represented an enormous sacrifice on Karamanov's part."

"Thank you, Comrade Bogdanov," said Malinivski, "for your reassuring report. As you say, it was a remarkable act of patriotism on Comrade Karamanov's part. He is a true soldier in the service of his country. . . . If there are no further questions for Comrade Bogdanov, I will now call on the last speaker before the general discussion, our distinguished scientific advisor and President of the Academy of Sciences, Pyotr Kapitsa."

"Thank you, Comrade Chairman," Kapitsa said, rising to his full six feet four and walking to the blackboard in the front of the room. "I have been assigned a difficult and responsible task, comrades: difficult because I will attempt to explain a theory to you that at present only a handful of scientists on this planet understand; and responsible because, depending on the clarity of my presentation, you will then decide on the feasibility of this undertaking.

"To begin with, I will reiterate what has already been said, that no matter whether you belong to the *fusillade* school, staking your safety on the off-chance that an enormous volley of missiles would decimate every bird, every insect, every enemy projectile in the sky, or whether you belong to the more fatalistic *megaboom* school, conceding in advance a fourth of our population but gambling that the heavy traffic in neutrons blasted off a hydrogen bomb would melt a missile's guidance system—the simple truth, comrades, is that neither alternative is acceptable. This, however, does not mean we have exhausted all possibilities. Fortunately, there remains a third approach, the one offered us by Comrade Karamanov.

"Those of you here who pioneered our missile program know that the major obstacle we had to overcome was the problem of reentry. Missiles traveling at the orbital speed of eight or twelve kilometers a second generate enormous heat on reentering the atmosphere. As our earlier experiences told us, such heat is of the order of a thousand to eleven hundred degrees centigrade, necessitating the use of a special, heat-resistant alloy in the nose cone to prevent incineration. The best alloy our metallurgists were able to devise was titanium with a maximum heat tolerance of twelve hundred and fifty degrees. Consider a moment, comrades, the implication in the last statement. Should the heat exceed twelve hundred and fifty degrees centigrade, the missile would burn up like a comet. And that is the crux of the matter—the third alternative."

Now that Kapitsa had furnished the group with the solution to the problem, he saw that some of them were nodding their heads in agreement; others shaking theirs in doubt. "What you now expect me to pose is the problem itself, how such a formidable step can be accomplished," he said.

Picking up a piece of chalk, Kapitsa drew a schematic diagram of the component parts of a missile and the forces acting on it during its descent from the stratosphere.

"What is needed, comrades," he continued, "is a means to increase the heat of reentry a mere one hundred and fifty degrees. This can be done in only one way: by increasing the friction. But is such a step possible? Again, we have but a single means: by increasing the density of the atmosphere. Theoretically, this can be done by increasing the force of gravity, and since the equation for such an interaction is F equals mg, where F is the force exerted on a particle by gravity, m is the mass of the particle, and g is the acceleration caused by the gravitational pull, the only approach is to increase the factor of mass.

"This, comrades, for all but Karamanov, was an insoluble problem, awaiting the physicists of the twenty-first century. To succeed where others, including Einstein, had failed, he had to leap the chasm where they had faltered, invent an entirely new mathematical system, and finally, derive the gravitational constant which represented the key to the intricate puzzle. And just as Einstein's monumental equation E equals mc^2 unleashed the power of the atom, so does Karamanov's equation relating gravitational and electromagnetic waves make possible an impenetrable missile defense system.

"Now, to bring the gap between theory and applicability, let me describe the system in its entirety. At its core is an electromagnetic wave accelerator that generates an incredibly powerful beam of photons to the edge of the atmosphere. Once triggered by heat-sensing devices detecting the reentry of a missile, the photon beam, in accordance with Karamanov's postulates, increases the gravitational pull of the atmospheric interface enough to increase the density by a factor of one ten-millionth. Astonishingly, such an infinitesimal change results in a heat increment of over two hundred degrees. The effect, of course, is instantaneous combustion of the nose cone.

"This, in essence, then is Karamanov's proposal. What is required to make it operational is a network of such electromagnetic accelerators strategically placed throughout the land—provided, of course, that the initial testing of the system under simulated attack conditions is a success."

"Is such a trial contemplated in the near future, Comrade Kapitsa?" asked Marshal Bresnavitch, chairman of the Supreme Military Council.

"Such a trial can be prepared in six months' time, should this committee sanction it."

"At what expense?" asked Chuikov.

"An initial expenditure of thirty billion rubles. Should this pilot venture succeed, the entire defense system would cost in the range of one hundred to one hundred and fifty billion rubles."

"Approximately half the cost of the conventional radar-directed system, then?"

"In theory, yes," interjected Marshal Zakharov, a leading proponent of the conventional system. "But what about in practice? What are the risks of failure, Kapitsa?"

"The risks are many, comrade, but so were the risks we took in developing the hydrogen bomb."

"Indeed so," Zakharov replied, "but we had no alternative. We knew the bomb was feasible. Do we know Karamanov's scheme is equally feasible?"

"His initial experiments, on an infinitely smaller scale, of course, proved his calculations were correct. The mathematics of it are incontrovertible. Whether all the components of the system will function in unison, however, remains to be seen."

"If I understand you correctly, Comrade Kapitsa," said Feodor Lermontov, Chairman of the Atomic Energy Directorate, "the basic interaction is the collision and capture of a photon by a neutron, momentarily increasing the density of the neutron and, as a result, the atmospheric interface."

"That is so, Comrade Lermontov."

"Has this been proven?"

"Karamanov has produced such a phenomenon in the laboratory, yes."

"You, yourself, have reviewed his data?"

"I assure you I have gone over every detail of it many times. Comrade Karamanov doubtless would be pleased to show it to you himself. You would first, however, have to comprehend his new mathematical system. That prerequisite alone took me three months."

"In lieu of that, I must accept your judgment, Comrade Kapitsa."

"So must we all," agreed Stakhanov.

"If what you are suggesting, comrades, is that I stake my reputation on the accuracy of Karamanov's calculations, I accept the challenge."

"I, for one, feel such a unique system is worth a try," declared Malinivski. "If need be, we can divert funds from the cosmonaut program. We must insure our children's future. . . . Are there any further questions for Comrade Kapitsa?" he asked, scanning the length of the table. "If not, then we will commence the general discussion."

A little over an hour later, Chairman Malinivski called for a show of hands. The vote went thirteen in favor of recommending Karamanov's proposal to the Central Committee, and one, Zakharov's, the unyielding pragmatist, against.

Thirteen to one, thought Bogdanov, replacing the report in his briefcase as the
jet approached Moscow airport for a land-
ing. An overwhelming majority. But that
was eight months ago. How many would
maintain their support now, in the face of
Karamanov's affliction? Who would dare?
Not even the eloquence of a Kapitsa could
sway them. Well, Kapitsa would survive.
His international reputation will insure
that. As for himself, his fate and Karamanov's were now symbiotically linked;
they were like Siamese twins.

3

B leary-eyed, unshaven, possibly with the odor of alcohol from last night's drinking still on his breath, Nicholas Sten made the five-mile drive from his home to the University Hospital in record time. A patrol car certainly would have tried to stop him if one had been around. But the ticket never would've been written. Mention of the name Adam Blair not only would have ended the delay but guaranteed him a police escort the rest of the way to the hospital.

Not many of the Madison police knew Dr. Nicholas Sten, but they all knew Adam Blair. They should. To them, he was not only one of the wealthiest men in the state, an ex-governor, but the cops' best friend. They all ate free and often at his

restaurant chain. Adam had represented a
meal ticket, a sizable one, to Nick, too—
but he was much more than that. His successful surgery two days ago had made
headlines throughout the state.

But now Adam was in trouble.

Since the early hours that Sunday morning they were both in trouble. A premon-
ition—something—had roused him from
sleep even before the hospital called. . . .

Nicholas Sten woke with a shiver.
Damned cold in here, he thought. Ann
must have left the French doors open. No,
not Ann, he reconsidered; his wife had
spent the night in the guest room again.
Wakening further, as the room began to
lighten into mopish shades of brown and
gray, he peered at his watch. Barely six
o'clock, and they hadn't returned home
from the alumni dance until after two!
Bone-weary with fatigue, he wondered if
he'd really slept at all. It wasn't likely.
The quarrel Ann had provoked over her
father had been a particularly vicious one
and the aftermarth had unnerved him.

Rising from bed, Nick slipped on his
robe and walked to the half-open French
doors in the east corner of the room. He
opened them full and stepped out to watch
the dawn complete itself over Lake Mendota.

The next moment, startling him more

than if it had awakened him from a sound sleep, the telephone rang. The caller was Jim Belmano, a senior resident in surgery.

"You wide awake?" asked Jim.

"What's up?" Nick said, sensing the urgency in his voice.

"Look you'd better get down here right away. I don't like the way our star patient is acting. What I mean is—he's hard to rouse and what little I can get him to say sounds slurred. He also has—or had—a right facial droop. I gave him a papaverine drip and it seems to have cleared. But you know what I'm thinking, so you'd better get down here pronto. He's too good a triumph for your old gas gun to lose now."

"Okay. Get him up to the operating room for a repeat carotid angiogram, quick as you can. Oh, and call Casey."

"I already did."

"Good . . . and I guess you'd better call Dudley Emerson to come in. Jesus. I'm beginning to sweat already. See you in ten minutes, Jim."

Nick slowed the car to within ten miles of the speed limit as he approached the hospital. His brain continued to race, however, digesting the information Jim Belmano had fed him over the telephone. Adam Blair, jauntily alert when he had left him the previous day, now lay stuporous. The vital artery recently repaired for

him had probably clotted, leaving him
hopelessly paralyzed—near death—as the
result. And though other possibilities
existed to explain his sudden deteriora-
tion, Nick knew better than to indulge
himself in the wishful or the remote.

Whatever had possessed him to operate
in the first place? Nick knew he saw himself as no ordinary surgeon, no stripper of
veins or hacker-out of gallbladders, but
was it anything more than an inflated self-
image? The old aphorism, "Big surgeon,
big incision," was passe. Nowadays, what
with open hearts and transplants, it had
become "Big surgeon, big risk"—and for
an ambitious man like him, Adam Blair
had been the biggest risk of all.

Dudley Emerson, Adam's private physician, had opposed the operation from the
beginning. Too experimental, he decreed,
and no amount of arguing on Nick's part
could dissuade him. The gas gun he had
pioneered for the prevention of certain
otherwise fatal strokes had been successful in seven of the first eleven patients he
had operated on. True, four of them had
died; two on the operating table. But in
defense of these fatalities, Nick could
justifiably claim that all four had been too
far gone before he saw them.

Still, Dudley had warned him that he
was staking a lot in tackling a patient as
well known as Adam Blair. "Don't be too

heroic, Doctor," the older physician admonished. "The man is seventy-two years old, has bad coronaries, and is a poor risk for any kind of surgery. . . . Remember, whatever the outcome, your reputation will be made—one way or the other. I wouldn't want you to be known as the hot-handed young surgeon who knocked off Adam Blair. I doubt if even his heirs would thank you."

The actual operation, performed Friday morning, had gone smoothly. For a time, Nick feared he might have missed snaring the uppermost portion of the obstructing clot with his forceps—and only after Adam had fully wakened from the anesthetic could he dismiss the nagging doubt from his mind.

Now, as he reached the hospital, the same doubt had grown to virtual certainty, and Nick prayed there was still time to remove the residual clot before any permanent brain damage occurred.

He rode the elevator to the operating room suite, changed into a surgical scrub suit, and hurried past the swinging doors into Operating Room One. Waiting there was his surgical team: Jim Belmano, his resident; Mike Casey, the pathologist who had helped him pioneer the gas gun technique; Alan James, a radiologist ready to take the necessary X rays which would tell whether the carotid artery was blocked;

and lastly, Adam Blair, looking lifeless on the operating table.

"How long has he been out like this?" Nick asked, perturbed by the cadaverish color of Blair's skin in the glare of the overhanging lights.

"It comes and goes," Jim answered. "Neurologically, the cranial nerves are intact, but he has a definite rightsided weakness. I went ahead and took a cardiogram, Nick. Looks okay—no change."

"Good. Let's get going."

After swabbing the skin with disinfectant, Nick took a dye-filled syringe from Alan James and probed into the base of Adam Blair's neck until he felt the needle slip into the left carotid artery. Once that was done, the X-ray machine was rolled into position so that, coincident with his injection of the dye, serial X rays could be taken.

"Want to wait and see them?" Jim asked.

"No," said Nick. "No time. Let's go ahead and expose the artery. We can always back off if we get lucky."

"You want an anesthetic, Nick?"

"Let's see." He jabbed Adam Blair's neck with his scalpel and was relieved to see him twitch in response. Quickly, at Nick's command, Jim filled a syringe with a local anesthetic and infiltrated the area under the intended path of his incision.

Working with deliberate speed, Nick exposed a two-inch segment of the ropy, grayish-white carotid sheath and was about to pause to wait for the X-ray report when Alan James came rushing into the room with the wet films.

"Well?" Nick asked impatiently, sweat beading his forehead.

"You may have lucked out, Nick. There's a block all right, but it's not intracranially. It's just above the suture line of your previous incision. You can get at it without cracking his skull."

"Yes, I feel it," Nick said, putting his thumb and forefinger around the feebly pulsating artery.

"Is it completely obstructed?"

"Maybe just a trickle of dye getting through. Can't really tell for sure."

"Want me to step up the gas gun?" asked Casey.

"No. We'll try a conventional clean-out of the clot. It may already be too late for that, but it's his only chance. Maybe, just maybe, he's getting enough cross circulation from the other side to keep him going. I doubt it though, knowing the condition of his arteries."

Swiftly, Nick and Jim dissected free the full length of the artery, inserted a plastic tube above and below its clogged portion to act as a bypass for blood to reach the brain, then cut into the vessel and

stripped the gelatinous red thrombus from
its wall.

"How long did we take clamping the
artery?" Nick asked Casey, referring to
the most hazardous part of the operation.

"Less than two minutes!"

Nick felt a sharp relief, knowing that
clamping the artery for more than three
minutes could damage the brain.

Working more leisurely now, Nick
sutured the skin incision in Adam's neck.
Before placing a bandage over the wound,
he again felt the carotid pulse. "Good and
strong," he said with satisfaction.

"Want to try and rouse him now?" Jim
ventured.

"Little early." Then, with a shrug. "Oh,
what the hell. Here goes!"

Gently, Nick began slapping the right
side of his patient's face. "Wake up,
Adam!" he shouted. "For God's sake,
wake up!"

Blair flailed out with both hands against
Nick's slaps. "Breakfast! What's holding
up breakfast!" he croaked.

"Good Christ! What a tough old bird
this guy is," Jim exclaimed.

"He sure as hell is," Nick said, smiling
under his mask.

Shortly before noon, as Nick was com-
pleting rounds on his other patients, he

heard his name paged over the loud-speaker system.

"Nick?" Ann said. "Have you been there all morning? I didn't hear you leave the house. Did you get any sleep?"

"A couple hours."

"When are you coming home? You didn't forget today's the day those reporters from New York are coming, did you?"

"Yup. Had a few other distractions, I'm afraid."

"Oh, I'll just bet. Well, come on home. After all, it's your show, my dear."

Nick winced as he heard her bang down the phone. He sank wearily into a chair and almost reached for an open pack of cigarettes on the nurses' desk before remembering in time. He packed and lit his pipe, loathing it. His wife's sarcasm also rankled. Whatever had triggered her tirade of last night, he hoped would have worn off by now.

Thank God, Founders Day comes only once a year, he thought, since his father-in-law, Mr. Wisconsin Alumnus of 1925, came with it. Not that Nick actively disliked Henry Guy Stratton. "Hank"—as he democratically insisted on being called—was outwardly a likable person. An extroverted, scholarly man who had first made his reputation as a near All-American end

at the University of Wisconsin before
going on to the Harvard Business School,
a fortune in New England textiles, a
socially advantageous marriage, and ultimately, as a reward for his tireless efforts
as fund-raiser and sage of the Republican
Party, an appointment as ambassador to
the Netherlands during the Eisenhower
Administration.

Now semiretired, Hank Stratton was a
popular figure on the Madison campus, an
exceedingly   valuable   contact   for
Wisconsin alumni in the East. Such popularity was not universal, however—failing to encompass his estranged wife,
Sarah, who made her summer home here,
or his only daughter, Ann. Nick momentarily reflected on the strange love-hate re-
lationship that existed between his wife
and her father. Hank had a compulsive
need to be involved in their lives; to prove,
if only to himself, that his daughter still
needed him. Though initially amused and
for a while tolerant of his father-in-law's
intrusive behavior, Nick soon tired of
seeing Hank play the doting parent and
Ann's needlessly cruel rejection of him.

Better get home, Nick mused stoically,
reluctant to leave this relatively secure
haven with its obedient women for the
more uncertain authority he possessed
with Ann. Still, he knew he'd have to do
something to mollify her before the

visitors from New York came. Otherwise, there was no predicting how she might act.

Nick parked the car in the driveway and wearily climbed the steep front steps. He found Ann in the kitchen.

"You look tired," she said.

"I am."

"Want some coffee?"

Nick nodded. The offer was mildly encouraging.

"Hank stop by before he left?"

"No, he called," she said. "I told him you were out and I was hung over, so not to bother."

"Why do you always get so uptight over his visits?"

"You know how I feel about him. Why do you always get so horny when he's here?"

Nick smiled. "The challenge, I suppose. You're even more inaccessible than usual. A few drinks in me and you're like a sexual Mount Everest."

"Stop it, Nick! You know what's behind my feelings toward Hank."

Nick did and he didn't. Having served as his wife's confessor ever since she had briefly been a patient of his in the hospital, he needed no reminder of the animosity she felt toward her father. In a way, he felt sorry for Hank Stratton and the tyran-

nical women in his life—his wife, Sarah,
who before leaving had humiliated him
with an affair, and his unforgiving
daughter, Ann. Though Sarah had gradually wearied, the loss of Ann's love had
come more suddenly.

"That thing on the Cape was a long time
ago," he said softly.

Ann's eyes narrowed. "Maybe so, but I
still feel penalized for it. Sex isn't like
surgery, you know. Practice doesn't
always make you better. Psychologically,
it's the first time that counts."

It surprised Nick that Ann wanted to
talk about it. They hadn't for some time.

"I still think you're being too hard on
Hank. It was a well-meaning lie."

"Well-meaning, hell! It's was vicious!"
Ann replied vehemently. "Playing on
every child's fear their parent is going to
die. . . . Oh, that pious bastard!"

"You weren't exactly a child then."

"No, not physically. But emotionally!
You know how my mother and father used
to behave. Never any display of affection
between them. I wish to hell Hank had
divorced her when he caught her with that
Frenchman. But, oh no—not that maso-
chist! He kept her around ten more years,
till she finally got fed up and did it again—
this time with one of his best friends. . . .
Oh, sure I wanted love at eighteen. Why
not? There wasn't any at home and I was

curious. . . ." Ann's hand swept her fore-head, nervously patting down loose strands of hair. "Hank should've let me make my own mistakes. . . . Maybe he would've, if he wasn't so damned afraid I'd like sex so much I'd turn out like mother!"

Nick sipped his coffee. The incident Ann referred to had happened the summer after her freshman year at college. Whatever Hank's real motive, ostensibly he had lied to protect his daughter from the clutches of a beachcombing English-man, too young to be called lecherous but unprincipled enough by reputation to make Ann's maiden experience with sex an unpleasant one.

Hank had pleaded with her to leave her summer job on Cape Cod and go to Europe with him, but she'd refused; and when Ann's roommate told him that if she stayed on she'd almost certainly be seduced by that skirt-chaser, he lied to her. He told her he had a lump in his neck that was growing and believed to be cancerous. It was partly true; he did have such a lump, but it had been there since childhood and not changed a millimeter. Once safely in England, Ann found this out. Her revenge thereafter was swift and fitting. She had two affairs and possibly a third while in London, and two more the following fall in Boston. Hating them all for their emptiness, she swore an illogical, unremitting vengeance on her father for compelling her to seek them.

Hank Stratton, now Ambassador Stratton, was immensely relieved when Ann, after having broken off two engagements the previous year, met Nicholas Sten, then senior resident in surgery at Massachusetts General, and eight months later married him.

Nick held up his cup. "Mind pouring me some more coffee?"

"All right, but let's say we talk about something else. You're my husband—not my doctor."

"But if you despise Hank so much, why the hell do you defend him?" said Nick, referring to the matter they had quarreled over last night.

Ann shrugged. "All his cronies keep telling him what a big man he is around here, so let him add to his popularity by building a few buildings. It's his money. He should be free to spend it any way he wants."

"I don't give a damn how he spends it, Ann, as long as no one at the medical school thinks it's on my behalf. If I'm going to be made chief of the department, I'll get there on my own."

"And if you don't?"

"Then, I'll get out."

Nick knew how his wife felt about living

in Madison; her failure to make close friends here. Not that she hadn't tried, but her ebullience, her determination to excel in whatever project she tackled, had made the local housewives wary. He had promised Ann they'd move to a bigger city if he didn't make the promotion to chief.

"What time is your reporter-friend coming?"

"Around four. He's bringing someone from one of the women's magazines to interview you."

"So you said. I can't say I'm overjoyed. Oh, don't worry. I'll behave—as long as she doesn't try to get too personal. . . . Might even give her my Grace Kelly impersonation."

Nick looked at Ann. The vulnerability that had shown in her eyes when she'd talked about Hank was gone now. She had withdrawn her feelings from view like a turtle retreating inside its shell; reverted to her customary self. It was a defense of hers that left a need unfulfilled in Nick: his desire to give love—and in the early years, it had almost ended their marriage. But except for one lapse in his fidelity, he had stuck it out.

Later, as Nick tried to nap for a few hours, that one lapse was very much on his mind. Mark Tangley, the journalist who was coming to interview him, was one

of the few people who knew about Noelle—
and the anticipation of Mark's visit had
awakened old memories, old needs. Like
Hank's disastrous lie, Nick's affair with
Noelle had happened a long time ago, yet
its consequences lingered on. It rose in his
mind like a specter, an invidious comparison, each time he and Ann made love.

4

ot since Korea," Mark Tangley said
N in answer to Andrea's question. He
had last seen Dr. Nicholas Sten some fourteen years ago.

"Did you know him well?" Andrea
asked, as they rode a cab from the
Madison airport to the Sten residence in
Shorewood Hills.

"Nick?" said Mark contemplatively.
"Yes, I'd say I knew him pretty well."

Well enough, he thought, so that a des-
pondent Nick, waiting in the officers'
lounge of the Seoul airport for the MATS
plane that would end his tour of duty in
Korea, had confided in him.

What Nick had revealed during those
few, unguarded hours was hardly a confession—his involvement with Noelle Cardin

was a popular subject for speculation
among their mutual friends—but more a
privileged communication between two
men whose professions had trained them
to respect such confidences. And though
the possibility always existed that it was
merely the combination of circumstances
prevailing at the time—the fog-bound
airport, the full fifth of bourbon he had the
foresight to pack in his valpack—that
caused Nick to open up, Mark also felt he
had earned his trust.

"Well . . . ?" Andrea prompted, miffed
by Mark's sudden uncommunicativeness.
"What kind of guy is he? Hero or heel?"

A little of both, Mark started to reply,
then thought better of it. Though he and
Andrea worked for the same publishers
and were old friends, briefly lovers, he was
reluctant to share with her his more
personal feelings toward Nick.

"Oh, hell, Andrea. How should I know?
I haven't seen him since Korea."

"How about then? I find it rather
difficult to imagine any friend of yours
chaste instead of chasing."

Mark smiled. "No chasing I know of,"
he lied. "Besides, what business is it of
yours?"

"It helps me size up the wife."

"Explain."

"Well, if the husband is getting his
screwing on the outside and the little

woman gets wise, there goes the wifely devotion. From then on, if they stay together at all, it's strictly a business arrangement. Separate bedrooms, psychiatrist bills, and boozy brawls. Besides, the betrayed little wife usually lies like hell to cover up the cracks in her marriage. Makes it sound like the greatest love affair since Tristan and Isolde. I ought to know."

"Man hater!"

"Not altogether, huh, Mark? We get along pretty well, don't you think? At least, when we keep it business."

"So we do," he agreed, patting Andrea's knee, ruefully recalling her passive lovemaking after all the guile it had taken to get her knees apart.

Not like Noelle must have been, he mused, bridging the gap of fourteen years in his memory and recalling her proud, young beauty. Admittedly, such an assumption was sheer speculation on his part. No one, to his knowledge, had taken up with Noelle after Nick's departure, and his knowledge in such matters was near complete. Not that there hadn't been any takers. A vision of Noelle was doubtless the most called-upon sexual fantasy among the Seoul press corps that year: the undisputed, and after Nick, unattainable Astarte.

Actually, Mark had met her a day or so

52   Marshall Goldberg, M.D.

before Nick at a diplomatic reception.
Drawn to her immediately, he had managed to find out she was a Sorbonne-
trained child psychologist working for
UNICEF before she was whisked off to
meet more important guests. He had
called the French consulate the next day
hoping to date her, only to learn that
Noelle had fallen ill and was a patient in
the base hospital. Enter Nick, knightlike
in his white coat, and good-bye Noelle.
Only after that night at the Seoul airport
when Nick had confessed his true feelings
for her and what her loss would forever
cost him in the hard currency of regret, did
Mark relent in his jealousy.

The cab climbed the winding road
leading to the more exclusive, lakeside
section of Shorewood Hills and stopped at
the Sten address. Mark paid the driver,
instructed him to return for them at
seven, then helped insure his dependabil-
ity with a generous tip.

Nick greeted them enthusiastically on the
front walk. Following instructions for the
women, the four of them entered the house
and had a round of drinks at the bar.

"How long can you two stay?" Nick
asked.

"Not long enough," Mark replied.
"Actually, only a few hours. We have to
catch the eight o'clock plane back to
Chicago."

"That's a damned shame," Nick said, grimacing. "We have a lot of catching up to do."

"Fourteen years' worth."

"That long, huh? One war till the next. . . . Well, finish your drink and we can get started."

"Done," said Mark, gulping the last of it. "What say we go for a little walk while Andrea and Ann have their chat for the *Journal* readers? Show me the Sten estate."

Strolling along the edge of the lake, Nick and Mark were soon deep in remembrances of a small war.

"I know it's an unfair question," Mark began haltingly.

"Noelle?"

Mark nodded.

"What do you want to know?"

"Have you seen or heard from her again?"

"Nope. Nor have I made the effort. . . . Have you?" Nick asked with sudden intentness.

"No. Not a thing."

"I'm glad."

"Are you?"

"It's bearable that way, don't you see?"

"And your marriage?"

"That's bearable, too."

"One more question, Nick, and then I

promise to stop prying."

"Go ahead."

"Does your wife know about Noelle?"

"I don't think so. . . . At least, she's never brought it up. But there were a lot of newsboys in Seoul who knew about us. Her father might've heard something from one of them."

"Would he tell her, you think?"

"I doubt it. Still, I never know what he's liable to do in one of his moods."

"Your Ann is very attractive, you know. You have real luck that way."

"I've got a great pair of kids, too," Nick said, changing the subject. "Danny is almost seventeen now and the best high school tennis player in the state."

"And your little girl?"

"Deirdre's ten and a budding writer no less. She can type about thirty words a minute on her Olivetti."

"Impressive . . . Well, Nick," Mark began, sensing his friend's reluctance to explore beyond a certain well-guarded crossroad in his past, "I guess we'd better get down to the business at hand. As I wrote you, the *Post* wants to do a feature on the contribution modern physics is making to medicine. You know—the laser, cryosurgery, radioisotopes, and the like. And, naturally, being an old admirer of yours, I want to lead off with your gas gun."

"You've cleared this with the university, haven't you? They frown on this sort of publicity, you know."

"We cleared it. Our editor knows your president. He gave us the go-ahead, with the proviso that Dean Erikson approve the text prior to publication."

"Frankly," Nick said, frowning, "I would be just as happy to forego all this. I feel it's premature."

"Your gas gun works, doesn't it?"

"It works. At least, it's worked on eight of the first twelve patients. That's not a hell of a lot. I might just as easily botch up the next dozen. Besides, there are still a few bugs in it that have to be worked out."

"Then I'll play it down," Mark said. "Concentrate more on its potential than its actual use for the time being. That okay?"

"Fine—if you're sure to give equal credit to my coworker, Mike Casey. He's the pathologist who collaborated with me on it."

"Tell me."

"Well, as you know, since Korea my interests have been pretty much confined to the field of vascular surgery. Once the technique for reaming out the carotid arteries in the neck had been worked out, there still remained a small group of stroke victims whose clots couldn't be reached with that approach. They were

located too high up, as the artery entered
the skull. A couple of patients died on me
with lesions like that, so I began looking
around for some way to strip the clot off
the artery wall from below. Spent a couple
of years trying out an assortment of
reamers and corkscrews on dogs without
much luck. Then, about three years ago, I
just happened to drop around to the pathology department and passed a room
where Mike Casey was stripping the fat
deposits off a strip of aorta with a jet of
compressed air. If that jet could do such a
clean job on a piece of dead tissue, I
figured it might work on a patient's
artery."

"And it did?"

"It sure did. Actually, the beauty is—
it only strips off the inner lining, what we
call the intima, where the clot is attached.
Once the far end of the clot is freed, it just
stops. We can then reach up with a pair of
forceps and draw the entire plug out."

"Sounds simple enough. You'll have to
draw me a diagram of the actual setup
when we get back to the house. . . . By the
way, what's the potential of this technique
for treating clots in other parts of the
body?"

"Personally, I think it's promising. Especially for coronary arteries. I've already
tried it on a few dogs and it works like a
charm."

"And patients?"

"Not yet. Ferguson, our chief of surgery, won't let me. Wants to see more dog work first. Then again, there's a certain rivalry between his group and mine as to who gets the most papers published. He's due to retire in another year and there's an outside chance I might be offered the chairmanship of the department because of this work. But Ferguson's opposed. He's lined up his own man for the job. Probably get it, too. He's Wisconsin-bred like a prize moo cow. 'Not one of those smart alecs from up Boston way!' "

5

The two o'clock meeting of the Special Committee of the Council of Ministers was delayed thirty minutes by the tardiness of Lieutenant General Bogdanov. Upon his arrival, he saw twelve of the original members of the committee seated around the conference table and two specially invited guests: Dr. Valentin Chaikoff, director of the Moscow Institute of Neurosurgery, and K.T. Mazaurov, deputy chairmain of the Council of Ministers and Kosygin's personally appointed representative to the group.

Malinivski opened the proceedings with a brief statement. "We have been summoned here, comrades, because the Central Committee expects us to decide forthwith whether, after sanctioning an

initial expenditure of thirty billion rubles,
we should push ahead with Karamanov's
project, despite the grave risk it now
entails, or whether we should abandon it.
My instructions from the Central Committee call for a decision from us today. To
delay further can only weaken the confidence our leaders have placed in us. . . .
With that as a preamble, I would now like
to call on Professor Valentin Chaikoff to
inform you as to the state of Nikolai Pavlevitch's health.''

"Thank you," said Chaikoff, a thin, wiry
man with owlish eyes and a diffident
manner. "In a moment, I will display a
diagram for you, demonstrating the
precise cause and location of Comrade
Karamanov's illness, but before I do I
would like to spend a moment reviewing
his medical history.

"Ten months ago, Nikolai Pavlevitch
underwent something of a personality
change. His behavior became more erratic
and he suffered periodic attacks of weakness in his right hand. These, comrades,
are the classic symptoms of the condition
that only this morning we have diagnosed
in his case. I am referring to a blockage of
the internal carotid artery that supplies
the left, and for most of us, the dominant
side of the brain. Although, in retrospect,
it is clear that the symptoms Nikolai
Pavlevitch was suffering then were due to

this obstruction in an earlier stage, it would have been virtually impossible to deduce the cause at that time. Moreover, the X-ray procedure we use to diagnose such a condition is not without risk, so might not have been warranted. Such a procedure, what we call a carotid arteriogram, was, of necessity, performed on Nikolai Pavlevitch this morning. The findings are depicted on the diagram I will now show you."

Chaikoff reached into a cylindrical carrying case by his chair, removed a windowshade-sized chart, and unrolled it. "What you see illustrated in red," he continued, "are the four major arteries supplying the brain, and their many interconnecting branches, termed collaterals. When, in the process of aging, fat deposits accumulate inside these vessels, either a stenosis, which is partial, or a thrombosis, which is complete, results. A sudden blockage of one carotid artery usually results in a stroke or death unless, as happens in a minority of cases, the communications with the opposite carotid are abundant enough to provide the deprived area of the brain with enough blood to sustain it. If, however, the obstruction is only partial, a substantial number of these patients can be cured by surgery. What our surgeons can do, if allowed to intervene early enough, is to ream out the fat deposits inside the artery as one reams out a clogged pipestem. Advances in this field have come with great rapidity, considering that the first of such operations was performed in America a little over ten years ago, and in Moscow a few months later. The surgeons at our Institute have become so skillful in this procedure that our cure rate is probably the highest in the world, approaching eighty-five percent.

"I tell you this, comrades, only to provide you with some background in this technical area, not to raise false hopes. Regrettably, the obstructed portion of Nikolai Pavlevitch's artery lies in an unusual, and for all practical purposes, inaccessible location: as the vessel enters the bony vault of the skull. Any attempt to repair the diseased segment would necessitate a skull-splitting operation that few, if any, patients have survived."

Chaikoff paused to sip water. "In short, we are incapable of offering a cure. What remains is medical management. By putting Nikolai Pavlevitch on continuous anticoagulant therapy to thin his blood and reduce its propensity to clot, we may be able to retard the progression of his disease. *Retard* mind you, not reverse. By such means, together with a strict program of rest and proper diet, we may be able to prolong his life by several months. My experience with other patients on this regimen makes me reluctant to be more optimistic in this estimate. . . . Are there any questions?"

"I have one, Comrade Chaikoff," said Malinivski. "You said that, given special drugs, Karamanov's life could be prolonged several months. Would he be able to carry on his work during this time?"

"To a limited degree, perhaps. This, of course, would depend on his response. I can reassure you as to one aspect of his condition, comrades. Based on the interview I had with him this morning it is my firm belief that Nikolai Pavlevitch's mental processes remain as yet unimpaired."

"You mentioned, did you not, Comrade Chaikoff," said Zakharov, "that no operation your surgeons are presently capable of performing would be worth the risk. It was also your opinion that medical treatment would, at best, offer only a temporary reprieve. Do you not agree, therefore, that for all practical purposes, our unfortunate comrade is virtually a dead man? Certainly, no one who is likely to complete a project that would cost the Soviet Union upward of one hundred and fifty billion rubles."

"I do not feel qualified to make such a judgment, Comrade Zakharov. Placed on an intensive medical regimen, Nikolai Pavlevitch might survive one month or

one year. Beyond that, it is impossible to
say. Morever, the answer to your question
depends not only on the length of his
survival but on the length of time he will
require to complete his project and that, of
course, I cannot predict."

"Could you perhaps furnish us with an
estimate of sorts, Comrade Kapitsa?"
asked Malinivski.

Kapitsa appeared shaken by Chaikoff's
grim report and cleared his throat several
times before attempting to speak. "Please
forgive my emotional state, comrades, but
I was not aware until now of the terminal
state of my dear friend. I tried several
times today to learn of his condition but
was prevented, as I'm sure many of us
were, by Comrade Stakhanov's stringent
security ban. . . . How close is Nikolai
Pavlevitch to the successful conclusion of
his project? Very close, indeed. I reviewed
his latest data just four or five days ago
and can assure you he is on the brink of a
solution to the final obstacle: a means to
synchronize the pulse of the electromagnetic wave accelerator with the
tangential forces which will prevent it
from dissipating its charge before
reaching its target. It is an incredibly
complex and critical problem, but no more
so for a mind like Karamanov's than the
impossible ones that preceded it. Granted
the full use of his faculties, I would

estimate it would take him an additional four to six months."

"Should he falter, Comrade Kapitsa," asked Lermontov,"could you or any of your colleagues solve the problem for him?"

"Possibly I could, if I devoted ten years of constant effort to it. Possibly my colleagues could in a shorter time, working collectively. First, of course, they would have to comprehend his mathematical system. But eventually it could be done."

"Not a very encouraging prospect though, is it, comrades?" said Zakharov. "I have still not heard one convincing argument from either Chaikoff or Kapitsa that recommends to me we spend another ruble on this imperfect and obviously imperfectable system."

"Does anyone challenge Comrade Zakharov's pronouncement?" Malinivski asked, fearful there would be no other recourse but to abandon the project his committee had previously sanctioned.

"If you will permit me, Comrade Chairman, I would like to ask Professor Chaikoff a question or two?" said Bogdanov.

"Good. Proceed."

"Thank you, Comrade Chairman. The reason for my late arrival this arrival was that I was pursuing a solution to the very same dilemma Comrade Chaikoff has

posed for you with another professor at
Moscow University. His name is Yevgeni
Lenhov, and I'm confident Comrade
Chaikoff will vouch for his preeminence
among Soviet neurosurgeons. Once learn-
ing that Nikolai Pavlevitch suffered not
from a brain tumor, as was first believed,
but a severe blockage of his carotid
arteries, I sought Professor Lenhov's
opinion as to any remedy. Though admitting that a direct attack on the obstruction was beyond his capability, and the
capabilities of other Soviet surgeons, Professor Lenhov was not quite so willing to
concede that a surgical cure was out of the
question. He felt one more thing should be
considered: a new technique being developed by the Americans and the French
that employs a powerful jet of gas to act
as a bloodless scalpel. The technical name
for this procedure is gas endarterectomy.
Perhaps you've heard of it, Comrade
Chaikoff?

"No, Comrade Bogdanov, I'm afraid
not. Since my administrative chores
prevent me from attending many international meetings, I am not as up to date on
such advances as I might like. But please
continue. What you have to say is fascinating."

"Professor Lenhov felt he was not sufficiently familiar with the technique to
provide me with the full details. He did,

however, furnish me with the name of a friend of his who could, a French surgeon by the name of Marcel Marandat.

"Realizing, of course, the potential contribution such information might make to our present discussion, I immediately placed a call to Dr. Marandat's Paris office. Unfortunately, he was not there, and as might be expected, I encountered great difficulty in making the urgency of my call known to the Paris operators. Finally, a little before 1400 hours I reached him at his laboratory in the Broussais Hospital. The connection was a poor one and my French is labored, but despite these handicaps I managed to extract most of the essential details.

"The procedure itself was invented by two Americans at the University of Wisconsin, a midwestern university near Chicago, I believe. One of the inventors was a pathologist whose name he did not remember and the other, Nicholas Sten, a surgeon. Marandat, although borrowing the original idea from the Americans, has never actually visited them, but improvised a technique of his own. The basic procedure, however, is ingeniously simple. A small needle is plunged into the wall of the artery and several short bursts of gas are injected to separate the clot from the lining of the vessel. A small incision is then made in the artery and the clot removed with forceps.

"What Marandat told me that is especially encouraging is that both groups, the Americans and his own, developed the method primarily so that they could cure cases like Karamanov's. Sten has, in fact, now operated on eleven patients, seven of them successfully. Marandat has had poorer luck, saving only one out of six. He feels, however, that Sten has the advantage by using special instruments and is keen to visit with him to observe his technique firsthand.

"I might add one other bit of information I learned from Professor Lenhov. He has known Marandat for many years and assures me he is an active and devoted member of the French Communist Party who can be trusted to cooperate with us in any venture. I have not yet had the opportunity to verify this with our Third Directorate files but from the gist of our conversation feel confident it is so."

"All very interesting," said Zakharov. "But what is it you're really suggesting— sending Karamanov to America to be operated on?"

"Would not his genius be more valuable to us cured in America than left to die in Russia, Comrade Zakharov? I'm not, however, about to recommend such a trip. It would represent an insurmountable security task. No, there is yet a better approach: send him to Paris. Marandat himself could operate on him, or if he is unwilling to take the risk, the American surgeon could be invited over to perform the operation."

"Oh what pretense?" asked Lermontov.

"A simple invitation from Marandat to demonstrate his technique before a Paris audience might do it. If not, we could even arrange an international surgical meeting for that purpose. As a last resort, we could forego the Paris setting and invite Sten directly to Moscow."

"A brilliant scheme, Comrade Bogdanov," said Mazaurov. "Premier Kosygin will be most interested to learn of it. I have only one reservation. What if, through lapses in our security, the Americans learn Karamanov's true identity. What's to prevent their surgeon from deliberately killing him on the operating table?"

"Your reservation is a reasonable one," granted Bogdanov. "I cannot, of course, gaurantee either the invulnerability of our security measures or the humanity of the American surgeon. I do feel, however, that given sufficient agents to accompany me to Paris, Karamanov's safety can be assured at all times and in all places except one—the operating room. During those critical moments he would, of course, need protection of a special kind.

Perhaps, if Marandat himself does not
perform the operations, he could be
persuaded to serve as our watchdog.
Moreover, there is no reason why one or
more of our own surgeons could not be
present. Someone like Professor Chaikoff,
here, or Yevgeni Lenhov. Their only draw-
back is that they are unfamiliar with the
procedure the American will use and therefore unlikely to spot any deviance. Still,
there is no reason they cannot journey to
Paris a week or two in advance and learn
the precise technique from Marandat."

"My congratulations, Bogdanov," said
Zakharov. "Once again, you rise to the
occasion and make your preposterous
scheme seem almost plausible. You will, of
course, admit that what you propose is an
incredible gamble?" Waiting for Bogdanov to nod his head, Zakharov continued. "As much will be left to chance as
the flip of a coin. What you fail to see is,
that unless the coin improbably hangs in
the air, you lose either way. Heads, we do
nothing, and within a few months he dies
here in Russia. Tails, we ship him to
Paris, and if by some miracle he does not
die en route, the American surgeon kills
him. Can't you see, Bogdanov—should the
American CIA discover that their
inventive surgeon is operating on the
most brilliant physicist we have produced,
a physicist who, if allowed to survive a few

more months, will perfect a missile-defense system that would make the Soviet Union impregnable, they could not possibly permit his survival. They would do all in their power to assassinate him the moment he leaves Russia. If not in the operating room, then in the street. Remember, if the situations were reversed, we would do the same. We would have no choice."

"Your argument is a persuasive one, Comrade Zakharov," said Kapitsa, ". . .for the opposing view. Certainly, we all agree that, at this moment, Karamanov is doubtless the most valuable man on the face of the earth. He has within his grasp the most valuable gift a nation could possibly possess: a means to prevent war. Think of it, comrades, we are perhaps as close as a few months from achieving this extraordinary protection. . . . Is now the time to relinquish it? Abandon it without further struggle? Agreed, it is a gamble. Agreed, the likelihood is that we may lose. But how often is a nation like ours presented with such an opportunity? Not once in a lifetime. *Once in a century!*"

6

The rain began shortly before dawn, accelerating in short bursts of intensity as the morning progressed. Driving cautiously, as sheets of rain battered his windshield, Nick caught glimpses of crepe, tricolor banner whipping in the wind and cluttering the gutters the length of State Street. The storefront adornments reminded him that the annual Festival of France began in Madison today. Bantam-sized Eiffel Towers and Arc de Triomphes sprouted on every street corner and the dress shops displayed copies of the latest Paris fashions. It wasn't all pomp and pageantry, however, for inaugurating the festivities was the dinner party at the Fergusons'. Danielle Ferguson, Sam's French wife, existed for this gala evening, planning and plotting it year-round, deliciously anticipating the moment when she could shed her Americanized cocoon and flutter forth to greet her French *amis.*

The dinner party was black tie and de rigueur for members of Ferguson's department, and Nick, though grimacing at the prospect, planned to attend rather than risk an open break with his chief.

Nick was in his office working on the paper he had been invited to present before the New York Surgical Society the following week, when the phone rang.

"Monsieur le docteur Sten?" he heard midst a background of slicks and static. "This is Dr. Marcel Marandat callling from Paris. Can you hear me?"

"I hear you very well, Dr. Marandat. What can I do for you?"

"Do you remember my correspondence of a few months ago concerning your technique of gas endarterectomy?"

"Yes, I remember. You've received my reply by now, haven't you?"

"I have. It was most illuminating. Still, I am encountering difficulty. I've operated successfully only once in six attempts. An unenviable record, wouldn't you say?"

"I'm sorry to hear it. But as you already know, my technique is no secret. I'd be more than willing to help you in any way I can."

"Your generosity humbles me. It is more than I might expect from my own colleagues. And, to be truthful, I need your help urgently."

"In what way?"

"In person, Dr. Sten. To operate on a member of my own family. I realize it is an extraordinary request, but his condition is critical. The X rays show he has a seventy percent occlusion of his left carotid artery at the level of the siphon and an almost complete occlusion on the right."

"How symptomatic is he?"

"He suffered a stroke five days ago. Now, he is partially recovered, but for how long I dare not say. An operation is his only hope. And then only if you yourself perform it. Naturally, the family will meet all your expenses. Also, feel free to bring your wife and children."

Nick compared a vision of the sunlit Champs Elysees with the rain-drenched scene outside his office window. "I'd like to accommodate you, Dr. Marandat, but it's impossible to give you a definite answer right now. I have several other commitments for the month and these would have to be rescheduled. Also, I'd have to request leave from the university, and their permission to perform my operation abroad. That, in itself, might prove to be the biggest obstacle, so I'd better get started on it right away."

"Thank you, Dr. Sten. A very dear man's life is at stake: my uncle's. Only this winter was he allowed to leave East Germany. He deserves a few years of freedom. . . . How long will it take you to receive a judgment from your university?"

"A day or two at the most."

"*Bien.* I am relieved. That much of a delay he can afford. And I am optimistic that if God grants us your services, you can save him. For my part, I will do all in my power to facilitate the arrangements for your trip, and later, the operation itself."

"All right, then. Give me your address and phone number and I'll let you know at the earliest possible moment."

Nick scribbled the information on his desk pad, then repeated it back. His next words came out almost with a will of their own. "And one last question: would you possibly know a French psychologist by the name of Noelle Cardin? She's a woman in her early thirties. An old friend whom I haven't seen for years."

"Noelle Cardin? . . . No, I don't know her. But I shall make inquiries at the National Registry. We French are methodical record-keepers, you know. If she is still in France you will see her."

"Good . . . Then you should be hearing from me in the next few days."

"Thank you. I cannot but believe you will come. *Au revoir,* Dr. Sten."

Nick felt a surge of exhilaration as he hung up the phone. He envisioned a spring-fresh Paris, the challenge of Marandat's patient—and Noelle. There was now the hope he'd see her again.

Yet the prospect of that was not only perilous after so long a time, but slim. He would have to tell Ann of the invitation, Nick realized; take her with him. His research had prevented him from taking a vacation for over a year now, and after recently talking Ann out of going to Europe alone, it seemed unavoidable he bring her along.

Timing their entrance to allow sufficient bar time for two drinks each before dinner, Nick and Ann arrived at the Fergusons' a respectable half-hour late. They surrendered their wraps to the Fergusons' twelve-year-old and joined a handful of couples in the living room.

"Drinks, Nick!" Ann prompted, still exuberant over the news of Marandat's invitation. "A nice stiff bourbon and I'll behave like a convent girl all evening long."

"You'd better, if you expect to get to Paris. Ferguson seemed reluctant to even

consider it when I spoke to him earlier.
Thank God, the request came from a
Frenchman. Sam knows damned well what
his wife will do if he turns me down.''

"Okay, Nick—be nice to the Fergusons
or no Paris holiday. That being the case,
bring me a double.''

As Ann searched in her purse for a cigarette, she looked up to see Sam Ferguson
descending on her. She forced a smile,
overly friendly and therefore unconvinc-
ing, and extended her hand.

"Well, Ann, good to see you,'' Sam said,
starting to embrace her but changing his
mind as Ann took a leisurely puff of her
cigarette.

"Thank you, Sam.''

"Say—that painting of yours on display
at the Union is a mighty fine piece of work.
A real eye-catcher.''

"Thanks again, Sam.''

"Hey, what is this? Can't seem to get
much out of you except a few stingy thank
you's. What gives?''

Ann squinted. "Don't bait me, Sam.
You know what gives as well as I
do—Paris.''

"Paris!'' he scoffed. "Who's talking
about Paris?''

"I am. What are you talking about?''

"I'm talking about pressures, Ann.
Pressures on you from every angle, boxing

you in. Even for a man my age there's no letup. Paris trips. Million-dollar government grants. Medicine is so damned big business these days! Know what I mean?"

"Not entirely."

"I thought not. Hell, I'm not so sure I know myself. Well, the point is this. It's my responsibility—for a little while longer—to set the pace for my department. To speed a certain few up and slow a certain few down. So, the hell with pressures for a change. Nick'll go to Paris if I think he's ready, and he won't if I think he's not."

"Now wait a second. Just what kind of pressures are you talking about? Not Stratton pressures, I hope?"

"No, Ann. Not that I'm aware of."

"Then who?"

"Some other time," he said, spotting Nick approaching with their drinks. Ferguson lingered long enough to greet Nick and assure him he'd discuss the Paris trip with Dean Erickson in the morning, then left.

"What was all that about?" asked Nick. "You two looked thick as thieves."

"Oh, nothing much."

"Your eyes tell me different."

"What do my eyes tell you?"

"Paris. Do we or don't we?"

"That depends."

"Depends on what?"

"Whether or not he thinks you're ready for it."

"Oh? What's that supposed to mean?"

"It means this, Nick—are you ready to face up? Big failure as well as big success? It could go either way."

"Maybe so. But no matter which way it does go, I want the chance. I've earned it, and we both know at what cost: three years' work and four lives."

At 11:00 P.M., the nurse on duty on the fourth floor wing of University Hospital noticed the signal corresponding to Adam Blair's room light up on her console. Entering the room, she found her patient collapsed on the bathroom floor. A single glimpse of his ashen color, his stertorous breathing, told her his condition was critical. She rolled him face up, took a quick pulse reading, and was about to leave to summon help when his eyes focused on her and he reached feebly for her leg.

"Not here," he moaned.

Uncomprehending, the nurse jerked her leg from his grasp.

"Not . . . in the . . . damned bathroom!" he protested in a fierce whisper. "Get me out!"

The nurse's indecision immobilized her momentarily, then she complied. Gripping his frail body under the armpits, she

dragged him to the side of the bed. She
placed a pillow beneath his head, rechecked his pulse, and finally, futilely,
asked him what was wrong.

"Wrong?" Adam Blair replied incredulously. "The damned . . . damned infir-
mities!" he hissed, clenched his fists,
gasped, and died.

Ten minutes later, the news reached
Nick at the Fergusons'. Alerted to bad
tidings by the stutter in Jim Belmano's
voice (Jim only stuttered under duress),
Nick was nonetheless staggered to learn of
Adam Blair's death. Disbelieving at first,
refusing to allow the meaning of the words
to register; ready to claim hoax, nightmare, foul—he begrudgingly accepted the
known competence of his informant. He
grimaced with the effort it took him to
steady his voice and instructed Jim to
meet Mrs. Adam Blair on her arrival at the
hospital.

He returned to the dining room and
beckoned Ann to come out. She caught up
with him in the foyer.

"My God, Nick, what's happened?
You're pale as a ghost!"

"I just lost Adam Blair."

"Lost? You mean, died? Adam Blair
died! Oh, my God! Oh, Nick, how it must
hurt. What happened?"

"Don't know, damn it! They say he was
talking up until the end."

"Oh, that poor, sweet man. I know how much you thought of him."

Nick started to reply but remained silent, biting his lower lip.

"Are you all right?"

"I'm all right."

"Are you leaving right away for the hospital? Want me to drive you?"

"No, I'm okay. You stay and finish your dinner."

"Nick, I *want* to drive you. Be with you."

"I'm meeting Adam's wife."

"Good. I can console her better than you can. I'm a woman. Now you go ahead and pull the car around front. I'll make our excuses to the Fergusons."

Impulsively, Nick drew Ann into the half-hidden recess of the hall closet and hugged her, feeling a singular intimacy with his wife of nineteen years. "I'm afraid this means good-bye to Paris."

"Oh, who cares. I'd rather neck in hall closets any day."

7

Nick woke soon after dawn, looked out the window at overcast New York skies, and tried to fall back to sleep. He had barely drifted off when he was jarred awake by the ring of the telephone. He climbed grudgingly out of bed, stretched, and staggered over to the dresser, cursing the hotel management for its poor room planning.

"Major Nicholas Sten?" the caller inquired.

"Who is this?" Nick rasped, startled by the long-forgotten sound of the rank gladly relinquished fourteen years ago along with the tiresome discipline and, at times, the unparalleled sense of freedom.

"Major, this is Neil Canter calling. Captain Canter when you knew me in Korea.

You once drained an infected sinus for me.
Got a purple nose out of it instead of a
Purple Heart. But you had a ward full of
battle casualties to take care of at the
time, so I don't suppose you remember
me. . . . Well, how are you, Major?"

"A bit confused. Like why should you be
calling me up at seven o'clock on a Sunday
morning? And how'd you know where to
find me? Don't tell me war's been declared
and I'm being recalled to active duty?"

"No, nothing so drastic. Not yet, anyway. I just flew in from Chicago trying to
catch up with you. Wish I'd known ahead
of time about your talk on Monday. Would
have saved the government some airplane
fares and me a lot of hustling. . . . Your
wife told me where to find you. And now
that I have you, how about a little talk?"

"About what?"

"My fourteen-year checkup?"

"Get to the point," snapped Nick.

"Okay, okay. Forgive the tired attempt
at humor. I'm CIA now, and I want to see
you about CIA business. That's all I can
tell you for the moment. But indulge me.
It's rather urgent."

"All right. But give me some clue what
this is all about."

"Wouldn't make too much sense. It's
the sort of long, involved story you have
to tell from the beginning. What say I
grab a cab and meet you in your room in

fifteen minutes? I'll even buy breakfast.
Stop off at the Stage Delicatessen on my
way in and pick up some Danish. Or do
you prefer cheesecake?"

Nick sighed. "Okay, come along. But
I've put in a rough week and intended this
extra day in New York to get some rest. It
better be worth my while."

"It will be, Doctor. I promise you that."

Nick frowned as he hung up the phone.
What did the CIA want with him? Though
he had met CIA agents before, the desig-
nation held a vaguely sinister ring: an
organization of secretive men licensed to
operate outside the law and beyond the
public view.

Perhaps a friend of his at the university
was in the process of being cleared to work
on some top-secret government project
and they wanted his confidential apprais-
al? He had submitted to such an interrogation before and though it had left him
with misgivings, it was a tolerable ordeal.
If that's all Canter wanted, he would accommodate him.

But that *wasn't* all, Nick reasoned. The
CIA agent wouldn't chase him halfway
across the country for something as
routine as that. Nor would he be so
evasive over the telephone. . . . No, something more substantial was at stake and
he would simply have to wait for it to come
out.

Nick shaved and showered, then ordered coffee for two from room service.

A rap on the door interrupted him in the midst of dressing. Expecting the waiter with his coffee, Nick was surprised to see Neil Canter enter the room wheeling the service cart in front of him.

"I've already paid him, Doctor," he said with a cheerful smile. "Shall I pour?"

Nick appraised him in a glance: a tall, trim, broadshouldered man whose long face, receding hairline, and thick, horn-rimmed glasses bestowed a scholarly appearance. Nick remembered the face only vaguely, if at all. Still, he reclaimed certain impressions: a well-educated, fresh-out-of-college youth who suffered from an over-eagerness to prove his courage and a year-round allergic rhinitis.

They shook hands.

"I'll say it's nice to see you," Nick said, "if you'll do me two simple favors: stop calling me Major or Doctor—Nick will do —and stop stalling."

"Fair enough, Nick," Canter obliged, grinning. He wheeled the service cart between the end of the bed and the dresser, drew up a chair, and opened a box of pastries.

"Your government wants you to kill a man."

"Wh . . . What?" Nick put down his cup before it spilled. "Say that again."

"You heard me correctly. The firm—meaning your government—wants you to kill a man."

"What the hell do you mean? Kill who?"

"I suppose assassinate might be a more accurate description of the job," Canter amended with a shrug.

"Are you mad?" said Nick incredulously. The intent, half-amused look on Canter's face amazed, then infuriated him: "Listen, you lunatic bastard, either explain yourself in one big hurry or I'm going to throw you the hell out of here!"

"Take it easy, Nick," Canter urged, emphasizing his own calm by taking a bit of his Danish and washing it down with a gulp of coffee. "Look, it's a nasty world we live in. Cliche, right? Also happens to be true. And it's getting nastier every day. A computer at the Pentagon predicts the odds are fifty-fifty there'll be another war in the next ten years. But that's not your bag, is it? You're in the business of saving lives. Well, so am I—American lives! And just as dedicated to that aim as you are. Now we both know prevention is good medicine, don't we? That's what the National Security Council wants us to practice in this instance: a little preventive medicine. Unfortunately, it involves killing a man, a Russian physicist —a goddamn genius—and it involves you."

"How can it possibly involve me?" Nick protested.

"You've been invited to Paris to perform some surgery. Who invited you?"

"A French doctor by the name of Marandat. Why?"

"Marandat happens to be a dedicated Communist. Did you know that?"

"No, but so what? So are a lot of other Frenchmen. What difference does it make?"

"A very important difference, under the circumstances. Know who he wants you to operate on?"

"A relative of his. I think he said his uncle."

"Did he tell you anything else about him?"

"Not much. Something about his not being able to leave East Germany until just recently."

"Nice," said Canter. "A convenient cover-up. Might help explain why he doesn't speak French, only Russian or German."

"So?"

"So, we have reason to believe that the patient Marandat wants you to operate on is only the most important man in the Soviet Union today; ;a man who had the blueprints for an impregnable antiballistic missile system locked up in his brain. His name is Nikolai Pavlevitch Karamanov, and thanks to him, the Russians may soon far outdistance us in the missile field. Einstein gave us an early lead, and now they've got the equivalent in Karamanov. The big question, though, is—for how long? Our agents report he's critically ill, the victim of some kind of brain condition that only an operation such as the one you've pioneered can cope with. It must be something like that, or else they'd never have taken the incredible risk of inviting an American surgeon to get within a thousand miles of him. How much has Marandat told you of his actual condition?"

"Enough to know that it will be rapidly fatal unless an immediate attempt is made to open up the arteries feeding his brain. He's got a bilateral lesion, which not only makes it twice the surgical risk, but twice as easy to kill or permanently incapacitate him. He's already suffered one stroke. One more—and the likelihood's imminent—and they either have a dead man or a vegetable on their hands. He couldn't add two and two, let alone design a missile system."

"It's that serious?"

"If Marandat described his condition accurately, I could kill him off without even leaving the country. Simply refuse to go. Truth is, I hadn't planned to anyway."

"Why not?"

"Oh, lots of reasons. I doubt whether I could've obtained university approval, for one."

"That's already been arranged for you. We cleared it with your dean yesterday morning."

Nick glared. "Efficient little bunch, aren't you? What exactly did you tell him —that you want a hired gun?"

"We told him just enough to get you loose. Nothing whatsoever about what we had in mind for you and nothing about Karamanov. Believe me, he's the biggest secret we've got. No more than a handful of men in the whole country know we've tumbled to him. We had to jeopardize the safety of one of our key agents to learn as much as we did. Should the KGB get wise, it would finish him. And he's much too valuable a plant for us to lose now. You see, I've told you more than I really should've already. But I trust you. . . . I suppose the corollary to that is—do you trust me? After all, I haven't shown you any identification."

"Save it," Nick said. "You know enough about matters you have no business knowing to convince me. One question though—who's the operations officer? Are you making the minute-by-minute decisions, or are you passing them on to Helms?"

"No, I'm a deputy director. From here on, it's all ad lib on my part."

"Can you prove it?"

"Call Langley if you want. I'll get you through to the chief myself."

Nick sighed, momentarily doubting the reality of the situation. ' 'All right. It's simple enough," he said after a pause. "I'll forget the Paris trip. Forget our meeting ever took place. As far as I'm concerned, the last time I saw you was in Korea when I drilled a hole in your sinus. That ought to settle matters, shouldn't it?"

Canter started to answer, sniffled, and withdrew a rumpled handkerchief from his pocket. He blew his nose lustily.

"Well?" Nick prompted.

"I'm plagued with more damned allergies than the whole United States Army," he complained.

"Please answer me!"

"You asked a tricky question. I'm not sure I've thought out the best answer."

"What's to think about?"

"This, for instance: if you, personally, don't operate on Karamanov, it's a cinch he dies—right?"

"Right."

"Not quite," said Canter, shaking his head. "Ninety percent right, maybe, but not a hundred percent. And for an assign ment as crucial as this, it's got to be *one hundred percent*. We can't afford any last-minute miracles. For all you know, Karamanov may prove to be as hard to kill as Rasputin. The way I figure it, they're still left with two outside chances to pull it off. One, Karamanov may survive long enough to finish his work. All we know on that score is that he's close—awfully damn close—to adding the finishing touches. And two, if they can't get you to operate, they may decide to let some other surgeon wield the knife."

"Marandat?"

"Why not Marandat?"

Nick shrugged. "I suppose he might, if they pressure him into it. It triples the odds against Karamanov making it, though."

"Even so," said Canter, "any odds won't do. We just can't afford to chance it."

"Meaning?"

"Meaning we want you to go to Paris and guarantee that Karamanov dies of his disease. I know it's a hell of a thing to ask, but that's what we're asking. I only wish I had the necessary skills to do it for you."

"Do you?" Nick said with a wry smile.

"I wouldn't sweat much over it, believe me. You see, I know what's involved: one life in exchange for perhaps millions. Just look at what's going on now. The Middle

East crisis is at flashpoint. The latest estimate we've received from our agents in the area is that war is inevitable, months —maybe days—away. And don't think the Russians aren't in there somewhere stirring the pot. Then, there's the seventh rung of hell, the bottomless pit we're trying to fill in Indochina. What happens if we start winning that one and Red China sics a million *volunteers* at us, for no better reason than to practice a little birth control? Use our nuclear deterrent? Hell, no. Not unless we clear it first with the Russians."

"The Russians?"

"The balance of power. The only thing that's kept the Communists at bay so far is our ability to maintain nuclear parity with the Russians. Upset that, and see what happens the next time their interests and ours collide in some brush war. They'll replant their missiles in Cuba so fast it'll make your eyeballs pop. Turn Florida into another Death Valley."

"Even if it forces us over the brink?"

"Would it, though? After all, we're an eminently sensible nation. No national death wish like some of our Oriental friends. All the Russians would have to do is pick some barren chunk of real estate— a stretch of Siberia, say—and challenge us to test their defense system. And if we fail to score, their point is made. What good are all our Minutemen and Poseidon missiles then? It's strictly no contest. The war's won.

"Karamanov's system is so avantgarde, I'm told, that even with the counterpart of a Klaus Fuchs on our side, it might take us a decade or more to duplicate it. And the Russians won't wait. They've squirmed under our strategic superiority long enough."

"That's a pretty pessimistic outlook, isn't it? Since we know all this, what are we doing to counter it? Don't tell me we don't have our own plans for an antimissile network?"

"Of course we do, but compared to Karamanov's ours is right out of the Stone Age. The rumor is—he's found some way to harness electromagnetic waves. We don't know how or why, but he must know what he's doing. He's reputed to be one of the world's greatest theoretical physicists. In comparison, the best we have to work with for the moment not only is fantastically expensive—upwards of eighty billion!—but leaky as a sieve. We know at least five ways the system can be penetrated, and the Russians probably know a few more. Even if we decide to deploy our ABM's to the extent that it affords us token protection—cuts the estimated first strike casualties from ninety to thirty million—where do we dig up the eighty billion to finance it? At least, the Russians have the same problem. Their price tag may be a mite less, but it still adds up to around a hundred billion rubles. And just imagine the spot their economy will be in if their investment fizzles out along with Karamanov. Their reserves would be so depleted they'd be forced into increasing their foreign trade, and that might mean the end of the cold war for at least a generation." Canter sat back in his chair and smiled. "Wouldn't it be loverly?"

"Maybe from your point of view it would. I don't quite see it that way. Know the way I see it? Start with a sick human being who knows that unless risky surgery is performed by an American, a member of the enemy camp, he's had it. His only hope is to trust me. His doctors trust me. His family trusts me. Even the bloody KGB trusts me. So what happens? I put on my scrub suit, make my incision, have the blood supply to his superbly functioning brain in my hands, and then, standing Christ-like in judgment, starve it off, watch while that glistening mass of tissue shrivels and rots. For what? For God and country? Whose God? Think we have separate Gods—the Russians and us?"

"I don't deal in speculations like that. I deal in facts."

"What kind of facts? Little red pins on a

map? Is that all there is to your life,
Canter?"

"Get this straight—I didn't expect you
to pump my hand in thanks for the assignment I'm offering you. It's risky business.
Oh yes, risky as hell. The odds are, the
Russians have ordered a twin coffin for
you in case their savior, Karamanov, ends
up in one. I make no bones about it. So
why should you stick your neck out? Well,
the answer is pretty abstract, I suppose.
Abstract as God. . . . Patriotism, Major.
Love of country. There are always a few
around who'll settle for that. I'm one!"

Nick stared back in silence. There was
something about Canter's manner which
perturbed him, made him distrust the
agent's motives. He was obviously well
trained. Perhaps too well trained, too
drained of emotional impediments. He
went strictly by the book and the book
was explicit, miserly in its permissiveness.
Canter had the inured instincts of a
predator, but that alone didn't bother him.
What did was the evangelistic look on his
face; the projected message that Nick was
being offered the opportunity of a lifetime:
the chance to strike a decisive blow at the
enemy—and should not need any further
persuasion.

"What if I said no?" he challenged.
"What then?"

"No?" Canter repeated, eyebrows raised.

"A clear, unambiguous no. What are your instructions then? What pressures are brought to bear? After all, I'm the recipient of a quarter million dollars in government grants."

"No pressures at all. We're not a police state. Let your own conscience exert the pressure—every time you read the headlines in the morning paper."

Canter rose, replaced his chair under the dresser, and paused to straighten his tie in the mirror. When he turned around, his sanguine expression reappeared. "Think it over, why don't you? It's a lot to digest in one sitting. Should you want to talk some more, you can reach me at this number."

Canter wrote the number on the memo pad by the phone, took a last sip of coffee, and prepared to leave. "How long you planning to stay in the big city?" he asked.

"I'm leaving tomorrow afternoon."

"Okay, Major," Canter said, forcing a smile. "I'll be at home tomorrow between one and six. Call me to say good-bye."

8

In the abrupt silence that followed Canter's departure, Nick tried to compose himself. What an incredible performance, he marveled, recalling the agent's precipitous delivery of the punch line. No hesitation, no apology, no embarrassed throat-clearing; a clearly enunciated statement of fact; "Your government wants you to kill a man." No ambiguity in that, by God. Your government who has sheltered and nourished you these forty-five years, who has given you freedom of choice and limitless opportunity along with a sense of pride in its traditions of fair play, now wants you to unburden yourself of such restrictive beliefs, accept the plundering roots of its origin: the Darwinian Imperative, which, when invoked, refashions law and tradition to its own design.

Canter evidently belonged to a more adaptable species, not surprising in view of the agent's indoctrination and training —the antithesis of Nick's own. Yet, who was to say which of them practiced the greater morality? At what point on some arbitrary scale of survival did the welfare of the herd, the pack, the group supersede the God-given right of the individual to exist?

Though never so pressed for an answer, it wasn't the first time Nick had examined this thesis. He had heard it debated in Korea and debated it himself in the privacy of his thoughts. What if, instead of being there as a physician, he had been an infantryman, a common foot soldier who, in the tumult of battle, was ordered to leave his foxhole and advance in the face of devastating enemy fire: an assignment crucial to the outcome of the skirmish, yet carrying with it the risk of almost certain death. Would he refuse, thereby branding himself a coward for the rest of his life? Or would he, with the matchless grace of a Nathan Hale, repay his lifelong debt to flag and country in one final, heroic gesture? And though the choice, so clearly defined in the annals of American folklore, seemed self-evident, Nick could never fully bring hismelf to accept it; not because he lacked courage (he had accumulated a lifetime of lesser episodes to refute that) but because he lacked conviction: the belief that his life and the disposal of it belonged not to himself and his Maker but to his commanding officer and the expediency of battle.

Impulsively, he telephoned Ann.

"Wake you up, love?" he asked, as she answered sleepily.

"Pleasantly, darling. I was dreaming about you. You and me and nobody else— no kids, no hospital, no intruders—strolling the streets of Paris."

"Ah, romantic . . ."

"Anyway, I was going to phone you as soon as I got up. I ran into Lucy Erickson at the Union last night—and guess what? Without my even mentioning it, she congratulated us on the Paris trip. She realized, of course, she'd put her foot into it when I told her you hadn't received anything official from the university as yet. But I managed to assure her she wouldn't be turned over to a firing squad and got the rest of the story. Seems she spotted a memo on her hubby's desk informing Ferguson that as a gesture of goodwill, and in exchange for Jeanne Moreau, you were being loaned to the French."

"Anything else on the memo I should

know about?"

"Isn't that enough?" she said peevishly.
"I thought you'd be pleased as Punch."
Nick said nothing and she erupted:
"Damn it, what's the matter? Are we
going or aren't we?"

Nick's fingers clamped down on the
phone handle. He felt trapped, stymied,
witlessly devoid of an answer—knowing
he could tell Ann nothing of Canter's visit
and, in that way, involve her. "The truth
is," he began haltingly, "I haven't
decided. It won't be just a vacation, you
know. I'm expected to perform surgery.
And after what happened to Adam Blair,
I'm having second thoughs about it. Hell,
Ann, you know the sorry state of French
medicine. There's no way I can be sure of
the kind of help or equipment I'm liable to
get over there."

"Couldn't you insist on the Paris-American Hospital?"

"I did," Nick lied. "But Marandat
didn't think he could arrange it." Certainly not for Comrade Karamanov, he
thought ironically.

"Well, just how damned much equipment you going to need?"

"Oh, it's not that so much. What I need
is a team: anesthetists, internists, surgeons. People I can depend on for his post-
op care. Otherwise, I might end up having
to sit with him myself for six or seven

days. That wouldn't leave us much time for a fling, would it?"

"Maybe not. But that's not what's really bothering you, is it? There's something more."

"More? Oh, I suppose. Much as I hate to admit it, I'm afraid of a second, well-publicized failure. Especially after Adam. . . . God, how I dread going to his funeral when I get back! If only that damned biddy of a wife of his had signed the autopsy permit. The *post* might've established whether he died of a coronary or because I botched up his second operation. Now, of course, we'll never know—which leaves me fair game for my detractors in the department. Oh, the hell with being chief, anyway. I can live without the added pressures. And there's nothing holding us to Madison."

"Of course not," Anne quickly agreed. "You know my opinion of the place. Not the place, really—the people. The pygmy-headed people . . . Oh, damn it, I wish you were here right now so we could talk this out. I suppose I'm willing to go along with whatever you decide."

"Thanks. Even if we don't make the trip at Marandat's expense, there's no reason we can't go on our own in a few months."

"No, but I bet we don't. I think I know you well enough to know you won't have the stomach for it. Not this way. That's what puzzles me so much. I've never known you to run away from anything."

"Jesus Christ, Ann! Didn't you ever hear of a surgeon turning a case down before? I've already told you I don't think my reputation can stand two big failures in a row. Not with an experimental technique. And it's my reputation that concerns me right now. So let's drop it— okay? We can discuss the whole thing when I get home. . . How are the kids?"

"Oh, fine," said Ann subdued. "Danny made me promise to remind you to get him that gismo he needs for his chem lab: a Pyrex condenser, I think. Oh, and Nick, I nearly forgot—Hank will be in New York. He's flying up today to attend the UN session Monday and will get in touch. Wants you to have dinner with him and a few of his VIP friends at Pavillon."

"I'm not sure I feel up to it."

"Might be interesting. Avery Sinclair will be there, and I know you like him. Also a suave Frenchman, name of Phillippe Delorme. Got his face scarred up in the war—which makes him ugly and terribly attractive at the same time. I had sort of a crush on him when I was fifteen. Not just a schoolgirl crush, either—an *amitié amoureuse*. He reciprocated in a way. Enough so I didn't dare go anywhere alone with him. Oh, who knows, I might have imagined the whole thing. I'll let you judge for yourself when you meet him. Observe the lupine look on his face when you mention my name."

"I'll bring my Minox."

"Then you'll go?"

"All right, I'll go."

9

Nick stepped off the curb and into the back seat of his father-in-law's chauffeur-driven limousine. He accepted Hank Stratton's vigorous handshake, but shied away from the arm embracing his shoulder. Unperturbed, Hank said: "Glad you could make it, Nick. . . . Ann tells me you two are going to Paris."

"Oh," Nick replied noncommittally.

"Wasn't she supposed to?"

He shrugged. "No secret, really. I still haven't decided whether or not to accept the invitation."

"I see," said Hank, and changed the subject.

Arriving at Pavillon, they were immediately taken in hand by the maitre d' and

led to a secluded, quiet table in the rear.
Two of Hank's guests waited at the bar:
Vincent Teller, recently retired counsellor
of the American Embassy in Moscow, and
Phillippe Delorme.

Hank introduced Nick to Teller first, a
tall, stooped man with the erosion of too
many Russian winters imprinted on his
gaunt face, then to Delorme.

"My wife, Ann, sends her greetings,"
Nick said, scrutinizing Delorme's
response. His reaction, however, was not
in his face, but in his hands, reaching out
in the semblance of an embrace.

"Ah, Ann. What an exquisite child she
was. I feel a great loss not having seen her
again. Like reading the first chapters of a
particularly interesting novel and then
misplacing the book."

"Nick and Ann have been invited to
Paris the end of this week," Hank said.
"I'm trying to convince my busy son-in-
law he should accept."

"What madness! Of course you should
accept," Delorme urged, before being cautioned by a subtle change in Nick's expression. "The moment your plane arrives
at Orly I will be at your disposal."

"When are you returning?" asked Hank.

He shrugged. "When the latest Mid-
East crisis is over and I can estimate the
price of a barrel of oil. Your country, I'm

sure, is also interested in that commodity."

"Indeed, we are," Teller answered coolly. "Among more important issues at stake."

Avery Sinclair, the missing member of Hank's table, made his entrance just as the waiter was serving the soup. Avery's was a familiar face: a former professor of political science at the University of Wisconsin, he had been enticed into government service by John Kennedy, and much to his friends' surprise and against their counsel, had stayed on in subsequent administrations as Assistant Secretary of State for European Affairs. A rumor Nick had heard that Avery finally had had his fill of Foggy Bottom seemed confirmed a moment later when he was asked to relate what stance the State Department was taking in the fast-developing Mideast crisis.

"Stance?" Avery exclaimed with a disgruntled shake of his head. "Hah! No one's willing to stand still long enough to even make footprints. They're all bending over taking each other's rectal temperature. You'd think the fools might've learned something about the dangers of consensus from the Bay of Pigs. It's not original thinking they want. It's job security!"

"That bad?" asked Hank.

"Morale's bad. Some of the talk I've heard recently sounds like it belongs on a psychiatrist's couch. I do more hand-holding in my section than work. I'm not honestly sure what their problem is. If I had to guess, I'd say it was the home front: the great, self-indulgent society out there who just can't get together on what they want this country to do. They demand clear-cut choices—cowboy and Indian stuff—and there aren't any."

Sinclair paused to season his soup, then continued: "But don't worry. I have enduring faith. The cavalry charge usually comes in the nick of time."

Sipping his wine, Nick grew preoccupied with the thin thread of Avery's dilemma that connected with his own. His theme was much the same as Canter's, although more discriminating, more deeply felt. He wondered what Avery would do if the choice, together with the special talents, were his? Chagrined, he felt he knew.

" . . . Another incredible blunder on Thant's part," Nick heard Teller say, as he began to listen again. "What must the man have been thinking? Not that we'll ever know. Too inscrutable! . . . Well, Avery, what's it to be? Do we back the Israelis or don't we?"

"Oh, I'm with you," Avery said. "A commitment's a commitment. . . . Come to think of it, Phillippe—France signed that commitment, too."

"*Oui*. But our interests lie heavily in that part of the world. The Israelis have shown they can take care of themselves. So must we."

"A ruthless brand of diplomacy, wouldn't you say?" Avery replied dourly.

Delorme shrugged. "Perhaps. I really don't think so. In order to protect your interests, you must be prepared for all eventualities. It's a state of mind. Like a surgeon's state of mind when he contemplates a risky operation. Isn't that so, Dr. Sten?"

"A surgeon would be considerably more ethical, I'd hope," said Nick.

"It's not a question of ethics, my young friend—but expediency. We French, forced to survive many enemy occupations, have learned that expediency is the keynote to existence. We bend and buckle but we do not break. I grant you, we are not always proud of what we do. But we do it, nonetheless. Our heritage must survive."

"I imagine the Jews feel the same way," said Nick.

"*D'accord.* They have my deepest admiration. Regrettably, it's no longer in our best interests to support them. This time we shall act in our own best interest. After all, when you run with the wolves, you must howl with the wolves."

"That's a Russian proverb, isn't it?" Nick asked.

"Even so," Delorme conceded, "it seems to apply. I look at war as perhaps you look at surgery—painful and ugly but often beneficial in outcome. Mankind makes progress through war."

"Wanton killing isn't my idea of progress," said Teller.

"Oh, but killing is necessary. I myself have killed many. My own people even. Only those who've never fought in a war think killing is difficult."

"I saw enough killing in Korea," said Nick.

"And did you yourself participate?"

"No. The army was quite emphatic they wanted live doctors, not dead heroes, so I was spared that experience."

"Fortunate for you," Delorme said with a tolerant smile. "As a non-physician, I was never given that choice. The only justification we war-killers have is that we fought in a just cause. . . . Now the Israelis must decide. My sympathies go with them."

"But not your government's?" said Teller.

"No. By their very nature, governments are much more corrupt than people. Since we as individuals are often loath to act morally, we allow governments to choose the lowest acceptable standards for us. Self-interest is paramount."

"Maybe for governments," said Nick. "But doesn't each of us have his own conscience to answer to?"

"Perhaps so. But as we French have learned, those answers change. After all, morality is only what the majority at any given time agrees upon. It was once moral to burn witches at the stake. Who knows what will be considered moral a thousand years from now?"

Nick was bemused by the way in which the conversation seemed to parallel his thoughts. Was it coincidence, he wondered, or had he subtly directed it?

The table talk returned to the current political crisis and continued spiritedly until eleven o'clock, when the group broke up. As he prepared to leave with the others, Nick was detained by his father-in-law. "Let's have a nightcap together," Hank suggested.

"Fine with me," Nick said, wishing to postpone the time when he would be back in his hotel room with time to think.

"It's probably none of my business," Hank began, "but you look like something's troubling you."

Nick debated whether he dared take Hank into his confidence. Doubtless Canter would frown on it. Well, the hell with Canter, he decided. He needed some level-headed advice.

"Know anybody in the CIA?" he asked.

"A few people. Why?"

"Know a fellow named Canter?" A flicker of change in Hank's expression forewarned Nick what to expect next.

"As a matter of fact, I do. We were in touch the other day."

Nick struggled to contain his rage. "So, the plot thickens. . . . All right, Hank. No more pretend games. Tell me how much you know. Who's Karamanov?"

"A Russian physicist. They want you to operate on him—unsuccessfully."

Exhaling audibly, Nick gulped down the remainder of his drink and poured himself another. "Knowing as much as you do, what would you advise?"

"It's a brutal choice."

"It's murder! That's what it is. Maybe Phillippe could sanction it—I can't! His philosophy is completely distasteful to me. . . . How deep did they involve you in all this?"

"They only wanted Canter to sound me out as to how you were likely to react. I made no attempt to predict. I only went so far as to assure him that, regardless of your decision, you could be trusted to keep silent about the mission."

"But I couldn't, could I? I told you."

"I maneuvered you into it."

"Good Christ! Don't tell me the whole evening was for my benefit!"

"Calm down, Nick. I only meant I had Canter's permission to discuss it with you. If you hadn't brought it up, I would have."

"Then why didn't you—earlier?"

"I couldn't. . . . Look, I know how you'd react if I said you were like a son to me. So I won't. I'll spare you any maudlin sentiment. Let me just say, I care what happens to you. You can accept that, can't you? I'm willing to live with any decision you make."

"Easier than I," Nick replied with a wry smile. . . . "Say I *do* go—what about Ann? She can't possibly go with me. What do I tell her?"

"You've taken trips without her before."

"Sure. Only this isn't a trip to the Mayo Clinic she'd be missing. It's Paris!"

"Tell her it's a last-minute decision."

"She'll still want to go. . . . It'll lead to one hell of a brawl."

"Well, you've had those before."

"Oh, sure. But this time I may not be around later to patch things up. Canter made that clear. What happens to Ann then? My kids?"

"Ann and the children will be well taken care of. If worse comes to worse, they'll come live with me—just as when you were in Korea. They're my family too, God knows. I'll provide for them the best I can."

Nick stared. Hank's assurances had been offered so matter-of-factly that he almost suspected his father-in-law wanted him to die. Then Ann would finally be dependent on him. It seemed morbid, irrational—yet it was the one thing Hank acted irrational about.

"If anything *did* happen to me," Nick answered deliberately, "you'd be the last person Ann would turn to. She'd try to get as far away from you as possible."

Hank drew back. "What do you mean?"

"You know how Ann feels about you—about men in general. Oh, I don't blame you for her shortcomings—not altogether—but damn it, she's not your wife or your ward, she's your daughter! She's still waiting for you to treat her like a grown woman. . . . So she had a few affairs before we were married, stop trying to make her out a whore. She's hung up enough over sex already."

"Whose fault is that? Did it ever occur to you it may be more yours than mine?" Hank accused. "After all, you've been married to her for nineteen years—you might've remedied it by now. Maybe the reason she's unresponsive has more to do with your actions than mine."

"Meaning what?"

"Oh, I don't doubt your virility. But don't tell me in all your years of marriage, you've never given Ann any reason to wonder how faithful you've been?"

"All women wonder. Have anything more specific in mind?"

"Maybe I'm being unfair—"

"Be unfair! Come on, Hank. If you've got something to say—say it!"

Hank's innuendo sickened Nick with the taste of old, indigestible truth. Did he really know about Noelle? And if he knew, did he tell Ann? Nick suspected so, but was afraid to ask—knowing he could never face his wife again if she'd known all these years. It would be too humiliating.

"Well? . . ." he prompted.

"No, nothing." Hank said finally. "I know you've tried to be a good husband, Nick, just as I have tried to be a good father. I've tried every means I could to get closer to Ann. In your case, I'd say the opposite was true. You've never made Ann feel she's a very important part of your life. She's never been able to get close to you. Something stands in the way."

"What?"

"You're far too ambitious. There are people who say you operated on Adam Blair mainly to serve such ambitions."

Nick's uneasiness over Ann rapidly gave way to anger.

"I don't give a damn what they say! I operated on Adam because he needed operating on!"

"There are some who feel you'd have been better advised to wait. That your gas gun wasn't all that safe."

"The Russians don't think so! They're willing to risk the life of their greatest physicist on the premise I know what I'm doing."

"The Russians are desperate."

"So am I—all of a sudden! So far you've told me I've failed my wife, my patients, my profession! Now my country!"

"Easy, Nick," he urged, gesturing placatingly.

"Easy, hell! I don't have that choice anymore. Not if I'm foolish enough to get on that plane. Then my only choice is to be murderous or suicidal!"

"Then don't go."

"I didn't plan to. At least I didn't a few minutes ago. Now I'm not so sure. If I'm such a coldly ambitious bastard, why give up a chance to play God?"

"You don't mean that."

"Don't I? You might be more right than you think. Maybe all I do care about is myself. Ever since Canter visited me today, all I've thought about is me, my future, nobody else. I know I can't kill Karamanov—any man—and keep operating again. I'd be finished as a surgeon. I'd also probably be dead."

"You're overwrought," Hank said. "I beg you, think this over carefully."

"I don't know . . . I don't know what I think anymore. At least, you've convinced me of one thing: I won't be as missed around home as I thought. Ann will have you. My kids will have a Presidental citation to hang up—and maybe a future." Nick returned his glass to the bar and reached for his coat. "It's been quite a day."

"Lunch tomorrow?"

"No, afraid not. My talk is scheduled for 10:00 A.M., and I'm getting out of this crazy town as soon after that as I can."

Nick refused a ride back to his hotel in Hank's limousine and started to walk crosstown. Though the crisp night air felt refreshing against his flushed face, he still seethed with frustration and anger. The thought of a physician willfully killing his patient was repugnant to him; as repugnant as a priest axing down one of his parishioners in the middle of confession. Yet, if Canter were right—as probably he was—the Russians would use the Karamanov system to dominate the world; make the next small crisis the final solution to the ideological struggle. And

there went the Israelis, the Indochinese,
the Sten family, for the next hundred
years. Goddamn it! Nick railed, cursing
the circumstances that had entangled him
in this insoluable quandary, this Chinese
finger trap that the more you resisted the
tighter it gripped.

After crossing Third Avenue, his pace
suddenly slowed. Ahead of him, two
youths in satin jackets sauntered along
taking up the middle of the sidewalk.
Casting an insolent glance over their
shoulders at passersby, they intentionally walked slower whenever anyone
attempted to pass. Nick approached, just
as a bearded older man a step in front of
him was nudged off the curb.

Nick felt his cheeks begin to warm as he
fell into line behind them. Their pace
lagged even further on hearing his footsteps and they separated to cover the full
width of the sidewalk. Timing his forward
progress to coincide with the taller one's
drift to the right, Nick moved inside him,
colliding hard with his shoulder as he
passed.

"Excuse me,' he mumbled brusquely.

Before he could take another step, he
felt a hand grip his arm. "Hold it a minute.
Kinda crowdin' a little, ain't ya?"

Nick swung around, forcing his accuser
to take a backward step. He peered into

the sneering face. "You don't mind my using part of the sidewalk, do you?"

"If I'm using it—yeah, I do mind. Damn right, I mind! Maybe you'd better get back where you was." He gestured with his hand.

"If that's the way you want it," Nick said, stepping back slightly as if to turn away; then, as his weight came down on his left foot, pivoting sharply and driving his elbow into the youth's gut. There was a sudden whoop of released air, followed by the grunts and gurgles of retching as he doubled up and buckled at the knees. His shorter, stockier buddy stepped up to steady him. Nick saw his free hand drifting toward his jacket pocket and smashed the side of his fist into his elbow. He felt the crack of bone against bone and the arm went limp.

The squat one glowered at him through his pain. "We'll be looking you up later, mister."

"You just do that, punk," answered Nick, debating whether to hit him again but deciding to end it there.

A small crowd had begun to gather. Ignoring the questions blurted at him, Nick unhurriedly walked away. . . . Jesus, a street brawl! he marveled. What had possessed him? But the reason didn't seem to matter. He had been thwarted

once too often, and with the flush of
excitement still strong in him, he vowed
that no one, not father-in-law nor government agents nor sidewalk bullies, would
thwart him again. He hadn't experienced
such primitive, blood-lusting anger since
Korea.

Though he deplored a government using
a physician as a political weapon, this
issue alone no longer dissuaded him.
Counterbalancing it was the compulsion
he now felt to explore the limits of his
physical courage. He knew he had killed
people before. Unintentionally, of course,
but they ended up just as dead. A mistake
in judgment here, a laxity there—it all
added up. It added up to more than a few.
So why all the soul-searching over killing
one more: a menacing Russian? But could
he actually kill Karamanov? He wasn't
certain he could. He was considerably
more certain, however, that this was too
dangerous a man to let live.

Nick unclenched his teeth, realizing he
had reached some sort of preliminary decision. He'd call Canter in the morning and
tell him he would go to Paris, commit himself that far—but not all the way. He
would postpone making the more crucial,
bloodletting decision until some later date
and in that way preserve for the future
two of his most useful illusions: the
already shaky myth of his God-fearing

humanity, and the slim hope that, with the greatest of good fortune, Karamanov might yet die unassisted.

He didn't know if Canter would agree to such a hedging compromise, but he didn't intend to give him a choice; even if Canter should buy it, there was still the problem of what to tell Ann.

10

The pounding of Federov's fist on the thick oak door of Lieutenant General Bogdanov's Moscow apartment rended the early morning quiet and reverberated loudly within the dwelling. Inside the bedroom, Bogdanov stirred. A second volley of knocks wakened him fully and he tried to rise, only to find himself entangled in the willowy limbs of the girl sleeping beside him: his personal choice from among the ranks of the Ministry's language school to help him rehabilitate his knowledge of French.

With his right arm pinioned underneath her, Bogdanov reached out with his left, pushing her pliant breast and shoulder off him. He next tried to withdraw his thigh from its warm entrapment between hers,

but she refused to yield, tightening the
vise and returning her shoulder to its
former position with a sigh.

Gently but firmly, Bogdanov shook her
awake.

"Again, Denis? Yes, again," she pleaded
amorously. Her body suddenly tensed as
she heard the next paroxysm of knocking.

"Who is disturbing us?" she asked with
a quiver of apprehension. Disentangling
herself, she groped about on the floor
beside the bed for the blanket.

"Don't be alarmed, Yulyotchka," Bogdanov soothed. "You're as safe here as in
Kosygin's bedroom. Quick now, hide yourself, while I find out who's out there."

Switching on the bedside lamp, Bogdanov was momentarily amused to see her
nude backside scamper out of bed and into
the bathroom. He grabbed his robe off the
arm of the chair and barely had it on when
his visitor began to pound the beleaguered
door again.

"Who's there?" he shouted as he turned
the lock and opened the door on the latch.

"It's me, Federov, Comrade General."

"The devil take you, Federov!" Unfast-
ening the latch, he flung the door wide
open to confront his unwelcome deputy.

Federov, a powerful man with huge
arms and shoulders and a polio-weakened
right leg, stood transfixed by the hostile
glint in Bogdanov's eye. Shifting his

weight to his stronger leg, he assumed a posture of full military attention.

"Well, don't just stand there like an ox!" Bogdanov scolded—then relented as he saw the befuddled look on his deputy's face. "Come in, Yacov. Come in," he said, grasping his arm and ushering him into the living room.

Bogdanov turned and glanced at the clock on his mantel: a family heirloom that had not stopped ticking in his lifetime. Its eternal performance represented another of the Armenian superstitions passed on by his mother.

"You're three, four hours early!" he accused. "Our train's not scheduled to leave till noon."

"The trip has been called off. By direct order of Marshal Malinivski."

"What!" Bogdanov exclaimed, momentarily staggered. "Explain!"

"Are you alone, Denis?" Federov asked warily.

"No. My French instructress from the language section is here with me," he replied, briefly losing his harried expression. "We crammed late into the night."

Federov managed a grin. Lowering his voice, he said: "The treacherous Israelis have attacked Egypt. A massive air strike. We received word of it from Cairo less than an hour ago."

Bogdanov's brow furrowed as he

digested the news. Reaching into the pocket of his robe for a pack of Pimar Filters he withdrew one and, after accepting a light from his subordinate, seated himself on the arm of the couch. Federov, standing opposite him, awaited his reaction intently, expecting a sharp outburst. To his surprise, he saw Bogdanov smile.

"A fascinating development. It succeeded grandly, I presume."

Federov nodded. "The Egyptian Air Force was at their mercy. Very few of their planes got off the ground."

"Hah! What primitives they are," Bogdanov scorned. "Didn't their radar warn them?"

"The Israelis used some electronic trickery we didn't know they possessed to distort the radar pattern. A dozen airports were hit before our interceptors drove them off."

"Brilliant! And not so disastrous as you might think. Neither side can defeat the other, and as long as we and the Americans stay out of it again, it's unlikely to get far out of hand. So, with that in mind to assuage your patriotism, picture what another Israeli victory might mean to us. To you and me, old friend. . . . Don't you see, Yacov, the biggest loser to come out of this is likely to be our mutual devil—Stakhanov. Who else seemed more complacent over the outcome? 'This time the Arabs couldn't lose,' he predicted. The military advisors and superior weaponry we'd provided them made it all a foregone conclusion, according to him. . . . Well, we tried to warn him, didn't we? There are still a few intangibles that determine the outcome of any battle. Now, of course, Stakhanov's rash predictions are a matter of record. And so are ours. You see what a favorable position it puts us in? The only bothersome feature is how all this might affect Karamanov's surgery. What were you told of that?"

"Nothing directly. My only orders were to instruct you to remain in Moscow and report immediately to the Ministry. . . . Forgive me, Denis, I meant to tell you that sooner."

"No matter. It's inconceivable to me they'd cancel the trip, especially now when they face another confrontation with the Americans. But to delay our departure for even a few days might wreck our delicate timetable—risk the chance the American surgeon arrives in Paris before we've made the necessary preparations."

"Have you received word from Marandat yet as to the American's intentions?" Federov asked.

"There's that problem, too. My only encouragement is that he didn't refuse outright. How far along are you in preparing the good doctor's dossier?''

"I received additional information on him from our Chicago *rezident* just yesterday. It's in my office. A much more detailed report on Marandat is being completed.''

"It's Sten I'm concerned about!" Bogdanov snapped. "It's Sten that interrupts my sleep at night. I intend to know him as intimately as I knew my dear, dead brother. If not beforehand, then in Paris. But I need the additional time,'' he said, emphasizing the urgency he felt with the slap of his fist into his palm.

"I'll supply you with whatever I can.''

"I know you will, trusted friend,'' he said, squeezing his arm. "Now wait for me in the limousine while I dress.''

Watching his deputy's gaze shift to the bedroom, Bogdanov was abruptly reminded of his lissome guest shivering in the poorly heated bathroom. "Give me a few extra minutes. World crisis or not, I just can't throw her out. . . . Besides, there are still a few verb conjugations I want to run through with her,'' he added straight-faced.

After Federov's departure, he spent a pensive moment at the window watching the turbulent flow of the Moskva River and the soldier games of a handful of children near the entrance to Kremlin Park. Then, snuffing out the butt of his cigarette, he went into the cramped, closet-sized kitchenette, installed in such bachelor apartments by the economy-minded Ministry of State Housing, to brew a pot of tea. Once the kettle was underway, he reentered the bedroom and finding it vacant continued on to the bathroom. There, to his amusement, he found Yulya huddled in the tub, concealed up to her nose by the quilted bed comforter.

"My God, Denis," she said breathlessly. "What kept you? The place is as cold as an outhouse."

"The heat should have gone on at 6:00 A.M. The furnace must be out. But come now, get dressed. I must leave at once for the Ministry."

"No. I refuse to move until I'm warm again. Warm me yourself, Denis," she asked plaintively.

"I'm afraid there's no time. Don't be difficult, Yulyotchka."

Rebuffed, she stared petulantly for a moment, then announced: "I'm not moving."

"We'll see," said Bogdanov. He engaged her in a brief tug-of-war and yanked the comforter from her hands.

"*Cochon!*" she cried, and struggled to raise her unclad body from the slippery-cold porcelain surface of the tub.

He watched admiringly from the doorway as Yulya bent under the shower

curtain pipe and stepped out on the tile
floor, her firm, globular breasts bouncing
against her chest. She had provided him
with a pleasurable evening and, though
preoccupied with far more important
matters for the moment, he was reluctant
to see her go. After working tirelessly for
days planning the Paris venture, formula-
ting countermoves to a thousand unlikely
contingencies, the brief interlude with
Yulya seemed well earned. He had been
patient with her, allowed himself two
extra days to gain her confidence, and the
blossoming response he had drawn made
his sexless vigil of the past several weeks
well worth the wait. He could, of course,
have enjoyed her sooner, ordered her into
his bed with the same unassailable authority that could command her to salute. But
had he done so, she doubtless would have
been less of a woman, and he, in turn,
much less of a man.

Though the acquisition and proper use
of power had been a lifelong fascination,
Bogdanov used his own sparingly. His apprenticeship in the KGB was over: the te-
dious years spent as an embassy attache
in Ankara and the more eventful ones in a
Chinese prisoner-of-war camp on the Man-
churian border. It was during the Korea
War that Bogdanov had established his
worth as an intelligence officer. The
technique of total sensory deprivation he

had helped pioneer was, until the early
1960's, the most effective and devastating
means known to overcome an enemy's will
to resist. Nowadays, the method was
rarely used; it had been supplanted by a
new family of drugs that accomplished the
same purpose far more safely, and rather
than regretting its obsolescence Bogdanov was secretly relieved. The procedure, at best, had been too punishing, too
difficult to control. If carried beyond
certain ill-defined limits, the victim's
sanity was shattered along with his will.
Once fully aware of its perils, Bogdanov's
interest in the technique waned and he
could no longer share his Chinese
colleagues' enthusiasm for its continued
use. It became an episode in his life that,
useful as it had been to his career, estab-
lishing his capacity for ruthlessness at a
time in the Stalinist era when such a
display was mandatory for advancement,
Bogdanov found difficult to stomach. But
he had progressed far beyond that
experience now; he was a member of the
elite, as highly skilled in his special way as
was the American surgeon—and he was
determined to use all his considerable
craft to remain there, never to revert to
such grueling assignments again.

Lieutenant General Bogdanov's Chayka
limousine, chauffeured by Federov,

arrived at the gates of 2 Dzerzhinski Square shortly before 9:00 A.M. and was promptly admitted ahead of a procession of similar cars awaiting security clearance. Perfunctorily saluting the three sets of guards they passed en route from the subterranean parking ramp to the elevator leading to ground level, they entered a rear door of the drab, soot-caked building housing the headquarters of the KGB, together with a large portion of the world's most advanced electronic equipment.

The meeting site was a cavernous auditorium, slightly smaller than the orchestra floor of the Bolshoi Theater but with the same red velvet upholstery on its chairs. A large portrait of Lenin hung in the foreground of the otherwise windowless and bare-walled room. Federov separated from him to sit in the third tier of seats, while Bogdanov took the last remaining chair at the oversized conference table occupying the center platform. He was barely seated when he jumped to his feet with the others as Malinivski entered the room. Reseating himself as soon as the Defense Minister permitted it, he undid the top few buttons of his tunic enough to withdraw a small notebook and pack of cigarettes from his inside pocket and placed them on the table. The room was darkened at Malinivski's command and a screen lowered to receive a televised report of the latest developments in the Mideast crisis transmitted from the War Room of the Kremlin. Following the briefing, Malinivski took the podium and offered his own analysis of the situation, shifting the focus of his diatribe from the perfidy of the Israelis to that shown by his own intelligence service in failing to alert him to the surprise attack.

Malinivski continued in this vein until noon when his strident voice began to croak and he concluded with a stern warning: "Failures such as this cannot be tolerated! The fault must be shared by all, and all of you will suffer our wrath once assessments are made. Remember that when you return to work this afternoon, comrades. Remember it the next time you are tempted to place personal ambition above the welfare of the Motherland!"

Malinivski's parting innuendo lingered in Bogdanov's mind as he gathered up his notebook and cigarettes and searched for Federov's head in the moving crowd. He was about to follow after him when he was intercepted by Colonel Pavel Nederov, Malinivki's aide-de-camp.

"The Defense Minister would like a few moments to confer with you, Comrade General."

Bogdanov nodded. "Where?"

"Your office will be suitable. No transcript."

"Very well," said Bogdanov. "I will inform my deputy not to wait for me and meet him there directly."

A few minutes later, Bogdanov climbed the stairs to his second-floor office and unlocked the door. He had barely time to adjust his intercom when Malinivski was upon him and Nederov stationed outside the door.

"Shall I order a little lunch sent up?" Bogdanov offered.

"No. I have no appetite after this morning's debacle. I could use a drink, however. What beverages do you provide?"

Bogdanov removed his key chain and unlocked a file cabinet to his rear. "Vodka, kirsch and a half bottle of Canadian whiskey."

Malinivski beamed. "Let us proceed to finish off the Canadian. Paper cups will do."

Bogdanov removed two cups from the dispenser by his sink and poured them three-fourths full. He passed one to his visitor, then held up his own in anticipation of the customary toast.

"To Mother Russia," the Defense Minister said.

"To the Motherland."

Malinivski savored his first mouthful of the whiskey, took another, then rested his cup on the desk. "You were quite correct in your predictions of the Israeli response, but I needn't tell you that. Nonetheless, it is to your credit. We have a great need for bright young men like you, Bogdanov. We need them urgently. But before you allow such praise to swell your head, let me tell you my feelings about bright young men. I don't trust them. Admittedly, their breadth of vision is greater than mine, but they have blind spots where the enemy is concerned. Lacking precise knowledge, they show a deplorable tendency to gamble. . . . I presume, of course, you know what I'm referring to. The arrangements you've made for Karamanov's surgery represent a colossal gamble. I, personally, would never have had the rashness to propose it. To fail is to perish into the oblivion of the Anti-Heroes. . . . What will happen to that imbecile Stakhanov, after today, would be quite inconsequential in comparison to what we'd have in store for you. The two are related, however, as I shall explain in a moment." Malinivski paused to empty his cup. He nodded his thanks as Bogdanov immediately refilled it, and his own, from the bottle.

"Essentially, what I have to tell you is that Stakhanov is finished. He will be relieved of his command within the month. The members of the Politburo have considered only two men to replace him: yourself and Ivan Kharitom. You, Bogdanov, are their first choice—at least, for the present. Ivan Ivanovitch, however, is ready to leave his post in Vietnam and step in the moment you falter. Naturally, we all hope you don't. Your fate and Karamanov's are now inseparable. Russia needs both of you!"

"I pray I will be worthy," Bogdanov said resolutely. "I take it, then, the plan to transport Karamanov is still operational?"

Malinivski nodded. "The special train has been delayed only one day. It will leave at noon tomorrow."

"Good," Bogdanov said, draining his second cup of whiskey.

He remained at his desk another hour after Malinivski had left, waiting for Federov to return, and then left with him for his apartment. Arriving home, he was relieved to find only Sasha, his houseboy, there to greet him. Yulya, he was told, had vacated the apartment around midmorning. The expression on the houseboy's face indicated the two of them had exchanged words and Bogdanov was amused, half-wishing he had allowed her to stay but knowing he needed solitude in which to work. He would labor diligently through his reports, then invite her to spend the evening with him. The events of the day had suffused him with rampant energy and he could think of no better way of releasing it than sexually.

Dispelling Yulya from his mind with some difficulty, Bogdanov removed the unfinished dossier Federov had compiled on the American surgeon and began to read. He completed the brief document five minutes later, feeling no better informed about the man than if he had passed him on the street. It barely interested him to learn that Nicholas Sten was a competent surgeon—he'd assumed that —or that his ambition was to become chief of surgery at his university. What did claim his attention was a rumor that Sten might have become involved with a French girl during his military tour of duty in Korea. It was mere hearsay, according to the report; the gossip of correspondents in the area. But it could be true, he speculated, and if so, he might be able to use it. . . . Who is this Noelle Cardin? French, attractive, a psychologist —but what else is there to know about her? And where was she now? It was imperative they find out at once. If Sten did love her—loves her still?—might he try to contact her if she were in Paris? . . . The possibilities seemed numerous and of a sort Bogdanov knew how to make best use of. Together, they might provide him a glimpse into the complicated—and vulnerable—inner man.

Bogdanov returned the report to his briefcase and poured himself a drink,

sipping it by the window. Nicholas Sten,
he thought; next to Karamanov, the most
valuable man on earth. *I wonder if you
realize that, Dr. Sten?* . . . No, of course,
you don't. Not yet, anyway. But there's
always the possibility you might; the
American intelligence network might have
made greater inroads into our security
than I care to think about. And if that's
truly the case, then it will be you and I in
the arena, Dr. Sten. Just the two of us.

11

Adam Blair's funeral service began at 10:00 A.M. at the Frautschi Funeral Home West, the more decorative, suburban branch of the establishment, and concluded three hours later at the Forest Hill Cemetery. Nick, feeling he bore a special onus as Adam's unsuccessful surgeon, was thoroughly depressed by the proceedings. It upset him to think of so vital a man dead. A gambler to the last, Adam had been willing to stake the precarious few years he had left on the slim hope Nick could make him well again. The thought of ending up his life as a mute cripple, wheeled back and forth among the rooms of his rambling house by some hired attendant, was utterly repugnant to such a proud man. "The last concession I made

to age was to give up sex at the age of
sixty-four," he once told Nick. "This old
carcass of mine pulled itself together like a
thoroughbred getting his last crack at the
money and it was a damned fine time . . ."

"You're smiling," Ann whispered,
nudging him.

"I'm what?"

"Smiling," she repeated.

"Oh."

"What in the world are you thinking?"

"Nothing important . . . . How long do
you think this is likely to go on?"

"A good hour at least. The Governor
hasn't spoken yet. So settle down before
you start attracting attention."

"Everybody knows I'm here, love. You
can bet your boots on that."

Ann dropped Nick off at the hospital
before going on home and freshening up
for her dinner date with an old school
chum. Brigit Chatfield—"Bebe" to her
intimates, of whom Ann reluctantly considered herself to be one—had flown into
town that morning, fresh from Nevada
and her second divorce. Ann had helped
console her the last go-round and was now
expected to perform that function again.

"I should be back around nine—okay?"
Ann said to him as she pulled the car up to
the entrance.

"Fine," Nick replied, adding unwisely: "Don't drink too much."

"Don't operate *too* much!" she answered sharply: "*Chacun à son goût,* huh, Nick?"

The edge to Ann's voice surprised him. He wondered if it had anything to do with the unmentioned Paris trip. "All right, see you later," he said and climbed out of the car.

Nick spent the rest of the afternoon making the final preparations for his trip. He filled out a leave-of-abscence form, canceled his scheduled surgery for the next two weeks, and finally, resolutely, cabled Marandat that he would arrive in Paris on the ninth. Though he had managed to simulate a casual, almost buoyant pose while dictating the cablegram to his secretary, his face tightened into a scowl as soon as she left the room. The communication symbolized his active commitment to the mission. But he hadn't really made up his mind to kill Karamanov yet. He had postponed that decision, just as he had postponed dealing with Ann.

At six, just as he was preparing to leave his office, the phone rang.

"Nick? Jim Belmano."

"What's up?"

"You're having the damnedest run of

luck. They just wheeled Perlmutter into the E.R. Convulsed twice in the ambulance, I'm told, and once before I got here. Right now, he's comatose. Doesn't respond to painful stimuli so I guess he's pretty deep."

Perlmutter! Nick thought, shaken. A big, balding man and a brilliant aeronautical engineer. Next to Adam Blair, his most famous patient: a double lesion—the first one he had operated on successfully.

"Any localizing signs?" he asked reflexly.

"Neurologically, he shows bilateral Babinski's and flaccid extremities, but nothing focal so far. His pupils are dilated, too. They react maybe a millimeter or so to light, but no more."

"What do you make of it?"

"He might be postconsulvie right now, but I doubt it. Looks more like brain-stem involvement to me."

"Jesus!" Nick groaned at the grim pronouncement. "Has anyone gone over him medically?"

"Cramer, the medical resident, is here with me now."

"What does he think?"

"A brain-stem stroke, too. He's hitching him up for a cardiogram right now. Anything else you want done before you get here?"

"Just keep him alive. I'll be over as fast as I can."

What the hell was happening? Nick wondered incredulously. What kind of curse had he fallen under? First Adam and now Abe Perlmutter. His patients were coming back to him to die like a herd of stricken elephants!

"Room two, Dr. Sten," the duty nurse said as he entered the emergency room.

Nick picked up the chart on Perlmutter from her desk and read the medical resident's note. He was about to put it down when the temperature recording in the upper right-hand corner caught his eye: 96 degrees. Abe's body temperature shouldn't be that low, unless—hypoglycemia! But why should he have a low blood sugar? They had known at the time of Abe's surgery that he was a borderline diabetic, but since he was also grossly overweight they felt he could be managed with diet alone. Not so the physician who cared for him back home. Nick now recalled Abe had written he'd been advised to take a pill by the name of chlorpropamide and asked his opinion of it. He had opposed it, preferring that Abe lose weight first, then have his sugar level rechecked. But just how strongly he had expressed such opposition escaped him for the moment—and maybe Abe had not listened. He was a gourmet cook and a big eater, Nick knew, so instead of sticking to his diet he may have decided to try the pills—unaware of their potential danger.

Oh, merciful God! If only that were it, Nick prayed. If only Abe had taken an overdose of chlorpropamide and was now in hypoglycemic coma, he had a chance of coming out of it alive. Even more than alive, for his brain, now short-circuited by its lack of sugar, convulsing him with its unsatisfied demands, could also be salvaged if he received the proper treatment in time.

"How is he?" Nick asked, joining Jim Belmano and Cramer in the examining room.

"Still alive," said Jim.

"Good boy. Now get hold of the nurse and tell her to fill up a big syringe with fifty percent glucose. Got it?"

"Right," Jim replied, wise enough in the ways of his chief not to question a direct order.

Cramer, on the other hand, unaware of the personality change Nick underwent when he was severely stressed, made the mistake of challenging him. "Why glucose?" he asked, glancing back over his shoulder from his position at bedside.

Nick reached forward, spun him around, and lifted him almost bodily out of his way. "Let me borrow your stethoscope," he said, yanking it from his neck.

A flustered Cramer, his jaw seemingly unhinged by Nick's brusqueness, relinquished the stethoscope without protest and moved out of his way. It took him another few moments to recover his voice. "I still don't get it," he stammered.

"You don't, huh? . . . Here, hand me that reflex hammer. Well, I'll tell you something else you didn't get—a history! A history, Cramer, the most essential step in making a diagnosis."

"But he's unconscious!"

"Sure, he's unconscious," Nick said, testing Abe's tendon reflexes while he talked. "But Jim told you his name, didn't he? He had a wallet on him, didn't he? From that you might've found his telephone number. You might even have gotten to talk to his wife. And from her," he said, walking around to the opposite side of the table, "from her, you might've gotten some history."

"You mean, he's a diabetic?"

"I mean, he *might be* a diabetic. If so, what does that suggest to you?"

"It suggests . . . hypoglycemia. Oh God, what an idiot I am! Is that what you think's wrong?"

"I won't be sure until I get some glucose into him and he wakes up. But it fits. Convulsions, dilated pupils, hypothermia, a little froth around his mouth. Everything's there, except a bracelet around his wrist telling you, I Am a Diabetic. How long's he been out like this, anyway?''

"Hard to say for sure. He was found like this by the maid in his hotel room around five o'clock. The ambulance got him here by five thirty. I saw him about ten minutes after that, then called Jim.''

Nick glanced at his watch—almost six thirty. "Where the hell's that glucose?'' he shouted out the door, feeling an added sense of urgency.

"Find me a vein,'' he said a moment later. "A big, fat vein. Stick a syringe with an eighteen-gauge needle on the end into it and keep it open for me. I'm going to find out what's holding things up.''

"Will do,'' Cramer said.

Nick located Jim and the nurse in the treatment room preparing the glucose injection.

"Just about got it drawn up, Nick,'' Jim said, pulling the last few cubic centimeters of the syrupy solution into the syringe.

"Good. Give it here,'' he said, taking it out of Jim's hands and delivering it himself to the examining room. "Got that vein?'' he asked.

"Right here,'' said Cramer. He pulled back on his syringe until it was filled with enough blood for a sugar determination, then, grasping the hub of the needle with thumb and forefinger, steadied it so that the syringe Nick held could replace his own.

Nick made the switch and pulled back gently on the handle until a trickle of blood entered the barrel, then injected the concentrated sugar solution into Perlmutter's blood stream. "Jesus, look at the way my hand's shaking!" he exclaimed, as he pushed the syringeful past the halfway mark. "You'd never know I was a surgeon, would you?"

"You'd know," said Jim.

The three of them lapsed into a tense silence. The patient showed no response.

"How long's it been since I gave him the stuff?" Nick asked.

"Two minutes, I'd say," Jim answered.

"All right, let's try this." Leaning over the edge of the examining table, Nick began to slap Abe on the cheek, lightly at first, then more vigorously. A mental image of him doing the same thing for Adam Blair flashed across his mind and started his lips quivering. Abe's head rocked passively from side to side, but he remained unresponsive; Nick began to despair of ever rousing him.

One more, he thought resolutely. One good hard one in memory of big Abe. Arching his arm back fully, Nick unleashed a blow that struck his patient's face with a resounding slap and was followed almost immediately by a cry of pain.

Abe opened his eyes, blinked several times, and said in a perplexed voice: "Hey, you son of a bitch, stop hitting me! What's got into you?"

"Stop, hell!" said Nick. "I'm not stopping until I beat a little sense into you."

"What for?" Abe protested.

"For taking those diabetic pills without my permission."

"Diabetic pills? . . . I was going to tell you," he admitted sheepishly. "I'm also back on my diet."

"Are you?"

"Yeah, really. Believe it or not, I hardly had anything to eat all day."

"You believe that, Jim?" Nick asked, straight-faced.

"I believe it. I believe it," Jim answered with a grin.

12

The exuberance that filled Nick when, once again, life returned to a dying man sustained him all the way home from Perlmutter's bedside. He felt he could cope with Ann now. An opening strategy had already hatched in his mind and he was ready to spring it on her the moment he stepped through the door.

But he had counted on her being there. The absence of her car from their driveway disturbed him. Abe's aftercare had taken several hours and it was now almost midnight, far too late for Ann to be out without him.

Where was she at this hour? Where and with whom and how much was she drinking? Too much, certainly, and probably in

some dingy, dangerous hole-in-the-wall
that Bebe thought quaint.

Nick's irritation grew as he trudged up
the stairs, then gave way to a surge of
husbandly concern on entering the bedroom and sensing an echo of past loving,
past loneliness. A small fear flickered in
his brain: she was out drinking as well as
driving and the combination of the two
created a well-recognized hazard. She
might have cracked up on some deserted
side street, developed engine trouble along
a lonely country road. She might be in the
hands of the police, or hands far worse.
Damn her for worrying him like that! But
maybe he was judging her too hastily?
Maybe she had called while he was at the
hospital and left word with one of the kids
as to when she would return.

He crossed the hall into Danny's room
and found his son sleeping with the lights
on.

"Mom call?" he asked, nudging him
gently.

"Nope. Uh-uh," Danny muttered,
shaking his head. "Get the light for me,
will you, Dad?"

"Sure thing," Nick said, turning to
leave.

"Everything's okay, isn't it?" his son
asked, more awake now.

"Everything's fine. Go back to sleep."

So she hadn't called, Nick thought with

a resurgence of anger. Now what do I do—
phone the police and make a fool of
myself? No, call Bebe, he decided.

He dialed the Edgewater Hotel and
asked to be put through to Mrs.
Chatfield's room. Bebe responded after
several rings.

"H . . . Hello," she stammered huskily.

"Bebe?"

"Uh-huh. Who is it?"

"This is Nick Sten calling. Is Ann
there?"

"Ann?" Bebe puzzled. "You woke me up
from a sound sleep to ask that? What the
hell would Ann be doing here at this hour?
Where is she, anyway?"

"That's what I'm trying to find out."

"Gee, Nick," she said, more conciliatory,
"I broke up with her around nine, then
turned in for the night."

"Where'd you leave her?"

"I guess at the bar. Maybe at the elevator—somewhere around there."

"Did she seem okay to you? Fit to
drive?"

"Oh sure. A little moodier than usual,
but otherwise okay. The two or three
drinks she had shouldn't faze her a bit."

"Were you alone?"

"There was one fellow—a Brad something—who hung around for a little while,
then left."

Brad Rollins, thought Nick: a recently

divorced neighbor. He and Ann occasion-
ally played tennis together. "Okay. . . .
Well, thanks anyway. Good night."

He let Bebe's parting expression of
concern go unanswered and hung up the
phone. He debated whether or not to call
the bartender at the Edgewkater and decided against it. He knew the man and
wasn't particularely eager to confess to
him that it was past midnight and he
didn't know where his wife was.

He wandered about the house for the
next several minutes, from the TV set in
the living room to the bookcase in the den,
but remained too preoccupied over Ann's
whereabouts to be distracted for very
long.

"Son of a bitch!" he said aloud, slam-
ming the book in his hand against the
shelf, as the clock in the den chimed one.
His shirt felt glued to his back and he removed it, stripping down to his undershirt. His mental state, however, remained
overheated. If Ann didn't show up in the
next five minutes, they were going to have
one hell of a row, Nick vowed, momentarily forgetting the deception he planned
and slipping into the more familiar role of
irate husband.

He paced the floor for the arbitrary five
minutes, and then, when his wife nowhere
in sight, was about to swallow his pride
and phone the bar at the Edgewater when

he heard the sound of tires scraping against the gravel in their driveway. Certain it was Ann, he took a diver's deep breath, exhaled slowly, and went to the door to meet her.

Relief turned to surprise, then to dismay as he stared into the semidarkness. He saw Ann emerge from a mandriven car, not her own or a taxi, and stumble up the steps.

"Hi there, Nick!" she greeted him jauntily. Her hair was disheveled and a tail of her blouse hung outside her skirt.

"Where's your car?" he asked.

"Too drunk to drive. Had ol' Brad drive me home. You know ol' Brad, don't you?"

"I know him," Nick said, stone-faced.

Ann walked past him into the house, then turned. "Okay, so I'm drunk!" she said. "Don't look so damned disapproving! You're not so perfect either!"

"Keep your voice down," he said sharply. "You'll wake the kids."

"Say it once more, and I'll wake the whole goddamn neighborhood! What've you got to complain about anyway?"

"You! You were supposed to be home by nine. Where've you been the last four hours? You could've at least called."

"Why? So you wouldn't worry? Don't make me laugh! Since when did you start worrying about poor, inadequate me? No, I mean it, Nick. Since when did I come first? Not your job, not the kids—me?"

"Don't change the subject. I want to know what kept you out so late and why you didn't call."

"Okay, I'll confess. The thing is, my husband has little secrets he won't share with me. So I'm getting even. Tonight's my secret—what I've got going with Brad Rollins."

"Damn it, Ann, make sense! I'm the one who should be indignant, not you. What's behind all this?"

She stared disdainfully. "Okay—play dumb. Make me the patsy. The undeserving bitch-wife. Keep it up and neurotic ol' Ann will do your dirty work for you. The onus for what happens will be on me."

"Look, we've been at each other's throats for five minutes now and I still don't know what you're so mad about. I don't get it."

"No, but I bet you will. In Paris!"

"Paris-huh?" Nick repeated. "What's that supposed to mean?" A sense of uneasiness swelled up in him like the sound of screeching brakes while he was driving his car. How could Ann possibly know he was going to Paris? Hank? No, even for him a disclosure of that magnitude seemed inconceivable.

"Some other time, Nick. I'm tired. I'm going to bed."

"I want to know now!"

"That's your tough luck. The interrogation is over for the night." She turned and started up the stairs.

"Ann, come back here!" Nick followed, and put a restraining arm on her shoulder.

"Let go, damn you!"

"Not until you explain what this is all about."

"Let go, I said! Keep your hands off me, you phony, conniving bastard!" Twisting free, she climbed another step. He wrenched her back.

"Lousy bastard!" Ann rasped. Turning abruptly, she struck him in the face with her fist. He reeled back, stumbled on the bottom step, and fell to one knee. Ann's eyes widened with dismay as she looked at him.

Nick struggled up, steadying himself on the railing. A trickle of blood from his nose ran down the side of his chin and dripped on his undershirt. Ignoring it, he stared steadfastly at Ann, forcing her to look away. "Come down here," he said in a compelling voice.

"No." Ann slumped down on the stairs. She sat hunched over, her arms hugging her knees.

"Come down here, or so help me I'll drag you down."

"No. Leave me alone," she said in a thin voice. Though she had bloodied him, her eyes were moist and she looked the more hurt. "You touch me and I'll get even with you. I'll tell everyone at the hospital. Everyone!"

"Tell them what, for Chrissake?" Nick growled, though growing uneasy over Ann's regressive behavior: the frightened-child look on her face. "Come down here, I said!"

"No, don't touch me! You're all bloody."

Nick stripped off his undershirt, wiped his face with it and tossed it aside.

Ann cowered as he took a step toward her. He lunged forward, pulled her up and dragged her down the stairs.

"No, don't! Don't get your blood on me!" she wailed hysterically and struggled to break free of his hold.

"Ann, stop! For God's sake calm down!" Nick pleaded, but she was wild-eyed and her struggling grew more frantic.

"Let go! Let go!" she shrieked as his fingers dug into the flesh of her arms, keeping her elbows in and her nails from raking his face. He felt her trying to knee him through her tight skirt, then the lancinating stab of her high-heeled shoe on his instep. He grappled her to the wall and pinned her there with his weight, until—managing to twist sideways—she sunk her teeth into his forearm.

"Damn you!" Nick roared, held her off, and slapped her across the face.

Ann's head snapped back and she crumpled on the stairs. Her body pitched forward on the bottom steps and she fell face-down on the floor. Nick's neck muscles contracted in anguish as he heard her gag, try to retch into her hands, then grow silent, unwilling or unable to cry.

So he'd finally done it, he thought bitterly. He could walk out now—go to Paris or go to hell as far as Ann was concerned. Canter had had his way. . . . Yet, staring down at her, he knew he couldn't leave her so humiliated and defenseless. No matter what had triggered her outpouring of hate, she was his wife and he couldn't be brutal to her in this way.

He reached down and helped her to her feet. She permitted it without protest and he drew her to him. He heard her low whisper: "Oh God, what's happening to us? What are we doing to each other?"

"Baby, I had to," he said. "You were wild, hysterical."

Ann pulled back, stared at him. As if comprehending for the first time, she saw his blood-crusted nose, the bruised bite of her teeth on his arm. "What have I done to you?"

"It's all right," he said. "I'm all right."

"No, nothing's all right—not after this!"

"It will be," he soothed. "I promise it will. Don't think about it. Just rest."

Nick stroked her shoulders, sensed the

yielding of her flesh. There was so much he
wanted to tell her, but they had gone
beyond words; words were powerless to
heal in the wake of such violence. Impulsively, he pressed her to him, then released
her to caress her covered breasts, totally
unaware of her receptivity and totally vulnerable, but refusing to think beyond the
moment, repressing all visions of the
course he was still compelled to follow.
Slowly, he unbuttoned her blouse.

"It's all ruined for us," she whispered.
"After this, it's finished." She stared
down at his manipulating fingers. The
blouse parted and he tugged it from her
skirt. Gently, he dug his fingers under the
fabric of her bra and thrust it up. Her released breasts slipped out and down.

Nick felt strangely aroused, not only
with lust but with an overriding tender-
ness. And hope. Maybe Hank had been
right: the blame for Ann's frigidity lay
more properly with him—and he wanted
her forgiveness in a way he could never
hope to verbalize, could only convey by
tender, fulfilling love.

Saying nothing, afraid that a word, any
word, might change her mute acceptance,
he cupped her right breast in the V of his
hand and tentatively touched the tip of his
tongue to the nipple. He felt her arch
against him, her head turning back and
up. He moved his lips along the smooth

grain of her flesh to the brownish circle of
areola and gently closed his teeth on her
nipple. He heard her sharp intake of
breath and suddenly all his raging frustration and fear and guilt converged and sank
together, centered exclusively on the cone
of warm, swelling flesh in his mouth. She
slumped passively against him and he
eased her to the floor. His hand slid under
her skirt and he partially undressed her
with an economy of moves, still fearful
any abruptness on his part might shatter
the silent acceptance he was achieving.
His fingers unfastened her garter snaps,
pushed her girdle up, and drew her nylon
panties down. She fell back in the supporting yoke of his arms. He moved over and
upon her.

Nothing they had known had been like
this before. He had no vision, no vague
erotic fantasy of Noelle, now. This was the
woman he wanted—had always wanted.
Ann lay on the rug between the newel post
and the staircase wall, eyes vacant, mouth
slack, dark hair spreading loose. He trailed
her bare flesh with deftly stroking fingers,
over mounding breasts, below the twisted
girdle, along flat belly and between
trembling thighs. And now he realized he
was nearly there, the frustrated questing
of nineteen years of marriage about to be
appeased.

Ann cried out wordlessly as he penetrated her. He arched to enter her again, but she writhed back and away from him. With unbelievable strength, she pushed him off and rolled on her side, locking her thighs together.

"Ann, don't—" he groaned. Grasping her buttocks, he tried to turn and spread her again, until sudden self-disgust overcame and halted him.

He grimaced and released her. They lay back-to-back half-clad and panting like tired wrestlers. Seconds expanded into a prolonged silence before he felt able to speak again. "What made you stop?"

Her voice sounded dull, remote. "I don't know . . . exactly."

"It was going to be—could have been—so damned good." He remained faintly hopeful. "Was it the hard floor? The kids upstairs? Could we—would you want to try it in bed?"

She stared at him incredulously. "Go to bed? With you? I'd rather run naked down State Street and give it to the first hot-eyed kid I met!"

"You hate me that much?"

"The same way you hate me!"

"Hate? Oh, God, I could kill you right now, but I don't hate you. All I want is to love you, Ann."

"Love!" Her lips twisted loathingly. "I've had a bellyful of your kind of love.

No more, though. Not for this girl."

She rose to her feet and absently began to dress herself; to pull skirt and girdle down and brassiere up, to button her blouse. He watched her breasts, now slack and flaccid, vanish from sight.

Dumbly, despairingly, unmanned as never before, Nick followed. He pulled up his trousers and buckled them. "You did it deliberately then? Why?"

"To hurt you . . . maybe to hurt myself."

"What could *that* possibly mean?"

"It means—that with all the other neuroses you charge me with, I'm probably masochistic as well. All us Strattons are masochists when it comes to sex. . . . If you must know, it's because I was scared."

"Scared of what?"

"Oh, God, don't you know anything about female anatomy? If I'd let you keep it up I would've come. Yes—come. Like you've never been able to make me."

"And you stopped me? Just when you— Why?"

"Because I didn't want it this way. Not as some cheap going-away present. I won't have it!"

He groaned. "Ann, this is crazy. Why won't you?"

"Because I won't have sex without love.

And you don't love me, do you?"

"But I do. Or could. If only you'd let me."

"Oh, stop it," she said wearily. "Don't bother to lie anymore. I'm sick of being lied to. I know you're going to Paris without me."

"How do you know?"

"It's true, isn't it?"

He hesitated, then nodded.

"Why didn't you tell me?"

"Ann, I'm sorry. I was going to—"

"When?" she scorned. "At planeside tomorrow? . . . The airlines called around six. Your round-trip, *single*-space to Paris is confirmed for tomorrow's flight . . . Oh, why, Nick?" she suddenly cried. "Why won't you take me?"

"I can't tell you. I simply can't."

"Why not? What's waiting for you in Paris that's so important I can't be there, too? Not that I don't know—"

"Ann," he said despairingly. "I have this operation to perform, this terribly delicate, terribly important operation. That's all I can—I'm allowed to say."

"What do you think I'd do? Charge into the operating room in the middle of surgery? You make me sick!"

"I only wish—but I can't tell you. It would be too—" He started to say dangerous, but that would be too much and too little to say. It would only provoke her curiosity, incense her further. "Look, I know how absurd, how melodramatic this is going to sound. Right out of the late, late movie. But you're simply going to have to trust me."

"Trust you?" mocked Ann. "Trust *you!* How dumb do you think I am? Oh sure, I'll trust you. Just like I trusted you in Korea. Remember, Korea, Nick? Remember how trustworthy you were then?"

"What are you talking about?"

"Not what—who! That French slut, that sow, that Noelle bitch! She's the reason, isn't she?"

Nick blinked, dumbfounded. So Ann knew, after all. It seemed extraordinarily naive of him to have gone all these years and not suspected it until recently. Why hadn't she mentioned it? Because she lacked proof? Distrusted her source? He considered dissembling, protesting outraged indignation and innocence, but knew it was no use. His life was hopelessly out of control.

"You seem remarkably well informed about a number of things all of a sudden."

"All of a sudden? You call fourteen years all of a sudden?"

"How did you find out? Hank? Oh, skip that. I don't want to know. Just think, you've known it fourteen years. My God! Why didn't you ever say something?"

"Why? I thought I knew what a bad

time you had in Korea and didn't want
to keep punishing you with it. I even made
excuses for you. I blamed myself first, the
war second, and that French whore third.
But never you! Wasn't that generous of
me?"

"Was it?"

"No, not really. It was fear mostly—
fear that if I said something, made you
feel guilty enough over it, I might lose
you. So I convinced myself that all I really
cared about is that you gave her up and
came home to me. But no reruns. I won't
stand for it!" Her eyes glittered mockingly. "What's so special about French
girls anyhow?"

"Ann, stop! You're only hurting yourself. I swear—my solemn word—I have no
intention of seeing Noelle or any other
woman in Paris." He forced a smile, tried
to sound deprecating. "It's been fourteen
years, for Chrissake. She's probably a
middle-aged bag. What could I see in her
now?"

"And so am I a middle-aged bag. But
you just tried to rape me on the floor. You
must have a hangup about middle-aged
bags, you middle-aged lecher!" She
started for the stairs, then turned, swept
up in a sudden fury. "Go to her then, you
sickening bastard! Go screw your French
slut. But don't you dare come back here.
Because I'll fix you. You humiliate me like

this and I'll make you wish you'd never been born. We'll ruin you, my father and I. In this town and everywhere!"

13

Nick followed the harassed, perpetually smiling stewardess up the aisle and had hardly sunk down in his seat when the Boeing 707 fired its jet engines and began to taxi out. He loosened his collar, wiped sweat from his neck and brow, and fastened his seat-belt. It was his third and final plane that day and Canter's lengthy, last-minute briefing had damned near made him miss it.

Now that he was finally on the last leg of his journey, Nick tried to relax, to rid himself of the eerie, nightmarish pall that for the past several hours had overcome his senses in spurts of stop-start, time-distorted motion. It was a preposterous state of mind, he realized, but his government wanted him to kill a man, which made

170 Marshall Goldberg, M.D.

everything possible. Nobody resembling a
KGB agent had caught the morning flight
from Madison with him, or had been
among the few passengers changing
planes in Chicago, or had followed him to
the men's room at O'Hare. He blamed
Canter for those absurd preoccupations.
But Canter was such a convenient all-
purpose devil that Nick recognized he ran
the risk of over-using him.

He thought about Canter. . . .

The message for their meeting had been
passed on by a squat, pleasant CIA agent
who had turned up at Nick's office that
morning carrying a sample case labeled
Corn Products, Limited. His instructions
had sent Nick directly from the debarking
gate at Kennedy to the Airlines' VIP
Lounge on the upper desk. A notice on the
door said: Temporarily Closed for Redec-
oration.

Nick knocked. The door opened immediately and a cautious Canter waved him in.
Instead of speaking, the agent stood
facing the door. A moment later, Nick
heard the knob being turned. It rattled
twice more, before whoever it was gave up.
Canter turned to him and nodded. "It's
okay."

"What's okay?"

"You weren't followed."

Nick suppressed the urge to ask, by
whom? He felt vaguely reassured.

Canter gestured at the spacious lounge. "Make yourself at home. We've got the place all to ourselves for the next hour."

"What does the airline say about it?"

"Oh, they're cooperative. One of their top brass, ex-Air Force general, sets it up for us. They even let us use the bar. . . . Come on over. Time for one bracing drink before we get down to business."

Nick surveyed the row of bottles on the shelf and chose Crown Royal. Canter poured a double shot, added ice, and passed it over. He fixed himself the same. "Well, how did things go with the wife?" he asked casually.

Nick's eyes flashed anger. "I thought you'd know by now. Isn't my whole house bugged by Corn Products, Limited?"

"No bugs, Nick," Canter smiled. "We're not like those buggers from the FBI. Sounds like she gave you a rough time."

"Yuh—rough, rugged, and maybe for keeps. Don't worry, though, my marriage may be over, but your secret's safe. Just add it to the casualty list and get on with the briefing."

"I'm sorry to hear that," said Canter. "But it had to be handled that way. If it'd been up to me, I wouldn't even have involved your father-in-law. From what we know of him, he's not the most stable of characters. . . . One more question: how are you holding up? Mentally, I mean. Now that you've had a few more days to think things over, any change of heart? What I'm referring to, of course—"

"I know what you're referring to," Nick snapped, "and the answer is no. No matter how you dress it up, it's still murder, and it's still repugnant to me. I break out in a cold sweat everytime I think about it."

Canter's eyes narrowed, but he said nothing. He sniffled, took out his pocket inhaler and put it to his nostrils. It was a stall, Nick recognized; a mannerism Canter used to convey sinister implications. His victims were gradually condition by it until it became a prelude to a punishing blow. He would hate to be interrogated by Canter, Nick thought grudgingly. But damned if he would make it any easier for him. Let him blow a hole in his sinuses for all he cared.

"I'm not sure I like that," the agent finally said. "Not at this late stage."

"That's too bad. I don't much like what you're asking me to do any better."

"Then why are you here?"

"Well, I'll be goddamned! I thought you'd explained that to me already. I'm here, Canter, because I'm one of a kind. A *rara avis*. The only bird in captivity who can fly unscathed into the Russian coop. But remember, I'm still a rank amateur as an assassin. I'm just not the hero you'd like me to be."

Canter gulped his whiskey. "Well, at least you're leveling with me. Let me do the same with you. Karamanov *must* die. He must never be allowed to leave that French hospital live. Make no mistake, that's the real operation. And you're our surgeon—not theirs. Either you do it, or someone else will."

"Who, Canter? Who's your backup man?"

"We've got one, believe me. He'll never have the clean shot at him you will, but he'll go in."

"A kamikaze? A human missile?"

"Call it what you like. It has to be done."

"By whom? Who've you got that's so dependable?"

Canter thrust his face closer. "You're looking at him."

Nick stared. "You're bluffing. . . . You're bluffing and you know it."

"Am I? Is that what you're thinking? Well, think some more. Picture what's at stake—no minor cold war issue, but national security. Survival! And our survival hangs on Karamanov's. The two are mutually exclusive. Either you finish him off, or by God, I will."

"That's pretty noble of you, but I'm not convinced. What makes you such a zealot?"

"I have my reasons."

"What reasons? I'm afraid I need a little more persuading. You're a brave man, I don't doubt. Dedicated, too. But you're no fanatic. Your outfit doesn't hire fanatics nor let them operate loose. . . . You're one of their senior men. Why would they want to sacrifice you?"

"It was my choice. Mine alone."

"Why?"

"I had my annual physical a week or so ago. A spot turned up on my chest X ray. What they call a 'coin lesion.' You're a surgeon, Sten. . . ."

Nick pondered; Was Canter telling the truth? Or was he trying to manipulate him with a cleverly devised ploy, one that would have special meaning for a physician? His instincts argued against it. It all sounded too pat, too contrived. The doomed agent determined to make the *beau geste* for his country.

"All right, so you've got a spot on your X ray," Nick said. "So do a lot of people. It doesn't necessarily mean you've got lung cancer."

"So they tell me. Only this one's growing. It wasn't on the film they took a year ago."

"Even so, it might represent any number of things. Tuberculosis, for example. The odds are less than fifty-fifty it's cancer."

"The odds they quoted me weren't quite

that favorable. There's no calcification in it. None of those reassuring little flecks."

Nick frowned. Canter's knowledge was confirmatory, if not conclusive. He could have read it in any medical textbook.

"They skin-test you?"

"Skin tests, sputum exams—the works. It all turned out negative, which leaves me up in the air."

"You feel all right?"

"So far, fine. But that doesn't mean much either. I'm also a smoker—or was— until a year ago. A two-pack-a-day man. That's another strike against me."

"There's still no proof, one way or another. Even if it is cancer, it's early. It might still be resectable."

"It might. Fifty percent are at this stage, I'm told. Five to fifteen percent make it five years. These are the current statistics, aren't they?"

"It's still worth the operation. Makes a hell of a lot more sense to take your chances that way then get yourself killed for sure."

"That's your opinion. Only you and I look at it differently. You're medical. I'm charter-member CIA. . . . Strange, how fate caused things to bunch together like this. Your surgical invention, Karamanov's illness, my lung lesion. Makes you wonder. But it doesn't change anything. Karamanov's got to be stopped, and one of us is going to stop him. Who goes first is up to you."

Nick nodded.

"Your chances, of course, are vastly better than mine. Far more direct and subtle. The difference between a scalpel and a meat cleaver. The Russians know how critically ill Karamanov is. They can't expect you to perform miracles. If, as a result of a few deft manipulations on your part, he doesn't make it through the surgery, what can they do about it? . . . Don't you see, Nick, everything's in your favor? If it's left to me, not only is the risk of failing that much greater, but there may be hell to pay after. There's no predicting how far they'll go to hit back at us."

"And yet you still expect me to believe they've given you the go-ahead to kill him yourself?"

Canter withdrew his handkerchief from his pocket, put it to his nose, and decided not to use it. "Not yet. The reason should be obvious. I was waiting to hear from you. I'm still waiting. You or me, Doctor —who's it going to be?"

Nick sighed. "All right. You're pushing hard for an answer and I still don't have one—not one that will be firm and binding and relieve you of further doubt. The best I can do for the moment is to give you the benefit of my thinking. I agree that the

Russians are no more trustworthy or peace-loving than they were during Stalin's time. What they're doing in the Middle East proves that. I also agree that if Karamanov lives long enough to finish his project they'll be more ruthless than ever. I'm willing to buy that much, and it's because I buy it that I'm here right now. I suppose if you gave me a rifle and positioned me in range of him I might be able to squeeze the trigger. A bullet is so marvelously impersonal. But you're not asking that. You want me to kill him in the most difficult, incongruous place in the world for me—an operating room. And I know damned well my instincts won't allow it. I'll block first, freeze up, be incapable of holding a scalpel steady in my hand. I'm sure that's what will happen if I attempt it cold, without any personal knowledge of the man. I guess what I'm really trying to say is this: I can't give you a final answer until I meet Karamanov himself, put the man in perspective with the menace he represents, and then condition myself to kill him, if I possibly can."

"And if you can't?"

"If I can't, and I'm not convinced that without the operation his death is imminent, I'll let you know."

"Okay, Nick. We'll leave it open-ended like that for a while longer." He looked at his watch. "Jesus! Look at the time.

We've got a lot of important ground to cover in the next twenty minutes, so we'd better get started."

They moved to a table where Canter could show him the contents of his attache case. He unlocked both sides and removed a sheaf of photos. "These are the Russians you've going to meet in Paris. Look long and hard at them. Remember their faces."

Nick listened to the steady, whistling hum of the jet and felt a torpid, muscle-aching fatigue settle over him. Bleary-eyed, he weaved his way up the aisle to the toilet compartment and rinsed his face off with cold water. He returned to his seat, turned on the overhead light, and tried reading a magazine. But the light glaring off the glossy pages soon tired his eyes and he abandoned it to stare aimlessly out the window.

Minutes later, he perceived a flash of light over the wing, and soon after that, the glimmering first light of dawn. He watched the colors along the rim of the horizon grow in brightness and clarity; watched the spectral bands of light shift from red to magenta to orange against the backdrop of blue sea.

His contact in Paris was an agent named Frank Avila; Canter had shown him his picture. Though his face had a delicate bone structure, a Basque-like

nose, he was not Spanish but Puerto
Rican, according to Canter, and one of
their most dependable men. An elaborate
system had been devised for Nick to reach
him. His instructions were to dial a certain
number, let it ring exactly five times and
then hang up. The phone itself was located
in an empty apartment. A listening device,
constantly monitored, would pick up the
signal and have it relayed to Avila who
would then proceed to rendezvous with
him in the library of the American
Hospital in Neuilly.

A billowy carpet of clouds grew visible
out the window.

He wasn't the only one with problems,
Nick reflected. The Russians sponsoring
the surgery must be sweating out his intentions, too; their necks were all in the
same noose. Did he know Karamanov's
true identity or didn't he? That was their
own dilemma.

The most formidable opponent he would
face would be Bogdanov, the operations
officer of the KGB. His photograph had
sufficiently impressed Nick so that he had
no difficulty remembering it. From his
brush haircut to his slightly oversized jaw,
his face looked square and Slavic, yet
modifying such broad features were high
Eurasian cheekbones and prominent eyes.
His outward appearance accurately por-
trayed what Nick had been told about him:

athletic, ambitious, highly intelligent.

His gaze was again drawn to the window
as the sun appeared on the horizon: a
brilliant ball of incandescent orange and
gold lights, its rays reflected like star
points against the pane of glass. He
wished he could have taken a photo of it.
It would have made a striking picture for
his wife to paint.

Ann, he thought ruefully. What had her
response been when she woke and found
him packed and gone? She certainly
wouldn't take his leaving passively; she'd
made that clear in her tirade of the
previous night. He guessed she would go
on a drinking spree. And if not
alcohol—men. The thought of his wife as a
bar-fly pick-up, the target of prowling
graduate students or skirtchasers like
Brad Rollins, enraged him. He could
imagine killing Rollins far easier than
Karamanov. But that was exactly the
problem. The Russian was not a personal
enemy.

The jet veered inland and now he could
see farmlands: green and tan and
burgundy squares joined in a crazy-quilt
pattern.

He shivered with fatigue.

If ever he came out of this alive; if by
some miracle the diseased artery in
Karamanov's brain should clog before he
had the chance to operate, he vowed he

would set things right with Ann. He would
confess the whole incredible tale to her
and drag Canter along to vouch for him. If
Canter refused, he would get Hank. . . .
Interspersed among the farms, he could
see the green foliage of forests, a gray and
crumbling aqueduct, and coming up fast
now, the alabaster rooftops of surburban
Paris. . . . But it wouldn't happen that
way. He instinctively knew he would have
to kill Karamanov—or fail to kill him.

14

Nick met Marandat in the tapestried lobby of the Georges Cinq hotel. The French surgeon's appearance surprised him. Unlike his slender, pinched-faced nephew who had chauffeured Nick in from the airport, he was medium tall, thick-necked, and rotund. His pudgy face creased in a broad smile as he stepped forward to introduce himself.

"*Mon cher Docteur Sten,* I am Marcel Marandat. It's a grand pleasure to meet you."

They shook hands. Marandat had the grip of a farmer.

"I hope you've had the chance to recuperate from your journey?"

"Yes. I slept the entire afternoon."

"*Bien.* Transatlantic flights can be

fatiguing. But now that your mind is
rested, I hope you've developed an appetite."

"I'm famished."

Marandat beamed. "Excellent. I have
made reservations for us at La Mediterranee. Perhaps you are familiar with the
restaurant?"

Nick shook his head.

"Well, take the word of a fat Frenchman, its cuisine is superb."

La Mediterranee evidently was a favorite haunt of Marandat's. A shout from the
waiter at the door brought out the owner
who personally escorted them to a table on
the terrace. The decor of the restaurant
was pleasant but simple with the aroma in
the air of seafood in various stages of preparation and a spotlighted view of the
Theatre de l'Odeon across the street.

Nick permitted his host to order for him
and was rewarded with a tasty crab
bisque, a filet of sole with cheese and wine
sauce, and a bottle of vintage Meursault.

Their conversation remained light until
after the desert and coffee were served.
Marandat removed a cigar from his
pocket, offered it first to Nick, then lit it
himself.

"What a pity your wife was unable to
accompany you," he said. "Paris is particularly enchanting this time of year. She'd
have enjoyed it."

"I'm sure she would. But it couldn't be helped. The children are out of school now and she found it impossible to get away." Nick took a sip of the rich, slightly bitter coffee. "I had a great deal of difficulty arranging it myself. Much as I enjoy your city, I'll have to return home at the earliest possible moment."

"I understand."

"When do you wish me to operate?" asked Nick.

A curl of smoke from his cigar caused Marandat's eye to twitch. "Time, of course, is of the essence, but I leave that decision to you. Whenever you feel you are ready. Naturally, you'll want to familiarize yourself with the case first. Review his X rays. They are none too favorable, I warn you. An almost complete obstruction on the right, seventy percent on the left. . . . It's entirely possible that after seeing them you will be unwilling to operate. That, of course, is your right. It's not pleasant to watch your patients die on the operating table. I've already watched too many. And regardless of how dear this man is to me, I shall fully respect your decision."

"You mentioned he was a relative?"

"Yes, an uncle."

"And his name?"

"Kammerman. Dr. Werner Kammerman. He is not a medical doctor, but a professor of mathematics."

So it was to be Kammerman, Nick thought. Not too dissimilar from Karamanov. He might have expected them to be more resourceful. But why should they? Either he knew the Russian's true identity or he didn't. The pseudonym they chose for him didn't change that in the least.

"He was a brilliant man, a leading theorist in prewar Germany, but fate has not been kind to him. Because his wife was Jewish, the Nazis deprived him of his chair at the University of Leipzig and forced him to flee the country. He came first to Paris and lived with my family for a time. Then, after the fall of France, he made his way to England. The foolish Englishmen mistrusted his loyalties and refused to offer him a post at one of their universities. Here he was, a world authority on quantum mechanics, and the British turned him down because of his accent, because of his eagerness to serve their cause. They put him to work as a bookkeeper. Imagine, Dr. Sten, a factory bookkeeper! But he tolerated it until the next blow fell. His wife was killed in an air raid. That crushed his spirit completely. He withdrew from the tyranny of the real world into the precise, orderly world of mathematical figures.

"After the war, friends of his, former

students, arranged his return to Leipzig. He resumed his chair in mathematics and was content to teach for a while. But then, the East German government realized what a prize they had in him. Why bother to import scientists from Russia, or lure defectors from the West, when they had the brilliant Werner Kammerman under their nose? They tried to force him to do research for their military. He refused and, of course, was again deprived of his position. They allowed him to remain on at the university in a minor post only because his colleagues interceded for him. But otherwise he was a virtual prisoner. He was only permitted to leave the country after their physicians certified he was a doomed man."

Nick listened raptly. It was a clever fabrication, but for what purpose? To gain his sympathy, make it more difficult for him to refuse the surgery? Or perhaps it had a second aim: to explain Karamanov's abilities as a linguist. Either way, he gave it high marks for ingenuity. He studied his host's benign, fleshy face and grew more cautious.

Marandat paused to relight his cigar, then continued. "There you have the story, Dr. Sten. A depressing one, *n'est-ce-pas?* We live in depressing times. The Israelis have performed a miracle in staving off the Arab predators. But how many miracles does the human race have left?"

"I hope you're not expecting a miracle from me?" said Nick.

"Only a minor one," Marandat said with a smile. "Not a cure. His condition is beyond that—he has coronary disease as well as cerebral. But perhaps a short reprieve. A year or two to enjoy Paris; to walk the streets with an invigorating sense of freedom. That, in itself, is a priceless gift for a dying man."

"How extensive is his coronary disease?"

"For the past year he has suffered periodic bouts of chest pain which, I presume, is angina pectoris. They began at a time when he was pushing himself very hard to finish a mathematical treatise, getting little rest or sleep. Since then, he has taken better care of himself and the spasms occur less frequently. At most, once a week."

"No evidence of heart failure?"

"None. That is some consolation."

Nick frowned. "Not much, I'm afraid. It doesn't tell me how well he'll tolerate the anesthesia. Has his cardiac status been evaluated by an internist?"

"To a degree, yes, and it is as I have told you. I originally wanted Professor Soulie to consult on him. His name is perhaps familiar to you? He is not only chief of the cardiac service at our hospital but a recognized authority on heart disease. Regrettably, however, Soulie was not available. He is out of the country on a speaking tour. He sent in his place his *chef du clinic*, Dr. Valentin Chaikoff. Chaikoff is a Russian emigrant who did his post-graduate studies here in Paris and has been with us ever since. Though he lacks Soulie's presence, his knack for diagnosing the rare malady, he is quite a competent fellow in his own right."

Enter Chaikoff, Nick thought. The corners of his lips twitched as he suppressed a smile. First Karamanov, alias Kammerman, and now the watchdog surgeon with his Russian accent and training neatly explained.

"You will meet Chaikoff in the morning when you visit the hospital," Marandat said. "A conference has been arranged for 11:00 A.M. In the interim, I have prepared a detailed case report for you to study at your leisure. It's waiting in my car."

"Good. But I hope I'll be allowed a chance to go over the patient myself before the conference?"

Marandat plucked the cigar from his mouth and gestured with upturned hands. "But, of course, Dr. Sten. It's unthinkable that we'd ask you to commit yourself to such perilous surgery without your own examination. With your approval, I've scheduled it for nine o'clock in the morning."

Nick nodded.

"Then it's agreed. I will arrive at your hotel at half-past eight and drive you to the Broussais Hospital myself."

"I can just as easily take a taxi, if it's out of your way."

Marandat shrugged. "A short distance, perhaps. Not the three thousand miles you have come out of your way. I will not say more, lest my sentiments embarrass you. . . . Naturally, there is much more we should discuss about the surgery, but it can wait until tomorrow. I also have many questions concerning our comparative techniques of endarterectomy. My results, as you know, are hardly enviable." He paused, looking preoccupied for a moment, then went on. "I would hate to have to operate on my uncle myself. Even apart from ethical considerations, the personal involvement, I dread my miserable luck with the procedure."

Nick regarded the Frenchman warily. "But would you, if I refused?"

Marandat's right eye constricted as though he were sighting along the barrel of a rifle. "In that case, the nightmare would come true. I'd be left the choice of abandoning my uncle to his disease or—I don't know. . . . No, I would have to do something for him. If it came to that, Dr.

Sten, I would beg you to teach me all you possibly could about your superior technique. I'd practice it on dogs, on cadavers, and lastly, if my courage permits, on my unfortunate uncle. You'd leave me no choice."

Nor would the Russians, Nick thought. But he derived no particular pleasure from Marandat's dilemma, since it only worsened his own. As Canter had predicted, the Frenchman would operate if he refused, and the risk of his succeeding was clearly unacceptable.

"One more thing," Marandat said, swirling a cognac in his goblet. "When we first talked together on the telephone, you asked me if I knew an old acquaintance of yours, a Noelle Cardin. I didn't, but I promised I would inquire."

Nick stared down at the reflected streaks of light along the rim of his glass and steeled himself before meeting Marandat's scrutinizing gaze. "Go on."

"Yes. Well, I'm pleased to report that I finally succeeded in locating her. At first, I could find no trace whatsoever; no listing in the telephone book or the professional registry. My poor secretary wasted an entire day searching through the student archives at the Sorbonne. Their filing system is hopelessly archaic. I was about ready to abandon the search when I just happened to mention her name to my wife.

Simone. And what do you think? She actually knew your Noelle Cardin! They had been classmates together at the Sorbonne. My wife is a social worker and they had taken psychology classes together. A remarkable coincidence, is it not? How long has it been since you've last seen her?"

"Fourteen years. We met in Korea. Where's Noelle now?"

"Alas, that's the disappointing part. Your Mademoiselle Cardin no longer resides in Paris. The last word Simone received was that she's living in Algiers. She now has her doctorate, you know, and her work with war orphans has brought some acclaim. Simone tells me she heads her own clinic in one of the government hospitals there and has held this post for the past five years. Simone saw her in Paris two summers ago but not since. She could, of course, furnish you with her address in Algiers, if you would like to write her?"

The vision of Noelle's face that had fused in Nick's mind and flickered animatedly like the images of a kinescope faded with Marandat's last words. Though he realized her absence from Paris simplified his life, limited his sources of conflict, it did not console him. Until that moment, in some sequestered corner of his mind, he had kept alive the hope he would see Noelle again, take her to bed with him, and in those brief and glorious moments, recapture what it once meant to be a free and self-serving man again.

Nick cleared his throat of a growing full-ness and said: "Yes, I would like her address."

Marandat smiled. *"Bien.* I'll have it for you without fail in the morning."

15

The Broussais Hospital was located in the fourteenth *arrondissement:* a district of antiquated buildings and narrow, cobblestoned streets. The hospital exterior matched the drab neighborhood. Its entrance on the Rue Didot was a brick archway in the center of an eroded concrete wall that ran the length of the block. The front of the building to the left of the entranceway had been demolished so that its four floors gaped open above the street like a monstrous mouth.

Beyond its bleak facade, the hospital grounds were pleasanter. Marandat drove through the iron gate to a graveled courtyard containing the clinic buildings and a fleet of ambulances. A second archway to the rear led them to an interior boulevard

lined with blossoming trees and low brick
structures, each with slate roofs, red
awnings, and an amphitheater dedicated
to some illustrious figure of French
medicine. The most modern unit in the
complex housed the Clinique de Chirurgie
Cardio-Vasculaire at the end of the row. It
towered several stories above its neighbors and far outshone them in the glitter
of its marble and glass construction.

Marandat pointed it out with pride as he
parked his Citroen in a space in front
reserved for him by name. Slipping agilely
from behind the wheel, he walked around
to Nick's side of the car. "Well," he asked,
"what do you think of our unit? How does
it compare with what you have in
America?"

"It compares very well. How old is it?"

"A mere infant, constructed only three
years ago. A special dispensation from de
Gaulle himself after one of his ministers
chose to go to England for his heart operation." Marandat grinned. "Actually, there
is American money in it, too. Your
National Institutes of Health were extraordinarily generous in granting us Frenchmen research funds while our own tax
monies were squandered on a frivolous
H-bomb."

Nick smiled. He was beyond the looking
glass now, in the land of opposites. Last
night, Marandat had spoken contempt-

uously of the Communists, yet was one. He had probably been an admirer of de Gaulle as well.

Nick followed his host through the glass-paneled doors and down a spacious reception area to a suite of officers in the rear. They entered the one displaying Marandat's name and title on the door and exchanged their suit coats for French-style wraparound white frocks.

Marandat looked at his watch. "It is now five before nine. What is your preference, my friend: would you like to examine your patient at once? Or would you like me to take you on a quick tour?"

Nick chose the tour. He could feel the momentum accelerating and he was in no particular hurry to meet Karamanov. For one thing, Bogdanov would surely be there, along with other members of the elite palace guard. He'd not only be on stage in their presence but would have to master one of the hardest acting tasks of all: to act naturally when the mere fact you were acting made it impossible to know what your natural response might be.

As he followed Marandat, Nick's apprehension grew. From a medical viewpoint, he was well pleased with what he saw; the hospital looked adequately equipped and staffed. What puzzled him was that most of the rooms they passed appeared empty.

He hadn't spotted more than a dozen patients in the entire hundred-bed unit.

He asked Marandat about it.

"Your observation is correct, Dr. Sten. There *are* very few patients in the unit at the present time. There were none at all a week ago. In fact, we were completely shut down. I neglected to tell you this before because the reason is quite shameful: an infection rate of twenty-five percent! A quarter of all our open-heart cases were becoming infected postoperatively. And why? Typical French penny-pinching stupidity! No gas autoclaves—only obsolete and inadequate steam ones. No filters in the operating room air-conditioners. The result, of course, was cross-infection. While the staphylococci feasted, our patients paid the price for such archaic practices. Finally, a crisis was reached. On the first of June, the unit was closed, the faulty equipment replaced, and the surgical areas disinfected from floor to ceiling with carbolic acid. We started admitting patients again—the few you now see—only since the first of the week. We do not plan to approach our full census for some time. . . . I tell you this in the strictest confidence, Dr. Sten. The incident, itself, was shocking enough. You can understand our reluctance to inform the general public about it."

Nick understood perfectly. He had

wondered earlier how the KGB intended
to maintain their tight ring of surveillance
around Karamanov once he entered the
hospital. Now he knew. Marandat had
arranged to have the building he was
housed in closed off. Whether true or not,
the infection rate provided his excuse. It
also made sense to assume that the
handful of patients in the unit now were
not cardiac cases at all but healthy young
Russians.

The elevator returned them to the men's
ward on the fourth floor. Karamanov's
room was at the end of the corridor. Nick
followed Marandat through the door.

Karamanov—now Kammerman—sat up
in bed to greet them. There were two other
people in the room: one, a dark, pretty girl
whom Nick guessed was Karamanov's
daughter, and the other, a tall, watchful,
square-jawed man whose identity took no
guesswork at all.

So this was Bogdanov, Nick thought;
his opponent in a revolving cat-and-mouse
game. The Russian had the advantage
right now, but that would change.

Marandat took Nick's arm and led him
to the bedside. *"Eh, voila!* At last you
meet? Dr. Nicholas Sten, my dear uncle,
Professor Werner Kammerman."

Nick looked at Karamanov closely: a
frail, white-haired old man who appeared
much the same in person as in the pictures

Nick had seen of him. What difference
there was lay in his eyes: bigger, brighter,
warmer. Nick sensed a strange familiarity
in those eyes: not a mere photographic
similarity, but more compelling, more intensely personal. Did a special communion
exist between murderer and victim? He
wrenched the unnerving thought from his
mind.

"A pleasure to meet you, sir," Nick said,
shaking his hand.

"I am overjoyed, Dr. Sten," Karamanov
replied in heavily accented English.
"Allow me to present the other members
of my family: my daughter, Galina, and
her husband, Monsieur Emil Gessler."

Nick turned to Bogdanov. "Are you
French, Monsieur Gessler?"

"No, Swiss, Dr. Sten. I, too, am de-
lighted to meet you." He clamped down on
Nick's hand.

Nick smiled and squeezed back.

"We're so grateful to you for consenting
to operate on my father," Galina said.

"Thank you, Mrs. Gessler. But I'm
afraid I haven't consented as yet."

Galina looked puzzled.

"What Dr. Sten means," Marandat
interjected quickly, "is that, like any good
surgeon, he wants to examine his patient
first. After all, Galina, it is not the type of
operation one undertakes lightly. There

are grave risks. Your father understands this. So must you."

"I do, Marcel. I do. I'm sorry, Dr. Sten, if I have caused you any embarrassment."

"You haven't. I understand your concern."

"Would you like us to leave the room while you examine my father?"

"If you feel it might upset you."

"Not at all. I am entering my final year of medical studies."

Nick feigned surprise. "Are you? Where?"

Galina hesitated. "The . . . the University of Lausanne. I, too, intend to become a surgeon. A neurosurgeon."

"That's a hard life, especially for a woman. Many years of training, many disappointments."

"Yes, but I am determined. There is much yet to be learned in that field."

Nick grinned. "Well, I'm intrigued. We'll have to talk more about it later."

"The instruments you will need are here, Dr. Sten," said Marandat. He uncovered a tray on Karamanov's bedstand.

Nick surveyed its contents: ophthalmoscope, otoscope, tongue blade, reflex hammer, tuning fork, blood pressure cuff, and assorted pins. He removed his own stethoscope from his back pocket. "These will do fine. . . . Well, Professor Kammerman, if you're ready?"

"Yes." He removed his robe. "You may
be too polite to say it, but I would prefer
my opinionated daughter to wait outside
the room."

"As you wish, Papa," she said dispirit-
edly.

Bogdanov whispered something to her
at the door, but made no attempt to leave.

Nick's examination was quick, but thorough. As anticipated, the major findings
were in Karamanov's neck. His right
carotid pulse was absent; the left, though
full and bounding, revealed the hallmark
of a significant obstruction: a loud, low-
pitched, blowing murmur that sounded in
his ear like the rush of wind through a
tunnel. At that point, Marandat was
called out of the room. A moment later, as
Nick   inadvertently   compressed   the
already compromised artery with the bell
of his stethoscope, Karamanov suffered a
blackout spell. His eyes rolled up and he
collapsed back on the bed.

Nick moved quickly to palpate his pulse
at the wrist. He was watchful, but not
unduly   alarmed.   These   spells   were
commonly provoked by such maneuvers
and almost always transient. Karamanov
seemed fully recovered in the next instant,
when, to Nick's surprise, he clutched his
chest and shouted to Bogdanov: "*Schnell,
Gessler! Hole mir den nitroglycerin!*"

Bogdanov paled. He sprung out of his chair, took a faltering step forward, then turned and ran out the door.

Nick put his stethoscope to Karamanov's chest, but he brushed it away. Their eyes locked in an intense stare. "I have no pain, Dr. Sten. And we've little time to talk, so please remove that instrument from your ears and listen carefully. . . . Do you play chess?"

"Chess?" Nick repeated doubtfully.

"Yes, chess. Do you play?"

He nodded.

Karamanov smiled. "Good. I prayed you would. It's the only way. . . . When the others return, I will ask you that question again. Your answer will be the same. I will then suggest that we play at some unspecified future time, and you shall agree. We will not speak of it further. But the match *must* be at four, tomorrow afternoon. You *must* appear. There will be no other time."

"B . . . But I don't—"

"I know you don't understand. But I cannot say more. Trust me, Dr. Sten," he implored. "Trust me, as I trust you."

Nick heard footsteps resounding along the corridor. "All right," he said. "Tomorrow, at four."

Marandat rushed into the room with Bogdanov and Galina close behind him. *"Qu'est-ce qui est arrivé, oncle?"* he asked breathlessly.

"It is nothing, Marcel. A minor spasm. I have almost recovered."

"Do you want a pill?"

Karamanov shook his head.

"Very well. But as I have told you before," Marandat admonished, "you must keep your vial of heart pills with you at all times."

Karamanov sighed. "Another medicine to take. I am beyond repair. Don't you agree, Dr. Sten?"

"Not yet."

"You are an optimist. For that, I am grateful. But if there is to be an operation, I hope it will be soon. I am weary of doing nothing." Turning to Nick, he asked off-handedly, "Do you play chess, Dr. Sten?"

16

At the end of his conference with Chaikoff, Nick agreed to do the surgery.
He set no date, but promised to discuss it
with Marandat on Monday. He declined
an invitation to lunch on the pretext of
meeting friends and left. He walked
briskly through the hospital grounds.
Once past the gate, he debated whether to
hail a cab, but decided to keep walking;
walk and think. By some Herculean force
of will, he had managed to suppress his
preoccupation with Karamanov's mystify-
ing behavior while in the pressence of
Marandat and the others. Yet, even now,
with every fiber in his brain tuned to its
implications, he found it impossible to
comprehend. In the emotional heat of the
encounter all his preconceived notions of

Karamanov had congealed into a shape-
less mass. The man had progressed dizzy-
ingly from ruthless enemy to sympathetic
human being to fathomless enigma. It
seemed unthinkable that the physicist
would want to conspire with him against
his protectors, yet why else had he faked
an angina attack to set up a clandestine
meeting between them for tomorrow afternoon? Certainly, Karamanov had no
intention of revealing his identity; such a
confession would not only nullify all the
elaborate planning that had preceded him
to Paris, it would effectively seal his doom.
Nick would be forced to refuse to operate;
anything less would be an admission of
intent.

It must be a trick, he mused; a clever
ruse to forge a personal bond between
them and insure that he would go all out to
save Karamanov's life during the surgery.
Yet, even though such a formulation made
the best sense, Nick's critical instincts
rejected it. It seemed too devious for the
Russian   mind—even   a   mind   like
Bogdanov's   which   had   plotted   the
masterly strategy used thus far. But if the
KGB   wasn't   behind   it,   who   was?
Marandat made an unlikely culprit; he
would never dare defy the Russians. No
one could dare defy them—except Karamanov himself.

Waiting at the corner of the Rue Didot

for the traffic to pass, Nick conjured up an
image of the physicist's face, his bright,
penetrating eyes. The vision was rapidly
succeeded by a more Gorgonian one: the
silhouette of Karamanov's skull on the
X-ray film; the snakelike pattern formed
by tiny blood vessels filling thirstily from
the contrast dye trickling past the
blockage in his neck. Nick had been awed
and challenged by the extent of his
disease. But it was the workings of Karamanov's brain, not its X-ray appearance,
that perturbed him most.

He crossed the intersection and headed
north on the Rue du Château, past the
gutted remains of the old Gare Mont-
parnasse and the sterile-looking steel and
glass marvel rising in its stead. He walked
the length of the Rue de Rennes to the
Place St. Germain des Prés: a familiar
haunt. Reaching the Café de Flore, he sat
at a sidewalk table and ordered coffee.

An attractive young girl with long, dark
hair and serenely innocent eyes sat next to
him. Nick glanced at her intermittently as
she read a magazine. She reminded him of
a girl he had briefly loved in college. His
sensuality stirred. He wondered if she
were American; if she would talk with him.

Her half-amused eyes swept past him,
but he said nothing.

If only Noelle were here, he thought
wistfully. He wanted her with such

sudden, swelling ardor that it made his
groin ache. He took a last sip of his coffee
and went inside the cafe. He purchased a
jeton from the matron at the cashier's
booth, descended the stairs to the bank of
telephones opposite the toilets, and dialed
the number which would signal Avila.

Nick lingered at the Café de Flore
another ten minutes, then took a cab to
Neuilly-sur-Seine and the Paris-American
Hospital. He rode the elevator to the third
floor. The woman librarian behind the
desk peered suspiciously at him as he
entered. Nick introduced himself, won a
perfunctory nod, and then wandered in the
direction of the periodicals. He plucked a
surgical journal from the display rack and
sat reading it for the next half hour.

At one thirty, the librian left to eat
lunch. Avila arrived a few minutes later: a
slender, virile, stylishly tailored man.

"Dr. Sten? . . . Frank Avila. Nice to meet
you. Think you were followed?"

Nick shrugged.

"Well, it doesn't matter. Not this time.
You're a doctor. Shouldn't surprise them
you might want to use the library here.
But I'm a journalist and this is a little off
my beat, so we'd better talk fast."

"All right. Pass this on to Canter. Karamanov is a patient in the Cardiovascular
Institute at the Broussais. Marandat
managed to empty the place a week ago on

the pretext that over a quarter of their patients were becoming infected post-op. That may or may not be true. Either way, it's a damned convenient excuse to get rid of nosy patients and fill the beds with security guards—which they have. Right now, about a dozen. My guess is the place will be crawing with them after the weekend. . . . Marandat's involved in this up to his fat little ears, but I don't know whether he's acting alone or has the backing of his government. Do you?"

"The word so far is that no one at the Elysée Palace knows anything about it. Evidently the Russians feel they can manage without their cooperation. They may need it later on, however. If so, the logical liaison man for them would be Edgar Delouvrier, Minister of the Interior. He's more Fascist than Communist, I hear, but he controls the troops."

Avila looked at his watch and fidgeted. "Anything else?"

"One more thing. A real bombshell . . ."

The agent's brows creased as Nick described Karamanov's behavior to him. His sole comment at the end was a sharply exhaled, "Jesus!"

"What do you make of it?" Nick prompted.

"Damned if I know. It smells like a trap —but what kind of a trap? Why should they risk jeopardizing their whole setup

when everything seems to be going their
way right now? It just doesn't figure. . . .
All right," Avila said, standing up
abruptly, "you go find out what it's all
about, but be careful. Be close-mouthed
and careful. And get back to me soon as
you can. No, wait—not tomorrow. I'm
meeting Canter in Deauville. Make it
Monday morning. . . . Know any doctors
here?"

"One. Tom Hewes."

"Good. Arrange to have breakfast with
him, then sneak back up here, say, to
return a journal."

"What time?"

"Eight o'clock sharp. I'll either meet
you here, or if anybody's around, in the
men's room on this floor. Got it?"

Nick nodded.

"Stay here another ten, fifteen minutes
after I leave," ordered Avila. He took a
step toward the door, then turned. "A
second meeting between us is a risk. A *big*
risk. But no bigger, I suppose, than what
the Russians are pulling. . . . See you on
Monday."

Nick watched the agent look both ways
through the glass panels before walking
out the door. He imagined Avila still had
the same perplexed expression on his face
as he'd shown when he first heard of Karamanov's strange behavior. The agent's
discomfort, and that which Canter was

bound to feel soon, amused Nick—but only barely. The devious game they played had now, with Karamanov's inclusion, grown devious beyond all reckoning.

17

The day crept toward four o'clock under Nick's observant eye.

He now assumed he was being followed; he made no effort to confirm it, but grew watchful of his moves. He left his motel room at 2:00 P.M. and joined the Sunday strollers on the Champs Elysées. He walked from the Étoile to the Place Clemenceau, then back to the Rond-Point where he took a cab to St. Germain des Prés. At a kiosk there he bought a newspaper and sat at a sidewalk table on the Rue Bonaparte side of the Café des Deux Magots. He sipped a coffee and a Cinzano for an hour, watching the miniskirted yé-yé girls and their hairy escorts parading by. At ten to four, he stood up and in two

quick strides slipped into the back seat of
a cab standing at the corner.

As he walked past the gate of the Broussais Hospital, he felt something like the
trepidation of a bullfighter entering the
arena.   Two   bathrobe-and-pajama-clad
men, sitting on the bench in front of the
Cardiovascular   Institute   watched   him
guardedly as he passed.

He heard the clicking echo of his own
footsteps as he walked down the marble
floor of the reception area and took the
elevator to the fourth floor. As anticipated, the rooms adjacent to Karamanov's
were now filled with patients. His footsteps roused them from their beds and
they exchanged glances with him through
the glass doors.

He met a nurse and male orderly at the
nursing station.

"Monsieur?" the nurse challenged.

"Bonjour," said Nick. *"Je suis Docteur
Sten."*

Her nose wrinkled. *"Comment?"*

"Docteur Sten," Nick repeated, accentu-
ating   each   sylable.   *"Le   docteur   de
Monsieur Kammerman."*

"Ah, je comprends!" the nurse finally
said. *"Le docteur américain,"* she told the
orderly, before answering Nick in English.
"Welcome, *Monsieur le docteur.* What
brings you here on such an agreeable
Sunday afternoon?"

"I promised Professor Kammerman that I would drop by to play a game of chess with him."

"Chess? . . . Oh, I see. Very considerate of you. Please proceed. He is in his room."

Karamanov greeted Nick with simulated surprise. "Why, Dr. Sten! Come in. How pleasant to see you again."

"How are you feeling?" Nick asked.

"Well, thank you. . . . But what brings you here? Not another examination, I hope?"

Nick answered on cue. "To the contrary. I'm looking for a chess match—if you feel up to it?"

"A splendid idea! Of course, I feel up to it. I would like nothing better . . . but not in here. We would be fools to confine ourselves on such a sunny day. We'll play outdoors. On one of the benches."

The nurse intercepted them before they reached the elevators. "*Attendez, Messieurs!*" she cried out, and hurried to catch up with them. A row of faces appeared behind the glass door of each intervening room. "*Professeur, où* . . . uh, where are you going?"

"No need to concern yourself, Madame Michaud. We are merely going outside for a while to play a game of chess."

"But my orders do not allow you to leave the floor, Professor."

Karamanov flustered her with a stern

look. "I was not aware of such confine-
ment. . . . Fortunately, I have my doctor
with me to issue new orders. Is that not
so, Dr. Sten?"

"It's all right, nurse, I'll watch over
him."

"B . . . But," she stammered, then threw
up her hands in resignation and said: "As
you wish."

They set up the chessboard on the bench
farthest removed from the Institute.
Karamanov reached for the pawn in his
first rank and held it between his fingers.
"We have very little time to talk before an
audience gathers, so I will make the
opening move. . . . Do you know who I
really am, Dr. Sten?"

Nick looked up from the board into the
Russian's face. Their eyes drew together
like opposite poles of a magnet.

"Come now," Karamanov prompted.
"It's a simple question."

"I don't understand—"

An evanescent smile played on Karamanov's lips. He moved his pawn to
queen-four.

"I suspect you do. I have suspected it
all along and now I read it in your eyes.
But no matter. I shall not prolong the
guessing game. . . . My name is not Kammerman, but Karamanov. Nikolai
Pavlevitch Karamanov. It's whimsical we
share the first name, for in all other ways

we are different, in opposite camps. You see, Dr. Sten, I am not German, but Russian. Not a mathematics teacher, but a physicist. The greatest physicist since Einstein, if you will permit the immodesty. Perhaps greater, since I have succeeded where he ultimately failed. That must be of some interest to you. How much more do you need to know?"

A self-protective instinct surmounted the shocks of incredulity set off in Nick's brain. He countered Karamanov's move on the chessboard with deliberate calm. "I'm interested. Go on."

"Forgive my testiness," Karamanov said. "I was naturally curious to know whether I was facing my own murderer. You see, unlike my esteemed protectors, I have a more respectful opinion of the prowess of your intelligence service. But I understand your predicament and won't press you further. To admit, even now, that you had prior knowledge of my identity would be tantamount to confessing you had been contacted by your CIA, and I don't ask that."

"What do you ask?"

Karamanov looked around warily. "Two things. First, that you recognize, as I do—finally—the great peril your country is in if my project is completed. I refer to a perfect antimissile defense system. In a word, impregnable. And I can assure you

that, if I live another six months, the
research will be done. The system could be
made operational in a year. Once that happened, your mighty nuclear armada would
be neutralized. The balance of power
would shift and Russia, not America,
would emerge the dominant power. It's
that decisive. My first entreaty is that you
recognize it."

"And the second?"

"That you take steps to prevent such a
dangerous imbalance by killing me."

"Wh . . . What?"

"It is no longer murder. I will it."

Nick glared. "I don't give a damn what
you will! I'm a surgeon, not an execu-
tioner."

"Are you? Then, forgive my presump-
tuousness. I thought such a request would
solve both our dilemmas and I spoke out
in the interests of time."

"Why do you want to die?"

"I don't relish it, but neither am I afraid.
The French philosopher La Rochefoucauld
once said that neither the sun nor death
can be looked at steadily—so I have
devoted more thought to reasons why I
must not be permitted to live. I have
written them down." Karamanov reached
into the pocket of his robe, removed a
letter, and handed it to Nick. "Since I
could not be certain how much time we
would be allowed before my guards

descended upon us, I've put my arguments on paper. Please study them carefully. I don't wish to sound melodramatic, but they are as persuasive an incrimination as Hitler's *Mein Kampf.*"

"You intend to sabotage your own project?"

"Not as an act of treason—but of humanity. Science doesn't teach us to be heartless. And for a scientist, such behavior is not unheard of. . . . It's not generally appreciated how close German scientists came to beating the Americans in their race to develop the first atomic bomb. By the spring of 1945, they were on the brink of making the atomic pile they had constructed at Haigerloch critical. They failed. Why? Partly because they lacked the necessary funds and equipment. But partly because of the foot-dragging of a few of their key physicists. Werner Heisenberg, for one—a brilliant man. I knew him in prewar Berlin, and I can assure you he recognized the colossal error his chief, Bothe, made when he selected deuterium over graphite for the reactor. He realized the mistake and said nothing, dooming the experiment to failure.

"You see, Dr. Sten, with my infirmity comes conscience. World *angst.* Such misgivings prevent me from allowing the purpose and product of my life, the Kara-

manov equations, to be used as an instrument of world domination. Surely you can
understand that?"

"That much—yes," Nick replied. "What
I don't understand is why you feel the
great need to die? Didn't you say your
missile-defense system is still six months
away from completion?"

Karamanov nodded.

"Could your co-workers finish it without
you?"

"Eventually. But it would take years."

"All right, then. If you truly believe
what you've just told me, there's an
obvious alternative: don't complete it."

"Naturally, that solution has occurred
to me. Many times. Yet, each time I have
rejected it, and for precisely the adjective
you used. Indeed, it is obvious. *Too*
obvious. My government sponsors are not
fools. Nor are my colleagues at Dubna. My
deliberate lack of progress would not fool
them for long. . . . No, Dr. Sten, I refuse to
risk it. To go to my grave with the stigma
of traitor to my name is not pleasant for a
man who, in countless other ways, has
worked for the betterment of his country.
But it's endurable. What is not endurable
is the legacy I should then leave my
daughter, Galina: the certain knowledge
she would suffer the severest punishment
for it. That I could never allow. . . . You see

the terrible irony I face? It is not death I fear; it is now my ally. I fear only the uncertainty of its coming."

"I understand," Nick said.

"I thank you for understanding," Karamanov replied; then, in an impassioned whisper. "But it's not enough. You *must* do more. Either you must agree to end my life on the operating table, or you must leave Paris at once."

Nick stared, dumbfounded.

"Yes, immediately. The KGB has you under constant surveillance, so it will present some danger. But if you get help from your embassy it can be done. . . . I don't know what pressures were put upon you to come here, but I urge you to consider your own safety. After all, as a physician, your life is not without value."

Nick smiled briefly. "I share your concern for it. But if I leave, Marandat would be forced to operate."

"Marandat," Karamanov scorned. "I have seen his thick peasant hands. I doubt I would survive them. . . . No, Dr. Sten, let the onus for my death fall on him. Let him suffer my security guards' lethal revenge . . . . The man I introduced to you yesterday as my son-in-law is not that at all. His name is Bogdanov and he is deputy chief of the KGB. In some ways, a likable man. But he is ruthless, as all our present rulers are ruthless. How could they help not be? They all grew up in Stalin's house. They are all Stalin's children. A menace to the world with his demented philosophy.

"But I have been struck too late with such revelations. It took recent events to awaken them in me. The Arab-Israeli war, symptomatic of the disease, the 'War Is Possible' philosophy, that afflicts my country's leaders. Only with their consent did our intellligence agents disseminate false reports to the Egyptians and provoke them into war. They foresaw neither the Israelis' swift response nor their advanced technology. They miscalculated, as Stalin miscalculated in Korea. Like true Stalin's children. And now they depend on me. They implore: Give us your marvelous invention, Nikolai Pavlevitch, and we will defend our cities; we will safeguard them against the warmongers in China and America. The devil take them!"

Four bathrobed men emerged from the Cardiovascular Institute and sauntered toward them. Nick alerted Karamanov.

"Inevitable," he said. "But we have talked for twenty minutes—longer than I had dared hope. The rest is in my letter. I entrust it to you. Read it with utmost care, and then destroy it."

The quartet came within hearing distance.

"Your move or mine, Dr. Sten?"

"Yours, I believe."

Karamanov reached for his knight, a slight tremor in his hand.

18

Polse Bylo Lyublystse, thought Bogdanov; a haunting echo out of his youth. After hearing the folk ballad sung for the first time in years last night, he had wakened with the melody still in his brain. He hummed it again now as he stood in front of the Soviet Embassy on the Rue de Grenelle and waited for the gate to open.

The evening had provided a joyful release from the tensions of the day. The morning, in particular, had been a severe trial. Like a tightrope walker working without a net, Bogdanov had kept his mental balance through the stresses of Karamanov's heart spasm and Sten's belated decision to operate. Afterward, though limp with fatigue, he had put in a six-hour planning session with his men.

But he wasn't an automaton, Bogdanov had realized. His nervous system needed some relaxation, and he relaxed best in the company of a woman. He had chosen Galina, not merely to perpetuate the charade of their marriage but because the girl was intelligent and attractive, and her disdainful attitude challenged him. They had gone to the Praga for dinner and afterward to Djuri's, a small cabaret on the Rue des Canettes, off St. Germain des Prés.

The cabaret was a single room below street-level; dark, bare-walled, crowded. They squeezed into a corner table, ordered drinks, and listened with mounting excitement to the strumming and plucking of twin guitars, then to the rich baritone voice of Djuri Cortes, the Gypsy-born folk-singer and owner who sang in nine languages. They sat woodenly through Djuri's opening medley of Spanish songs, joining the rhythmic hand-clapping of the audience only at the end. Thereafter, their reserve dwindled as their enchantment grew, until it was abandoned entirely on hearing the familiar strains of "*Padrushka Milaya*," the song of an old droshky driver, and its galloping refrain.

At midnight, and again at 1:00 A.M., Bogdanov suggested they leave but, upon Galina's urging, agreed to stay until the next intermission. He felt blissfully relaxed, more intoxicated by the music than by the vodka he had drunk. As the minutes passed, his eyelids grew heavy and his brain began to emit a soft, soothing buzz. He was about to succumb to his lethargy when he heard Djuri strum the opening chords of his next number and a sharp tug of memory shook him awake. The ballad was *"Polse Bylo Lyublystse,"* his mother's favorite, the one she had sung him to sleep with so often in his youth.

Bogdanov had not heard the song played for so long he had almost forgotten its existence. Since its sentiments were rooted in the old Russia, not the new, the commissars of Soviet culture considered it decadent, an unwelcome reminder of their prerevolutionary past. But the past was not so easily voided for men of Bogdanov's upbringing. It lived on, a time of triumph as well as tragedy: the dark, glorious night of their Russian soul. A nostalgia for those halcyon days flooded his brain.

Bogdanov listened as if transfixed to the lilting melody until his blood began to throb with the faster tempo and he could no longer listen alone. His hands exploded in a volley of claps, more resounding than the rest, and as the clapping diminished a voice rose in his throat to join Djuri's in

singing the last few bars of the chorus. His
half-realized voice, submerged at first in
the amplified echoes of the guitars, grew
louder until it captured Djuri's attention.
He nodded encouragingly, softened his
touch on the strings, and gestured for
Bogdanov to rise.

And buoyed up by his ebullient mood,
Bogdanov had risen with his head held
high and sung out the lyrics of the old
ballad in a deep, full voice that bespoke
the pride he felt in his Russian heritage.
Incredibly, he, a general in the KGB, had
done that. But he suffered no regret. A
part of him, the most vulnerable part,
lived in the past, only to emerge in such
odd, unguarded moments.

He and Djuri harmonized on a final
stanza, a final, rousing refrain, and then
Bogdanov sat down, acknowledging the
crowd's spirited applause with a wave of
his hand.

Galina stared at him curiously. "You're
a strange paradox, Denis," she said,
addressing him by that name for the first
time.

"Oh? Does such exhibitionism surprise
you?"

"I wouldn't have expected it—no. Not
from a man as self-possessed as you. That
old ballad must hold some special association for you. What association is it? A
woman?"

"Please—spare me your psychological insights. I'm the interrogator, not you."

"Yes, but I am a woman and have a woman's intuition about such things. Tell me, Denis. I beg you."

"Hush, before I lose my patience."

Galina pouted. "No, I won't be silenced so easily. It was a woman, wasn't it?"

Bogdanov sighed. "Yes, a woman. But she's long dead. And as the ballad says, 'I never meant to love.'"

The embassy gate was opened by a security guard dressed in the leather apron of a porter.

"Are the others here?" Bogdanov asked.

"Yes, Comrade General. They are gathered inside."

Bogdanov followed him up the walk, past another pair of guards at the door, and into the library where five other men awaited him. He greeted Zorin, the Soviet ambassador first, then the others in order of rank: Rokhlenko, chief *rezident* of the GRU, Ghorikova, intelligence officer of the Ministry of Foreign Affairs, Malashin, the embassy's chargé d'affaires, and Kolesnikov, his second-in-command in the KGB.

"A drink, Comrade General?" Zorin offered, moving over to the portable bar in the corner.

"Many thanks," said Bogdanov, "but

not now. Let's save the toasts until after our work is done for the afternoon."

"Very well. Business first," Zorin agreed, replacing the decanter. "I'm most anxious to hear how the mission is progressing."

"We have already surmounted our greatest obstacle. The American surgeon has agreed to operate."

"When?" asked Zorin.

"He's set no date as yet, but will do so on Monday."

"And what's your opinion of the surgeon himself?"

"A competent man. I'm satisfied with him."

"Are you?" challenged Rokhlenko, his closest military rival. "What assurance have you he can be trusted, that he will do his utmost to save Nikolai Pavlevitch's life?"

Bogdanov silenced him with a stern glance. "He's a doctor, Rokhlenko, not an infantry officer. Necessity teaches us we must trust such men." He smiled. "As we must trust each other. My greatest concern for the moment is not the American, but the French government. How far have we progressed in our dealings with them?"

"I met with Delouvrier Thursday morning and informed him that an important Soviet citizen, a scientist, had arrived in Paris to undergo brain surgery," said Zorin. "Naturally, Delouvrier was curious to learn more, but I explained that the nature of his work was highly technical and beyond my comprehension. Still, I'm worried as to how much his probing into Karamanov's background might uncover."

"Not a great deal," Bogdanov replied confidently. "We checked into this carefully before instructing you to divulge his correct name. The last series of papers Karamanov published was five years ago and concerned the properties of liquid helium. From the beginning, his work on his wave theory has been a closely guarded secret."

"I'm relieved," said Zorin.

"Perhaps prematurely," Bogdanov cautioned. "I know the record of this Delouvrier and I don't like it. He's the most dangerous of political animals: an intellectual whose great love is power, not ideas. Don't you agree?"

"I'll let Malashin answer for me. He knows him better than I."

"Your assumption is correct," Malashin said. "As you know, Delouvrier was a mere professor of political science at the Sorbonne in 1958 when de Gaulle came to power. A book he wrote that year castigating the premiers of the Fourth Republic was evidently to de Gaulle's liking, since he took him into his government. Following a brief apprenticeship in the foreign ministry, Delouvrier was sent to Algeria as First Secretary for North African Affairs. His assignment carried far beyond that, however, since he was given special authority to oversee the counter-insurgency function of the Deuxiéme Bureau.

"An interesting fact emerges from this period. Though I'm convinced that Delouvrier was one of the founders of the Cagoule Noir, the secret society of extremists dedicated to keeping Algeria under French rule, his career didn't seem to suffer for it. And this feat of political legerdemain leads me to conclude he was a plant, a government informer—which, if true, is doubly remarkable since I'm convinced his sympathies actually lay in their cause."

"Such behavior is the mark of a blindly ambitious man," remarked Zorin.

"Yes," said Bogdanov. "He bears close watching. Kolesnikov, how many of our agents have infiltrated his ministry?"

"Four, Comrade General. One is on his personal staff."

"Good. Good. They must remain alert to his every move. I want a daily report."

"It shall be done, Comrade General."

Bogdanov nodded, then turned to Rokhlenko: "As we discussed in a preliminary

way the other day, Colonel, the plan is to
have my men deployed inside the hospital
and yours in the street. I will now hear
your report."

Rokhlenko removed a map from his
briefcase and spread it out on the foot rest
between them. "The key intersections are
these . . ."

Bogdanov listened closely to the plan
for several minutes before his thoughts
began to wander. That infernal folk ballad
still played in his head. He leaned forward
and forced himself to concentrate as
Rokhlenko moved on to another phase of
his report.

A moment later, they were interrupted
by a knock on the door. Zorin rose, opened
it and took a message from the guard. "A
telephone call for you, Comrade General.
From Major Ivanov. Do you wish to take
it in here?"

Bogdanov hesitated. Since Ivanov knew
the importance of this meeting, it was unlikely he would bother him with anything
trivial. "No, I may want a transcript. I'll
take it in my office."

Bogdanov descended the stairs quickly
to the room assigned him in the maximum
security section of the basement. He
picked up the phone, shut off the recording device attached to it, and told the
operator to put through his calls.

"Comrade General, this is Ivanov."

"Yes, Ivanov. What is it?"

"Please, forgive the interruption, but I thought this should be reported to you at once. Karamanov has left his room. The American surgeon came by to visit him and they went outdoors to play a game of chess."

Bogdanov's sense of relief was acute, but momentary. "I see. Your men accompanied them, of course? They have them under constant guard?"

"From a distance—yes."

"A distance!" roared Bogdanov. "What protection are they at a distance? I want them surrounding him, you incompetent oaf! A human wall! I want a wall of flesh shielding him from an assassin's bullet at all times."

"Y . . . Yes, Comrade General. I'll order them out at once."

"Pray you are not already too late."

"I will, Comrade General. . . . I beg your forgiveness for my shameful delay. My only reason for not acting sooner was that I didn't want to arouse the American's suspicion. I wanted your judgment on the matter first."

"Enough talk! Each wasted moment increases the danger. You have your orders, now act! I'll join you there as soon as I can."

Bogdanov returned to the library and with deliberate calm adjourned the meeting until tomorrow. He lingered long enough to join Zorin in a toast to the success of their mission, then left for the hospital.

Once underway in an embassy car, Bogdanov lit a cigarette, inhaled deeply, and pondered their latest crisis. A chess match! he marveled. Who could have anticipated such a harmless pastime might set the stage for Karamanov's undoing? But then, who among his American counterparts had predicted the possible outcome of their President riding past a book depository in Dallas, Texas? Assassination basically was a patient man's game; and if patient enough, he always won. Sooner or later, the inevitable lapse in security was bound to occur.

Just his wretched luck that their chess match had to be played on a Sunday afternoon when the hospital teemed with visitors, any one of whom could be concealing a CIA-issue weapon. For all he knew, Karamanov's head might be in the assassin's sights this very minute; the muffled bark of the silencer, a searing pain, then nothing for Russia's foremost genius, chaos for all others concerned.

19

For the second time that hour Bogdanov felt a sharp sense of relief as he strode through the hospital grounds and saw no unusual activity. Nor did he see any chess players. He looked at his watch: four thirty-five. Ivanov's call had reached him shortly after four, which meant that their match had lasted no more than thirty minutes. It also meant vastly more: a half-hour's interval of unguarded conversation between Karamanov and Sten.

He approached two of his men on the steps of the Institute and was about to speak to them when he saw Nicholas Sten come out the door.

He simulated surprise. "Why, Dr. Sten, what are you—? Has anything happened to my father-in-law?"

"No, no. He's fine. I just paid him a social call."

"That is all?"

"That's all. I made the mistake of challenging him to a game of chess. It was child's play for him."

"I'm relieved. Seeing you here, I naturally feared there had been some emergency."

Nick smiled. "Fortunately not. Your father-in-law's condition appears stable for the moment."

"Yes, but we all realize he lives a moment-to-moment existence. My wife and I are beginning to feel the strain. We will not breathe easy until after the operation. Have you chosen the date as yet?"

"No, but I will decide tomorrow after talking with Marandat. All depends on how soon he can gather up the necessary personnel and equipment. You know the risk we're taking. I want to be prepared for all eventualities."

Bogdanov nodded soberly. "Yes, that is wise. . . . By the way, my wife and I are staying at the Hotel Terasse in Montmartre. Please call us, if you have a free evening. We would like nothing better than to entertain you."

"Thank you, I will. . . . Well, nice running into you again, Monsieur Gessler."

"*Au revoir,* Dr. Sten."

After stepping aside for Nick to pass, Bogdanov stood a moment watching his retreating figure. Their brief encounter left him with a vague sense of uneasiness: the vibrations of a sixth sense that probed beneath the surface like an X-ray beam. Though the sunglasses the American wore had prevented Bogdanov from studying his eyes, the way he shifted his weight from foot to foot had betrayed Sten's inner tension. And while their conversation had been friendly enough, he now held the distinct impression they had been dueling with words. Or was he overreacting to such subtle stimuli?

Perhaps not, Bogdanov decided. His advancement, his very survival in the KGB, the most perilous of professions, had depended heavily on the attention he'd paid to such hyperacute instincts. And though a chess match seemed innocent enough on the surface, he had long ago learned that the only true innocence in life resided in the acts of birth and natural death.

Bogdanov's suspicions were further fed during his conversation with Karamanov. The physicist had accepted his scolding passively, protesting only that it was maddening to be confined to a hospital room twenty-four hours a day. But again Bogdanov had perceived the small signals. Though slight of build, Karamanov was an

imperious, strong-willed person, disdainful of the military and their regimented
mentality. Bogdanov had learned that
much firsthand during the long train ride
from Moscow to Paris. Yet, Karamanov
had taken his rebuke calmly, almost
placidly, and he equated such atypical
behavior with only one thing: guilt. Guilt
over what? It seemed insane to speculate
that Karamanov had divulged his true
identity to Sten. Such a revelation could
only represent the enactment of a death
wish—national as well as personal. But,
terminal insanity, even suicide, were not
unknown   occurences   among   Soviet
scientists, particularly the hard-driving
eccentrics like this one. The bedazzling
bright light of their genius blinded them
to all earthly conventions, all loyalties,
except the pact they made with their
goddess, Nature. Nothing else mattered
but their obsession with her secrets. . . .
And this is how the world would end, Bogdanov had long believed; not by a military
confrontation, but by the earth-shattering
miscalculation of one of these madmen.

Yet, though his suspicions were
aroused, Bogdanov realized they might
still prove illusory—the product of
paranoia, not omnipotent intuition. He
needed something far more tangible before
he dared accuse a man like Karamanov of
death wishes or disloyalty.

* * *

At six, Bogdanov left the hospital and took a cab to the Hotel Terasse where he and Galina were registered as man and wife, though he slept nights at the embassy. He phoned from the lobby and invited her to have a drink with him at the *brasserie* next door.

When Galina joined him a few minutes later she greeted him warmly, a girlish twinkle in her eyes.

They sat at a sidewalk table out of range of possible eavesdroppers and ordered apéritifs. Bogdanov smiled faintly as Galina hummed the refrain from the folk ballad he had sung last night.

"Why so glum?" she asked.

"I saw your father this afternoon. . . ."

Galina tensed. "And?"

"He seemed well, physically, but in a peculiar frame of mind. It's difficult to describe."

"What did you two talk about?"

"Oh, what started out as a discussion of minutiae, the weather, French toilet fixtures, ended up as a hot political debate . . . I'm sure I don't have to tell *you* what's bothering him, Galina?"

"You mean, the Arab-Israeli war?"

Bogdanov nodded instantly. "Yes, exactly. Your father expressed very strong opinions about it."

"I know. It's upset him greatly. Es-

pecially the role he believes our leaders
played in instigating it. The role played by
men like you, Denis. . . ."

"Yes, I suspected as much. I sensed his
personal hostility as we discussed it." He
smiled. "The truth is, Galina, I opposed
our latest involvement. Opposed it vigorously. But my opinion went unheeded.
Still, my opposition is on record. Malinivski himself acknowledged it. When my
ministry is purged, it will probably save
my skin."

"Did you tell my father this?"

"No. Naturally, it is confidential. I
shouldn't even be telling you. . . . But I've
already compromised myself in your eyes
by my display last night. Might as well
hang for stealing two pigs, as one."

"I'm glad."

"Glad of what?"

"That you opposed it. Our provoca-
tion."

"I did so out of caution, not conscience.
But your father—why has he reacted so
strongly?"

"My mother, you know, was a Jewess.
My father had no interest in that religion
or any other, but because he loved her so
he was always tolerant of Jews. He felt
they were a productive people and should
be left in peace. The latest outbreak upset
him, but he believed the official Tass
version that, once again, the Israelis were

the aggressors. His present anger began
to mount when he read the accounts of the
crisis in the French newspapers."

"And what was his reaction then?"

"The recklessness of the Politburo in
allowing such adventurism appalled him.
He called them 'primitives,' 'Stalin's
demented children.' " She paused to sip
her drink.

"Did he say anything else?"

Galina's eyes, showing above the rim of
her glass, grew wary. "No, nothing. Why
should everything he said concern you so?
Surely you do not suspect my father of
unpatriotic tendencies—because that's
absurd! Laughable! For years now, he has
forsaken all personal pleasure and slaved
for the safety of the Motherland. You
know that—you've investigated him."

Bogdanov nodded.

"You shouldn't be concerned about my
father's intentions, only the American's!
How much do you really know about this
Nicholas Sten? His motives for coming
here? Does he intend to save my father or
murder him?" Galina reached out, covered
Bogdanov's hand with her own, and
squeezed it. "I swear to you now, I shall
insist on being in the operating room
during my father's surgery, and if any
attempt is made on his life I will kill this
Nicholas Sten myself. With a scalpel in his
back!"

* * *

Galina was right, Bogdanov later
decided: Karamanov, despite his quirks,
was above suspicion. It was Sten who
deserved his total attention; Sten who
might have set up this afternoon's rendezvous. Yet, for what purpose? If he were
truly in the employ of the CIA, why cast
needless attention on himself by such a
move? It made little sense, even as the act
of an amateur. Still, he shouldn't dismiss
the possibility so glibly; its very openness
might, in itself, be a deception. Bogdanov
resolved to put Nicholas Sten under a
microscope; to devote this evening, and
every evening until the day of Karamanov's surgery, to his systematic study.
The tapes, films, reports his men were continuously gathering on him must be painstakingly reviewed.

And he'd need help. Bogdanov realized;
he would need Federov as an extension of
his eyes and ears and instincts. Chary of
what Stakhanov's response might be
when he heard rumors of his impending
dismissal, he had left his deputy behind to
keep him posted on Kremlin intrigue. But
now such a precaution seemed super-
fluous. His future, what remained of it,
would be decided in Paris, not Moscow,
and to safeguard it he needed Federov and
all his peasant cunning.

He decided to cable "Center" for him
tonight, along with a hundred extra
security troops.

20

The hotel switchboard operator woke Nick at 6:00 A.M. Still groggy from sleeping pills, he tried to stand up but fell back on the bed. His muscles felt flaccid and a numbness stupefied his brain. After a moment, he rolled onto his stomach, drew his arms under him, and with a supreme effort pushed himself up and over into a sitting position. He rubbed his eyes and peered at the room, shadowy and silent except for raindrops tapping the window, then picked up the phone and, dry-mouthed and thick-tongued, ordered croissants and coffee. Slowly, almost painfully, he began to dress for his journey to the American Hospital.

By the time he was sharing a second breakfast at the hospital with Tom Hewes, an internist on the staff and a friend from his Boston days, Nick was feeling brighter. They talked over old times and then Tom let him into the still locked library with his key.

Avila entered promptly at eight. The dapper agent shook his head and led Nick to a table in a corner of the room.

"Canter sends his best," he began.

"His best what?"

Avila smiled. "We're all on the same side. We're here protecting our own. . . . What did Karamanov have to say?"

"Quite a bit."

Avila sat so he could watch Nick and the door at the same time. "Go on, Doctor. I'm listening."

Nick wondered how to begin. He decided to give Avila a taste of Canter's shock tactics. "Okay, listen then. The highlights are these: one, Karamanov told me who he really is. Two, he suspects the CIA is wise to him and wants me to kill him. And three, he wants to die."

The surprised look on Avila's face resembled a grimace. He blinked, stared, than slowly nodded. "We guessed something like that was a remote possibility, but we never figured—"

"Never figured what?"

Avila's eyes darted toward the door. "Time's short. Suppose you tell me the rest of it first."

"All right." Nick gave him the gist of Karamanov's conversation, repeating the Russian's words accurately and unemotionally. He omitted only Karamanov's letter, withholding it until he could better gauge Avila's reaction. The agent's eyes were aroused, wary, compassionless. "Well, that's it," Nick concluded. "Do I take the next plane out or don't I?"

"Not just yet."

"Why the hell not? You don't expect me to kill him now, do you?"

"No, I don't," Avila said calmly. "And neither does he."

"Meaning what?"

"Meaning that if you go through with the operation now, he knows damned well you won't try to kill him. He's home free."

"He is? How do you figure that?"

"By figuring him; his motives for telling you all that he did. Just remember who you were talking to—not some lackey, some second-rate official, but *Comrade* Nikolai Karamanov, Russia's foremost physicist. We know this man's record. He's been a dedicated Communist all his life. Winner of the Stalin Prize and a dozen other decorations. A man like him doesn't betray his country. It's as hard to believe that as it is to believe one of our top scientists, a Van Allen or a Linus Pauling, would go over to the Reds. The small fry

may defect, but never the really big ones.
They can't be bought or blackmailed, and
no matter how peace-loving, how 'better
Red than dead' they are, that's not enough
motive."

"What's Karamanov's motive?"

"Depends. Do you think his condition
might have affected his brain so much
that he's cracked up? Sees himself as some
kind of a savior of world peace?"

"No. Not a chance. He's as sane as any
man I've ever met."

"Okay, then. That still leaves two alternatives. Either he meant what he said,
which I doubt, or he had a much more compelling reason for disclosing his identity."

"What reason?"

"The CIA knew about him, didn't they?
Even though Karamanov and his work are
the biggest secrets the Russians have, we
still know about them in advance. How?
Obviously because we've managed to
sneak one of our men into their inner
councils. A feat like that shows we're
pretty good. Well, so are they—and
usually what we can do they can do. Now
suppose, just suppose, the Russians have
recently tumbled to our man. They know
that we know about Karamanov, but what
they don't know is whether we've gotten
to you to kill him. That puts them in a hell
of a bind. They realize Karamanov hasn't
much of a chance if you don't operate. But

they also realize he has no chance at all if they let you go in there and finish him off."

"So?"

"So, their only out is to have him tell you who he really is, win your sympathy, then let you decide for yourself whether you want to go through with it. Don't forget, the Russians are master psychologists. They know how hard it must be for a surgeon like you to kill your patient. And this way they've deprived you of your one real motive. If you believe all Karamanov told you, then he's no longer a threat to our national security; his project dies with him. Not only that, they've robbed you of your one advantage—surprise. You're out in the open now and either you go through with the operation on their terms or you clear out."

"Oh, that's brilliant," Nick snapped. "A bit contrived, but brilliant. Your idea or Canter's?"

"It's a possibility," Avila said stiffly.

"Sure. So's cutting off your head to cure a headache. It's that absurd. The whole premise is absurd. Look, I admit I'm an amateur at all this, but I'm no fool! And neither are the Russians. Especially a cagey operator like Bogdanov. I just can't believe they'd go to all the trouble of transporting their man to Paris, take over part of a French hospital, and get me over

here to operate on him, only to risk
blowing their whole setup by a crazy, last-
minute stunt like that. I don't care how
shaky they are over my intentions, why
scare me off? It doesn't make sense.
Besides, I've met Karamanov and you
haven't. The man is a scientist, not an
actor. What he felt compelled to tell me
was damned difficult for him. I watched
him sweat over it—and I believe him.
Every word."

"You believe it because you want to
believe it."

"What's that supposed to mean?"

"Simply that he told you what you
wanted to hear. That you could relax now,
give your troubled conscience a rest.
Instead of being the ruthless scientist you
thought he was, he's a pretty decent guy.
A lifelong Communist who's finally seen
the error of his ways. No traitor, mind you,
but a humanity lover, willing to die first
before setting off a third world war. . . .
Oh, for Chrissake, Doctor. Is that what
you really believe or are you merely
indulging in a little wishful thinking? Me,
I'm not so trusting of the Russians, and
Canter's worse! He'll want a signed
confession from Karamanov as well as the
arm he signed it with, and unless you can
come up with that, we're sticking to our
original plan."

Nick hesitated, the lines in his face deep-

ening as his thoughts focused on Karamanov's letter. Though realizing it would
extricate him from this treacherous affair,
he could not bring himself to reveal it. He
rejected the temptation, even as a self-
protective instinct within him railed and a
more cogent voice warned of the price he
might have to pay for misguided loyalty.
His brief contact with Karamanov, even
more than the contents of his letter, had
convinced him of the Russian's integrity,
his towering spirit. He felt he had been in
the presence of greatness; a man not
cowed by impending death but infused
with added strength and purpose—and
Nick knew he could no more betray such a
man than murder him.

"How about it?" Avila prompted.

"I'm still not convinced."

The agent sighed. "Look, Doctor, I
admit we see things differently, but we're
a lot alike, too. We're both professionals
and we both deal in life-and-death matters.
Your training as a surgeon teaches you
when to suspect cancer and how to deal
with it. Well, so does mine—and, believe
me, the Russians are just as malignant, as
hard to eradicate as any cancer. While
their diplomats have been lulling us into a
false sense of security with talk of wanting
to reach some mutual understanding on
the limitation of antiballistic missiles,
those Kremlin bastards have been

plunging full speed ahead. That's how
trustworthy they are. Only this time
they've   overextended   themselves.
They've sunk their life's blood into Karamanov's system, and we intend to see
them bleed! We just can't take Karamanov's word for his change of heart.
Since he already wants to die, you'll
simply have to oblige him."

Nick heard Avila's last words with his
eyes closed. He could be listening to
Canter, he thought ironically. Different
faces, accents, but the sasme fervid look,
the same self-righteous ring of conviction
in their voices. *We're both in the business
of saving lives—American lives!* he remembered Canter saying. And now Avila
playing up the same higher call to duty.
No wonder Canter trusted him to handle
such a crucial assignment. The two even
thought alike. A remarkably uniform
breed. They were also much more than
that: brave, intelligent, selflessly dedicated men. But were they right? Was
their ruthless pursuit of the enemy better
than the compassion he felt for one worthy
man?

Nick gestured futilely. "I don't know. . .
I want to hear that order officially first."

"You will. Canter's moved up. I'll be
talking with him this afternoon." The
agent took a business card from his wallet
and scribbled a number on the back. "A

pay phone," he said. "Call from another pay phone at exactly 7:00 P.M. I'll let you know."

Nick examined the card. Avila's name and affiliation with *L'Express* were printed on the front. "All right," he said, "but tell him this, too. Tell him I'm shaky as hell right now. Tired and depressed and fed up with this whole dirty business. Tell him I love my country and want to protect her, but I also remember the lesson of the Eichmann and Nuremberg trials and know I have to decide for myself what's right or wrong. Tell him that despite your best efforts I haven't decided that as yet, and may never decide it. I might grab a plane out of here first. Tell him I'm sorry to keep him dangling, but after all, I'm the one chosen to kill and I just might not have the guts or the will for the job. So, in case I chicken out he'd better be prepared to step in. Better a hero's funeral for him than me."

Avila's stare hardened. "Okay, Doctor," he said curtly, "you've had your say. The choice is still yours. Just be grateful you live under a system of government that gives you one." He rose abruptly and gestured. "This time you leave first. I'll follow."

21

The morning rain had slackened off into thin drizzle by the time Nick returned to his hotel. A liveried doorman stepped forward to open the door, but instead of entering he turned and continued walking down the avenue toward the Place de l'Alma. The prospect of being shut up in his room for even an hour with his heavy, brooding thoughts seemed unbearable. He ducked under the fringe of an awning marked "Chez Francis," went inside the bar and ordered a *café crème*. He watched it sputter forth from the *percolateur* in a hiss of steam, then carried it outdoors to a dry table.

Nick stirred the coffee, feeling the swirl of his own emotions. The dizzying spiral continued until his anger, a last defense, gave way and despair spilled over. He felt submerged in it; a drowning man. He had been used so indiscriminately by so many people: Marandat, the Russians, the CIA, now even Karamanov, he could no longer function. He was used up.

Nick spread his surgeon's hands and stared down at them until their image began to blur and he experienced a sudden, sinking feeling. He shut his eyes, but the giddy sensation lasted until he knew he had reached some sort of bottom: the limit of his endurance, the bedrock of his emotional being? For the first time in his life, he was giving up on himself. He was beaten. Too much to think about; too little conviction for too many demands. . . But before he would blindly serve any of his masters, he was getting out.

He would get a few hours sleep, Nick decided, then phone Avila at his office. He expected the agent to denounce, possibly even threaten him, but it made no difference. His final disintegration had been brought on by indecision, not fear, and he knew he was beyond reach of such persuasion.

Nick sighed. A gray peace, gray as the morning sky. From under the awning, he could see the facades of stately gray buildings across the Pont and the soaring spiderwork of the Eiffel Tower truncated by low-hanging clouds. He watched an *agent de police* in box hat and shiny raincoat saunter by and followed his progress until he noticed a woman emerging from the Metro exit at the center of the square. He could see only a vague outline of her profile at that distance, yet something in her cheekbones, the tilt of her head, gave him the first, faint intimations of a dawning familiarity. Subconsciously, the recognition signals grew until the connection was made—Noelle! The name crackled through his brain like electricity. As he strained to see her in the dim light, the sun glimmered through a break in the clouds and the scene took on a surreal quality, the color of twilight.

Impossible, he thought; he was dreaming, wildly hallucinating. Noelle couldn't be here. She just couldn't be conjured up on demand to fill the demoralizing emptiness within him. Yet the force of his logic left the apparition unchanged. She stood diagonally across the intersection now, her features blurred as cars passed between them. Finally, she moved, came within twenty feet of him, and as he saw her face clearly the reality could no longer be denied.

He rose abruptly, almost knocking over the pedestal table. He shouted, *"Je reviendrai,"* over his shoulder to the waiter, and plunged into the intersection. Momentarily losing sight of her as she

turned the corner, he panicked and broke
into a run. He felt his heart pounding, not
from exertion, but from the promise of a
second chance with Noelle, a second life,
after ending the first with an act of
cowardice moments ago.

He caught up with her as she was entering Givenchy's. *"Mademoiselle!"* he called
out, reluctant to speak her name.

Noelle paused and looked over her
shoulder guardedly, prepared to snub an
unwelcome admirer. *"Mon Dieu, Nicholas!
C'est impossible!"* she gasped, her
features dissolving into dazed incredulity.
She swayed and he reached out to steady
her. His heart leaped. A different Noelle,
no longer twenty-two, thirtyish, yet no
less beautiful. Her face was thinner, the
youthful fullness gone from her cheeks.
But her eyes seemed larger, brighter, and
the symmetry of her bone structure still
flawless. She was that rarest of aesthetic
gifts to him: a mature woman whose
beauty had been deftly sculptured by the
years. He ached to embrace her, but had
forfeited that right fourteen years ago, put
oceans and continents between them. Still,
the wrong was another's: a younger,
weaker predecessor who had been
punished enough for it before his recent
death.

She stepped back and Nick released her
arms. Wordlessly, she turned, took a

halting step toward the Givenchy entrance, paused before a reflection of herself in the glass, then turned again and shrugged. "Well, Nicholas, what should I say? Nice to see you after all these years? You gave me a bad time once, but welcome all the same?"

Her flat words chilled him. He felt witless to answer.

"Well, what is it you expect?"

"Talk."

"Talk!" she exclaimed. "I thought we did our talking fourteen years ago. We had quite a remarkable talk then—remember?"

Nick nodded.

"What's left to say? Surely, you don't want to have a nice little *tête à tête*, and reminisce about old times? No, Nicholas, that's not for us. We weren't friends, we were lovers—wartime lovers—a notoriously unlucky breed. I'm sure you remember better than I. The man always does."

"Yes, I remember." His voice cracked. " . . . Hour by hour. Day by day."

Noelle frowned. "How touching. Was I your grand passion? If so, I pity you. It's too late to mean anything to us now."

"Is it?"

"Of course. You're still married, aren't you? Still an ambitious surgeon?"

"Yes."

"I'm not surprised. That says it then. We've talked enough. I don't know what you're doing here or why you have that sad, exhausted look on your face—and I don't want to know. It's all quite hopeless. *Fini.* Still, I don't regret meeting you like this. It's comforting to know how little you mean to me, after all." She extended her hand. *"Au revoir."*

Nick stared, humiliated, at her out-stretched hand, the blackness of dream's end in her glove. Suddenly, his expression changed, the corners of his mouth turned up, and he laughed.

Nonplussed, Noelle reacted angrily. *"Vous êtes fou!"*

"No, not crazy," he answered. "Just inept. Totally inept. A dumb, duped American who's taking one hell of a pounding because he still doesn't realize the hopelessness of the trap he's in."

"What do you mean?"

"I let you put me down pretty hard a moment ago, didn't I? Bludgeon me into a futile submissiveness until I was ready to crawl into some hole with my guilt feelings and let you have the satisfaction of getting back at me. Well, revenge yourself all you want. I deserve it—hugely. Only that's not important now. What's important is this," he said, seizing her arms again. "You've haunted me for years, and here you are, more beautiful

than ever. But are you happy—content—
or as miserable as I am? Answer that, and
I'll leave, if you insist, or buy you a cup of
coffee."

Noelle's eyes darkened with his image.
She stayed in his arms, oblivious to the file
of passersby, and stared back searchingly.
Finally, she capitulated. "Not just coffee,
you incorrigible swine, you heartless
cretin—but breakfast! Eggs, sausage,
ham, as much as I can eat. Caviar, too, if
they have it. I haven't had an appetite for
days and suddenly I'm famished. How
would you explain that, Major Sten?"

Nick grinned. "Just plain doctor now.
Major Sten, the military misfit, no longer
exists."

"Oh? Does it make a difference? Make
you feel freer to by yourself?"

"Can you be yourself?"

"What do you mean?"

"Husband, family, other entangle-
ments?"

Noelle looked up sharply as they crossed
the street. "What if I said no—not for the
moment. Would that please you?
Encourage you to want to resume our
affair?"

"Yes."

"Simple as that?"

"No, not simple at all," Nick said, after
seating her at his cafe table. "What we
had was never simple. If we hadn't met

when we did, do you think two people like
us would've ever come together? . . . I
doubt it. The war created our need, and
afterward I became afraid of the effort it
might take to sustain it. The price scared
me, too.''

"The price is still the same," she said.
"Does it still scare you?"

"Yes, but not as much. What scares me
even more is letting you get away again.
My life's not entirely my own anymore. I
know   how   odd—melodramatic—that
sounds and I can't explain it any better—
at least I don't want to right now. But
whatever's been left me, that portion is
mine. And that part—that extraordinarily
free part—wants you.''

Noelle smiled, the same wistful, uneven
smile he had been trying to remember for
fourteen years. "That part you're talking
about sounds very devoted. It intriges me.
I think I'd like to kiss it—depending, of
course, where it is. . . . But I'm not sexy so
much as incredibly hungry. You haven't
explained that to me yet, have you? Some
kind of strange transference, I suppose.
You also haven't explained why, at a time
I was making clear to you what a *cochon*
you were, you laughed. What gall! Here I
was doing my best to despise you and succeeding—or   so   I   thought—and   you
respond with a totally inappropriate
laugh. Why?"

The waiter came to take their order. An older man, he beamed at Noelle's hearty appetite, assured her that her eggs would be properly poached, and in the vanishing tradition of gallant French waiters, appeared happy to serve them.

"Why?" Noelle persisted, a moment later.

"Cyrano de Bergerac."

"Cyrano?" she puzzled. "Why do you mention him?"

"My old hero. 'A man does not fight merely to win!' Even if I lost you again, I had to face it like a man."

Noelle's eyes glistened. "How typical of you. How touching and romantic and how vain! You and your masculinity. I remember the times it nearly got you killed in Korea . . . . What is it now? Why are you here?"

"To perform an operation. I was invited over by a French surgeon by the name of Marandat. I believe you know him."

"Marandat, yes. His wife Simone and I are old friends."

"He told me. In fact, he gave me your address in Algiers."

"What else did he tell you?"

"That you had your own clinic there and were famous for your work in child psychology."

"Nothing about my personal life?"

"No."

"But, naturally, you're curious."

"No . . . I only care that you're here.
That I still have a chance with you."

She shook her head. "No, Nick, too glib.
You expect too much. I'm not the same
person anymore. After you, I followed the
wars . . . Indochina, Algeria. You know the
kind of woman who follows the wars? You
know how it drains them? I'm as tough as
an old hen now. I'm like you were: all I
really care about is my work and my
children—all my children."

The waiter brought coffee and a basket
of brioches. After he left, Noelle's face
softened. "All right, a truce. A truce to
last through breakfast. Tell me why
Marandat invited you here?"

"To operate on a relative of his. A very
delicate, dangerous operation."

"And you intend to perform it?"

Nick hesitated, looked down at his
hands, then nodded. Was it bravado? he
thought. His masculinity again? No, much
more. It was right, it would be right
centuries from now after Russians and
Americans ceased to exist, and it was
what he really wanted to do.

"Why you? Why not a French
surgeon?"

"I pioneered the procedure. It's called
gas endarterectomy. I use a jet of gas to
clean out the clot in an artery."

"How dangerous is it?"

"In this patient—very. He has a heart condition as well as blockage of both carotid arteries. His chances of ever waking up from the anesthetic are pretty slim."

"Yet, despite such risks, you still intend to operate? Why?"

"Because I'm a surgeon, a good one, and because he deserves to live."

"Nothing more?"

"No. Why?"

"You look so haggard, so worn out. What have you been doing nights?"

"Thinking," said Nick. "About the operation, about my patient, about myself. Especially, about myself. . . . No answers, though. Just more questions."

"And after the operation—what?"

"I haven't thought that far. The operation is an end-unto-itself. After that, it depends—"

"On what?"

"On you. On what sort of a patch-up job we can do on the feelings that might be left after fourteen years. Maybe I don't even deserve the chance? That's up to you."

Noelle gazed at him appraisingly as she sipped her coffee. "How can I answer you? Since you dropped from the sky ten minutes ago, I've run through every possible emotion. . . . I need time to think."

"What are your plans for the day?"

"My plans? I have some shopping to do, then a conference to attend at the Faculté de Médicine at one. And you?"

"I promised Marandat I'd drop by the hospital to discuss final plans for the operation. Organize my surgical team."

"When will the operation be?"

"I'm going to try to get it scheduled for Wednesday."

"So soon?"

"The sooner the better. The less time I have to think what can go wrong . . . Where can we meet afterward?"

Noelle shrugged. "Oh, where you like. Where are you staying?"

"The Georges Cinq. And you?"

"I've sublet a small apartment on the Rue de Courcelles. Perhaps we should meet back here?"

"No," said Nick. "Your apartment."

Her eyebrows lifted. "Why there?"

"Do you object?"

"No, naturally not. But why?"

"It's the one place I know you must come."

Noelle smiled. "I'm glad to hear you're not overconfident, Nicholas. It's better that way."

22

Nick left Noelle and took a taxi to the Broussais Hospital. He found Marandat in his office. "*Bonjour*, Dr. Sten!" the French surgeon exclaimed and came around the corner of his desk to shake hands.

"How's our patient this morning?"

"Well, A quiet night. The nurse tells me your visit yesterday cheered him greatly. How thoughtful of you."

"Not at all. I enjoyed talking with him. As you say, he's a brilliant man."

"And what did you two discuss?"

"Oh, nothing of any consequence. . . . A philosophical discussion, mainly." Nick yawned.

"You look fatigued. All goes well, I hope?"

"Oh, fine. Since I'm in Paris alone, I've

become a *noctambule*. I'm just short on sleep."

"*Ah, je comprends!* . . . Knowing what a strain the operation places on you, I'm glad you've found time for some relaxation."

Nick grinned. "Perhaps, too much . . . But I promise to be well rested for the surgery."

"What day have you chosen?"

"Wednesday. Day after tomorrow. Depending, of course, if you feel this gives you enough time to set things up?"

Marandat exhaled. "Tell me what you need and, naturally, I'll do my best." Returning to his desk, he picked up pad and pencil.

Nick sat opposite him. "First of all, I want an anesthesiologist—the best you can find. Preferably a man who's not only had experience with neurosurgical cases but open-heart as well. Know someone like that?"

"Yes, of course. Armand de Musset. I have operated with him many times. His associate, Pierre Delavigne, is also quite good. . . . But why open-heart surgery?"

"I'll tell you why," Nick answered grimly. "I have no illusions about this case. None. Neither about my ability nor his chances. Cleaning out his left carotid will be tricky enough, but we both know the big question is his cardiac status. He might not even tolerate the anesthetic, and if his heart doesn't stop then, it might when I start manipulating those carotids. No matter how lucky we get, it's still going to be one hell of an obstacle course from beginning to end."

Marandat wrung his hands. "Yes, I know."

"All right, then. I want to be prepared to go all the way. If his heart stops, I want everything there to get it going again: drugs, defibrillator, intravenous, pacemaker, aortic balloon. And if that's not enough, I want a heart-lung pump in the room and a team of cardiac surgeons ready to put him on bypass."

"A wise precaution. What else?"

"I want him constantly monitored. Not just blood pressure and pulse, but pH, gas studies, the works! And I want a volume-cycled respirator standing by in your intensive care unit for his post-op care. He might never make it that far, but just in case, I don't intend to stop there."

Marandat finished writing the last item and sighed. "You shall have them all, I guarantee it. I'll use what influence I have and gather them together by Wednesday."

Nick shook his head. "No, too late. An operation as difficult as this requires teamwork and I'm calling a rehearsal of the team for two o'clock tomorrow afternoon. Can you arrange it?"

"God knows, I'll try. It's the very least I can do compared to your tireless effort. Even so, it hardly seems enough. It's—"

"It's enough," Nick interrupted. "Two o'clock, then?"

"Yes, two o'clock. . . . Shall we go up and visit my uncle now? I'm anxious to tell him the good news."

They found Karamanov sitting in a chair reading a French magazine.

"Ah, good morning!" he said, extending his hand without rising. If Nick's presence came as any surprise, it did not show on his face.

They spoke casually for a few minutes, then Marandat announced they had set the date for his surgery.

The magazine slipped from Karamanov's grasp. "When?"

Marandat exchanged glances with Nick before continuing. "We are agreed, Uncle —it shall be on Wednesday."

Karamanov gazed at Nick, his eyes remote and glassy as only old eyes could be. "I know you have considered this step very carefully, Dr. Sten."

"I have," said Nick.

Karamanov scrutinized him a moment longer. "Yes, I see. . . . I wish you well."

Alone and uneasy with his thoughts,

Nick wandered through Noelle's apartment. The five-story sandstone building rising up in the Rue de Courcelles might have once been the *hôtel* of a Parisian nobleman or a merchant prince. Now it was divided into numerous modest flats. Small as Noelle's apartment was—living room, alcove kitchenette, and tiny offset bedroom with bath—it seemed sufficient for a woman alone. Yet it struck Nick as oddly impersonal; hardly lived in. Except for a faint scent of perfume hanging in the air, there was nothing to suggest that anyone in particular, certainly not the vibrant Noelle he remembered, made this a house. Even her library, that infallible index to individual character, revealed little. The antique escritoire in the corner held only a few psychology texts, a biography of Freud, a Simenon thriller, and a novel by Camus. The lone periodical visible was a month-old copy of *Le Canard Enchaîné*, the satirical French weekly.

Idly, Nick flipped the magazine pages. They fell open to a caricature of the angel de Gaulle, winged like Jehovah, admonishing a diminutive Frenchman: "Build an ark, my son." He was about to put it down when the caption under the drawing caught his eye: *Apres le deluge—Delouvrier?* The name sounded familiar. He vaguely recalled Avila mentioning it in some connection with Karamanov. Nick translated laboriously.

> Edgar Etienne Delouvrier — what har-
> money in the name! It rolls off the
> tongue like a popular slogan: Liberty,
> Equality, Fraternity—or, if you prefer—
> Ready, Aim, Fire! Not since Charlemagne
> has the French politic known such a melli-
> fluous name. Whose can compare? Say
> Maurice Couve de Murville and the
> mouth twists, Georges Pompidou and it
> pouts. But say Edgar Etienne Delouvrier
> and—*helas*—you must smile. Think what
> his ascent to the presidency might mean:
> a nation of smiling Frenchmen! The
> American tourists would return in
> droves. But what manner of man is the
> possessor of such a name? Alas, he is no
> longer the outspoken professor, the
> apostle of students of the right. He has
> become secretive, inaccessible. He hides
> from the public eye like a lizard under a
> rock. Nonetheless, our spies are every-
> where; they permit us to speak for him.
> We present him to you now in truth and
> absentia. . . .
>
> Q. *My dear minister, why are you so
>   adverse to being interviewed?*
> A. The public is not yet ready to hear my
>   ideas.
> Q. *Then what brings you here today?*
> A. I'm not here. You are imagining it.
> Q. *Your former colleagues hint darkly
>   that you are a Fascist in your phil-
>   osophy?*
> A. No. A Bonapartist.
> Q. *What is the difference?*

A. A French one.

Q. *But you believe, do you not, in a strong concentration of power in the presidency and little for the Assembly?*

A. I believe that given the sensitive and congenitially disharmonious nature of the average Frenchman, one mind will serve him better than many.

Q. *What do you see in store for France now?*

A. A brief power struggle, another interim government, a further splintering of political factions, then a gradual acceptance of de Gaulle's logical successor.

Q. *Logical, in what sense?*

A. A man who thinks like him, dreams like him, and has the good sense to tighten his control over the internal security forces during this difficult period.

Q. *But looking beyond that, what does a man with your prophetic vision see as France's role in the coming decade?*

A. A crucial one. First, to grow—economically, militarily, politically, so as to stave off the threat of the German industrialists. Then, to lead the way for Europe to unite, to stand as a third force between the hegemonies of the Russians and Americans.

Q. *Do you see this as a hope or a reality?*

A. Under de Gaulle, it remained a hope; under me, it will become a reality.

Nick wearied of translating French at

this point and tossed the magazine aside.
An overpowering lassitude spread
through him, jumbling his thoughts. He
found himself drawn to Noelle's bed. Removing coat, tie, and shoes, he stretched
out on the coverlet. This was rash
conduct, he realized. Above all, he must
not fall asleep. Whatever Noelle's intentions had been when she gave him the key,
to come home and find him sleeping in her
bed would be brazen effrontery. . . . He
made his heavy eyes study the frieze of
ornamental molding that ran along the
walls and the cracked plaster ceiling.
Green, like the color of an operating room.
He thought of the surgery to come: the
taut, pale skin of Karamanov's neck
parting under the slash of his scalpel. His
brain dulled. He slept.

   . . . the eternal dust of treeless Korea
gritty on his lips during the long jeep ride.
Summer sun blazing on the war-riven
Land of the Morning Calm that in winter
became Frozen Chosen . . . Finally, Pu-san
and the hilltop hotel above the shining Sea
of Japan and Noelle's sweet, smelling
ardor in the night . . . Chance had thrown
them together, the lovely French
psychologist working for UNICEF and
the American Army surgeon who, after
ten harassing months in a forward field
unit, had been reassigned to the base

hospital near Seoul. High time, too, for by
then Nick was almost a casualty himself.
Too many bloody stumps and frag-torn
faces and airsucking chest wounds in too
many American boys putting their fright-
ened trust in him. Toward the close of the
nightmarish episode, Nick was steadying
his hand for scalpel and suture work with
lashings of medical alcohol in canned
grapefruit juice. So they brought him back
to Seoul where chance put in his way the
lissome French girl, this coolly aloof white
woman in a sea of Oriental females that so
many rear-echelon officers and embassy
personnel had vainly tried to seduce . . .
Maybe, he pondered after it was ended,
when Noelle had become a distant, not
quite believable memory of aching sweet-
ness, he simply happened to come along at
the right time. In Korea, even noncombat-
ants suffered their own peculiar kind of
battle fatigue. After seeing too many
orphan babies with their war-haunted
eyes, Noelle might have been ready to give
herself to the next man who asked.

Chance and the right time and their
mutual need and the flooding memory of
her first surrender. Pu-san and the
bamboo hotel perched on stilts above the
sea. Whitebearded Papa-san and doll-like
chambermaids shyly smiling at their
lovers' happiness . . . They talked little.
Not nearly enough, he later knew. Gasping

murmurs in the hollow of his shoulder and
the fragrant spill of her dark hair on the
pillow, but never enough talk. There were
things that Noelle had a right and a need
to hear from him, but with the taste of
ultimate betrayal already in his mouth,
Nick's tongue was tied . . .

Fathoms of time receded, and Nick,
drifting through the once forbidden
dream, felt unsurpassed contentment.
That time with Noelle had been the acme
of his sexual life and now that he had
found his way back again he never wanted
to leave . . . An intruding noise, a door
closing, a footfall, made him stir—swirling
the waters. Breathlessly, he resisted, until
sudden oxygen lack made him break for
the surface. His eyes slitted open. Above
him, Noelle's incomparable face.

"You take much for granted, *mon vieux*.
Too much by far."

Echoes of Noelle's faintly accentuated
voice rippled in his ear. Wake up, he
thought, answer her. But like a patient
under the mask, his head swimming from
the pungency of the ether, he sensed the
helplessness of his position, the opening
void, and fell on the mercy of others.

He said nothing, shut his eyes in search
of the dream, and when there was only the
afterglow of pale light on his retina,
opened them again and with strange

detachment (who had willed it?) reached for her hand. His fingers anchored around her slim wrist and his form floated up. Boldly committed now, his arms encircled her, pressed her cashmere-covered breasts against his face, and feeling her stiffen, waited for the judgment which he knew would either ressurect or destroy him as a man.

He waited through a breath-holding eternity, waited until whatever punishment he might have merited for his sins had been met by the waiting, and then, gathering courage from her silence, pulled her down with gently insisting fingers. She sighed, a surrendering sound, and Nick's taut muscles relaxed. His fingers tugged sweater from skirt and roamed silk undergarments until he clasped her firm, full breasts. Then he paused, reflecting and remembering. . . .

More than love, which he felt, and out of dreams older than this one, existed this oddly coupled need: desire in the presence of death. Nick had first wakened to it his freshman year in medical school when, after dissecting a cadaver all day, he'd felt this compelling urge to make love to a woman. Perhaps because sex with all its ritual pretensions was the antithesis of death, or whatever the reason, this association had lingered in his psyche ever since. In Korea, where daily dying made the compulsion strongest, Noelle had fulfilled him, and after that, in those nights made long by a patient's death, a reluctantly accommodating Ann. Now, he felt the strange pairing again: the act of love had conjured up death—and he could only wonder whose death, his or Karamanov's, this gift of Noelle's was meant to console.

He groaned with brief, bursting pleasure and she had slipped away from him. The bed shifted with the easing of springs. He opened his eyes to the sight of her bare back vanishing behind bathroom door. A sound of water rushing. A gurgling away into the bowels of hundred-year-old French plumbing. Nick listened and grinned. Romantic, he thought. The flushing of a bidet.

He stretched luxuriously, feeling the accumulated tensions of the past nine days seep out of his muscles. Nine days— a second lifetime! Canter had first approached him a week ago Sunday. But he preferred not to think about Canter, only Noelle.

The bathroom door opened and she emerged wearing a knee-length peignoir.

He gazed at her eyes, serene and adoring. No longer alone in this comfortless land, this devil's outpost of his mind. He smiled, hoping it would coax a smile from her. Her mouth twitched slightly, but her face remained impassive. Rashly, he murmured, "Thank you."

"*Service!*" she snapped, and with that her fury spilled out like bitter emesis. "Oh, damn you! Damn your beseeching eyes and your colossal ego. I didn't want this . . . want to be so easy for you."

"Then why did you?"

"Why? The woman never asks why— only the man!"

"Answer me."

"Not what you think, my dear Nick. What you might smugly assume. Oh no, something far more ordinary. Don't you know all women feel lust once in a while?" She shrugged disparagingly. "Why not? A rainy day, an unplanned opportunity, a phallic handyman in the bedroom—it's all too banal!"

Nick sat up. "I see you're not through punishing me. What happened just now was something I never thought—never dared hope—would happen again. But banal! I don't believe you."

"You are a child!"

Nick reached out and fingered the hem of her gown. "Perhaps with you. Otherwise, I can assure you there is nothing childish about the life I lead."

She snatched the thin fabric from his grasp.

He looked up curiously. "Why did you bother to put this on?"

"Because I feel cheapened. And ashamed."

"Is that what you feel?" His voice rose. "Look at me. Does my love make you ashamed, too?"

"Love! Oh my God, the man's mad! This delusion he raves about is back. There may have been something once, a long time ago. But if there was, it was all mine—not yours. Pride, of course. How could I give myself so wantonly without love? But you! You never even pretended."

"Oh, Jesus God! Didn't you know—couldn't you sense—I loved you?" Nick grimaced; there was to be no rest, no respite, to his life anymore. The climb was straight up. " . . . All right, so I ran out on you. I had a wife I didn't love. And a son—an infant son—I did, so I left. I've regretted it ever since. . . . But I'll try to make it up to you. The rest can be for us."

"The rest of what?"

"Our lives. Yours and mine."

"*Our* lives, you and I!" Her lips curved mockingly. "You dare offer that now? Do you think the world has stopped spinning these fourteen years? That, like Sleeping Beauty, I've waited in suspended animation for your kiss? No, *mon coeur,* no such magic for us. It's you who must wake up. Look!" Noelle stripped off her peignoir and revolved before him like a couturier's mannequin. "What do you see, *monsieur le docteur Sten?* What does my body tell you?"

Nick frowned. He should have seen it before, but he had barely opened his eyes. Now, it was telltale and obvious: a suprapubic incision mark, faintly livid against her paler belly flesh. "Cesarean?" he said.

"Yes."

"You have had a . . . a child?"

"A son. A fine, sturdy, ten-year-old boy, Alain. He is spending the summer in Bretagne with my mother."

"I see . . . You have a son." Nick's stomach contracted. He drew a sheet over his nakedness. "And have you a husband I've never heard of either?"

"Had," Noelle answered softly, "I'm a widow. Did you think I bore an illegitimate child?"

"No, of course not. . . . Tell me about your husband."

"Why?"

"Because you were his wife and it saddens me, and because that is what you want."

"He died in a place called Massif de l'Aures—a very picturesque spot. In case the name's not familiar to you, it's in Algeria. The French once fought a war there."

"Algeria. He—your husband—was a

soldier?"

"No—an archaeologist. A dedicated scholar. And then, pouf! Terrorists killed him in a cafe with a *bombe plastique*. . . . The sad part is he died a month, a mere month, before his son was born. They withheld the news from me until weeks after—but I knew. By some strange, terrible instinct, I knew he was gone and that the cycle of my life was over. . . ." Noelle's voice trailed off. Her chin trembled and her breasts rose. Hugging her arms around her, she lost her proud, straight carriage, her defiant nudity, and for a moment looked as frail and defenseless as a sick child.

Nick slipped out of bed and went to her. She accepted his embrace passively for a moment, then inserted her arms between them and pushed him back. "No, stop. Please let me go. Put some clothes on."

"Why?"

"So we can talk, talk sensibly, without our bodies to distract us. . . . We must talk if anything between us is to be settled."

Nick nodded. He picked her peignoir up off the floor and handed it to her, then slipped on his pants.

They moved into the living room where Noelle poured drinks, cognac for him, Cointreau for herself. Nick sat beside her on the couch, gently stroking her hand. Her eyes opened to his probing look like the edges of a fresh wound.

"What do you want of me?" she asked softly.

"These hours, this peace. To find some purpose to my life by loving you."

Noelle stared. "You're so different now, Nicholas . . . You say you've not thought past this operation you intend. But what will you do?"

"Do? I don't know. It really doesn't concern me that much. Not the way you, us, the surgery itself concerns me."

"You talk so strangely, so fatalistically about this operation. A man like you must have performed hundreds. What makes this one so unusual?"

Nick argued with inner voices whether to tell her. She was strong-willed, intelligent, a psychologist who knew war and death and human conflict. And he loved her, felt this vibrant, ennobling love that dispelled all distrust and doubt. But was it fair to involve her in such a murderous affair? . . . Yes, he thought, for she is involved with me.

He drained his drink, then said: "You're right. It's not just an ordinary operation. The patient is not an ordinary man."

"Not ordinary? What then?"

"He is a scientist, a great mind, and—" His glottis contracted.

"And what?"

"An enemy . . . a Russian."

Her eyes widened. "A Russian! You are operating on a Russian? Here in Paris? That's incredible! . . . Who is this Russian?"

"His name is Karamanov, only here he's called by another name. His is a physicist, a missile expert. Another Einstein, I'm told."

"Told? Told by whom?"

"Some fellow Americans. They would prefer him dead."

"They told you this?"

"Oh, many times. They were quite emphatic about it. You see, they knew enough about his plans for an impenetrable antimissile system to consider him the most dangerous man alive . . . . They want him dead at all costs."

Noelle frowned. "They want *you* to kill him? But how could that be? How can they expect you—a surgeon—to kill your own patient?"

"They have their arguments: love of country, the Red menace, the balance of power. . . . Oh, many."

"And you agreed? No, I can't believe it."

"Agreed? Not a first. I was appalled, horror-stricken. But that wasn't all. There was a certain fascination to it, too. A sense of great drama. Here I was, a surgeon, a man of action—and this made me absolutely unique—the only man among the earth's billions who could perform this delicate operation. Even the Russians have heard of me. The two most powerful secret services in the world, the CIA and the KGB, were both after my services. It was heady stuff for a surgeon from Wisconsin with a frigid wife and a jealous chief holding him down. I agonized over it, beat my breast, but at the same time felt incredibly self-important and alive. Who wiser than I could make such an awesome decision? So, in the end, I convinced myself I could do it. For love of country, I said. The common good."

Noelle smiled wanly. "Yes, love of country. We are all taught that at a very young, very impressionable age. I know. At the age of eleven, I served as a runner for the *maquis*."

"I didn't know—" Nick said, surprised.

"No, I've told few people. Sounds adventurous, perhaps? It wasn't! Still, my father and brother were already dead and I did what I was asked. It left scars; deep, psychic scars that ruled my life long after. Then you. All too briefly, you—a man I could respond to—" Her face grew wistful, then she shrugged. "Now, of course, you have more urgent matters to concern you. What will you do?"

"Do? Before I met you I had just about decided to do nothing. Get the hell out. I knew I couldn't kill this man—any man—and I thought I might be able to live with it if I ran. But I can't. Not with you. . . . Besides, the time for running is over. Karamanov's life is in my hands and there's no letting go." He smiled ruefully. "The irony is, it would be so damned easy to kill him. I could do it any number of ways. But if the CIA wants him dead, they'll have to do it themselves. Maybe it's pride, simple humanity, but I'll try to save him."

Noelle's eyes misted. "Yes, your CIA has misjudged you. They have chosen wrong. A true Frenchman lives with a sense of history. *La mort avant le déshonneur.* There is little else to his foolish existence, so he does not question it. But you are a complex man, my dear Nick, and finally, a compassionate one. Evidently, there are worst fates for a man like you."

23

Again the peremptory ring of the telephone, the eye-dilating orientation to darkness, and Nick woke to Wednesday, this crowning day, with a pervasive inner calm. He rose from bed, drew back the drapes, and stepped out on the balcony. Inhaling the rain-fresh air, Nick thought back to the many times he had stood out on his own balcony to gaze reflectively at the thinning white haze over Lake Mendota. Now he was homeless, free-drifting, responsible only to himself—but perhaps it had always been meant to be that way, and he felt no overriding regret. He felt little of anything, as though a protective sheath had overgrown his nerves during the night. Still, he went back inside and composed a long letter to

Ann. He wanted her to know the truth
about his ordeal. He didn't trust Canter to
tell her and Hank's knowledge was incomplete. He wrote, too, of his accidental
meeting with Noelle, his need for her, and
his intention to remain with her no matter
what the outcome of the surgery. He
urged Ann not to blame herself, only him,
and asked her to explain it as best she
could to the children. He signed it love and
regret, and felt both in sharp measure
until, later, the letter slid down the
mailbox chute and he strode through the
archway of the Broussais Hospital to
more impending concerns.

The entrance to the Cardiovascular
Institute, the reception area, the sixth-
floor cafeteria, all contained clusters of
young, alert, Slavic faces. Though he had
anticipated it, their very openness disturbed him—as if their presence were
meant to serve notice that the game was
nearing a conclusion and all subterfuge
had been lifted.

The harsh cafeteria lights glared off the
white tableclothes. Nick joined an
unusually tense, sweating Marandat and
five other members of his surgical team at
the back table. He surveyed their faces;
only the anesthesiologist was missing.
"Where's de Musset?" he asked.

"A regrettable occurrence," said
Marandat. "He was stricken with severe

stomach pains during the night and put in
the hospital. His gallbladder, I believe."

Nick frowned. De Musset had impressed
him: a quietly competent individual who
spoke fluent English and appeared the
type who could keep cool-headed under
pressure. He wondered if de Musset's real
trouble was with his gallbladder, or the
Russians? But if they didn't trust him,
why the hell hadn't they replaced him
earlier? He had already spent hours
instructing the anesthesiologist in the
special hazards of the procedure. Now he'd
have to rush through the briefing with a
new man, and he didn't like being
harassed in this way.

"Armand called me himself late last
night," Marandat continued, "and recom-
mended a replacement."

"Who?"

"His associate, Pierre Delavigne. I've
operated with him before. He's young and
tends to be a little temperamental, but
otherwise a good man. In another year,
he'll be a full professor at the Faculté de
Médicine."

"Where's Delavigne now?"

"In the operating room. Setting up his
equipment."

Nick glanced around the table; five
somber faces. Evidently, his Russian
cohorts didn't care much for the last-
minute substitution either. "All right," he

said. "I'll go talk to him."

Marandat rose with him.

"He speaks English, doesn't he?"

"Of a fashion—yes."

"Good. My swearing is limited in French."

Delavigne looked more Germanic than French, Nick thought on meeting him: a tall, heavyset man with flaxen-blond hair, blue eyes, and thick lips. Possibly, an Alsatian. He listened attentively to Nick's operative plan, asked the right questions to prove he understood it, and expressed his pleasure to be working with him on such a new procedure.

"Don't thank me yet," Nick said. "You may be in for a rough morning."

"Yes, I suspect so."

"What time are they bringing the patient down?"

Delavigne looked at his watch. "Any moment now. I personally gave him his premedication at seven thirty."

"Okay," Nick said, "I guess that about covers it . . . Just remember I want the gas-oxygen mixture controlled precisely. And go easy on the Fluothane. Carry him light as you can on it after you induce him. His heart is bad enough without the gas depressing it further."

Delavigne's fingers restlessly drummed a beat on his clipboard as he listened. "I understand perfectly," he said curtly. "It shall be as you wish."

Nick followed him out of the small anesthetists' office. Lagging behind, he watched Delavigne bang open the double doors to the operating room suite. He sighed: the last thing he needed was a temperamental French anesthesiologist in the operating room with him. He would have vastly preferred a phlegmatic Russian, he thought wryly.

Nick walked through the doctors' lounge to the tile-floored dressing area to the rear. He removed his street clothes and put on a white scrub suit. Out of habit, he transferred his watch from his wrist to his ankle, then laced on a pair of rubber-soled cotton boots. He had always enjoyed the routine of dressing and scrubbing, even as he imagined actors enjoyed applying their makeup. But now he was too preoccupied by a host of forebodings to notice: Karamanov's heart condition, the fate of his antimissile system if the physicist should survive, the peril to his own life if he should not; most disconcerting of all, the portent he now felt toward the plans of his fellow countrymen. What had happened to Avila? he asked himself for possibly the hundredth time. As instructed, he had called the number written on the agent's card Monday evening. No one had answered. He had phoned twice more than night, to no avail.

He had even considered calling the emergency number Canter gave him, but hadn't really thought out what he would say and the deception was distasteful to him.

He stood up, stretched, and was about to leave when Marandat came to fetch him. "All is ready, Dr. Sten."

Nick stared appraisingly at the pudgy, perspiring Frenchman. "You look nervous, Marcel."

"Ah, *oui*. Intensely. I'm glad it is you who will be operating, not I."

Nick smiled, picturing the cordon of flinty-eyed Russians in and around the Institute. "Yes," he said, "I can understand why."

Nick raised his mask to his face as he entered the operating room. Karamanov had already been wheeled in. Taking hold of the draw sheet, Nick helped Delavigne and two orderlies transfer his frail body from the stretcher to the operating table and strap him in. The sudden lifting and tugging barely seemed to rouse him. His face appeared a pasty gray under the arc of overhanging lights. Nick turned to Delavigne. "You've got him pretty well snowed, haven't you?"

"*Comment?*"

"Exactly how much premedication did you give him?"

"The usual—one hundred milligrams of

merperidine and four tenths of atropine. That is standard, I believe." He shrugged. "Evidently, he is quite sensitive to the drugs."

Nick palpated Karamanov's pulse at the wrist, checked the color of his nailbeds, then gently slapped him on the cheek. His eyes blinked open, he muttered something Russian-sounding, and smiled.

"All right," Nick said. "have the nurse prep him."

"Both sides of the neck?"

"Neck, chest, and groin."

"As you wish," said Delavigne. He instructed the nurse in French.

Nick looked up at the overhead clock: eight five. "I'll use his left arm for my cutdown. You can start your IV in his right."

"Very well, Dr. Sten. Shall I proceed?"

"Go ahead. I'll scrub."

Nick held the operating room doors open as the two cardiac surgeons on his team wheeled in a cart containing their heart-lung machine. He nodded as they passed, then continued through the doors to the adjacent alcove containing the scrub sinks. He cleaned out his nails with an orange stick, then picked up a small, hard bristled brush and began a thorough cleansing of his forearms from elbow to fingertips. Marandat and Lenhov joined him before he finished.

Marandat looked flustered. "Galina has

spoken with me again."

"And?"

"I told her quite emphatically that you would prefer not to have her in the operating room, but she insists."

"Oh, Christ! Doesn't she know it will be crowded enough in there as it is? Why can't she watch from the observation gallery?"

"I suggested it. Many times. But, alas, she's adamant. She realized the extreme danger her father is in, and if these are to be his last moments she wants to be closer to him."

"Okay, let her," Nick agreed reluctantly. "But keep her out of my way."

He rinsed his forearms a final time, let some of the water drip off, then turned with his elbows extended and backed through the operating room doors. He dipped his hands in a basin of alcohol, dried them on a sterile towel, and plunged them into a pair of rubber gloves held stretched out by the nurse. The moves were as automatic as breathing. All else, from the French labeling on the monitor panel to the Russian faces peering down from the gallery, was unique and unsettling.

Karamanov's body now lay exposed on the table, an intravenous salt solution dripping slowly into his right arm.

"Cover him," Nick ordered brusquely,

and the nurse draped a sheet over his middle.

Holding his gloved hands up, Nick watched while Chaikoff and the nurse attached electrocardiographic leads to Karamanov's arms and legs and plugged the connecting cable into the monitor. After a brief lag, a series of triangular waves began sweeping across the face of the oscilloscope and the room filled with the static-like *kik kik kik* of the audio signal. "Look all right?" he asked Chaikoff.

"The Russian nodded. "For the moment —yes."

Nick moved to Karamanov's left, where his arm lay extended on a board. The nurse lifted it while Nick slipped a sterile towel underneath and swabbed the wrist with a reddish-brown disinfectant. He draped more towels on either side, filled a syringe with local anesthetic, and infiltrated the tissues surrounding the radial artery. Karamanov's hand jerked slightly as Nick jabbed the hypodermic needle under the skin, but his eyes stayed shut and he remained silent. Too heavily sedated, Nick thought, but decided to say nothing more about it.

Picking up a scalpel, he made a small slit across the inner wrist. He probed the wound with the jaws of a hemostat until he saw the whitish-yellow sheath of the artery. He slipped two nylon sutures underneath, tied the lowermost one, and holding his blade with a light, steady touch made a short nick across half the artery's circumference. Blood immediately spurted like a geyser, flooding the wound. Nick sponged it away and, exerting tension on the artery by pulling up on his ligature, threaded a thin plastic tube a few inches into the rent. Chaikoff attached its other end to a strain gauge whose moving stylus produced a continuous recording of Karamanov's blood pressure.

Marandat entered the room, donned gloves and gown, and stood opposite him, assisting in the suturing. Once a compression bandage was taped to the wound, Nick straightened and looked around. The operating room was now crowded with people and equipment; the observation gallery filled. He glimpsed a grim, tight-lipped Bogdanov in the front row and a barrel-chested man next to him whom he guessed to be Federov. Their scrutiny left him unperturbed. This was his milieu, his special world, and he knew he could breathe better in it than they could. If only he could feel as sanguine about the intentions of the equally determined Canter, Nick thought.

He saw Galina in a nurse's frock, the bun of her black hair showing in back of her cap, slip into the room. "Put on a gown, Mrs. Gessler," he snapped.

"Yes. At once, Dr. Sten," she said.

"Are you ready for the induction, Dr. Sten?" Delavigne asked.

Nick felt a twinge of anxiety; he anticipated trouble at this stage. "Get out the defibrillator paddles," he told Chaikoff, "and lubricate them."

A black rubber anesthetic cone now covered Karamanov's face. Intravenous solutions trickled into both arms. His chest rose and fell with his slow, rhythmic breathing. Nick felt his own warm breath recirculating under his mask. He gazed at the X-ray view box attached to the wall. A profile of Karamanov's skull glowed with a bluish-gray light. He took a last look at the almost complete, funnel-like narrowing in the carotid lifeline rising out of the neck before turning away. The stark silhouette of skull, that bony carapace for blood-hungry brain, reminded him of the imminent presence of death more than anything else in the room. Still, he remained calm. He had tormented himself with all of this long enough. Now was the time to force an ending. "He's all yours, Doctor," he said to Delavigne. "Just go easy on the pentothal."

The anesthesiologist nodded, his eyes glacial above his mask. He took a fluid-filled syringe from his tray and inserted it into the hub of a three-way stopcock connected to the IV tubing. "I shall now proceed to inject two hundred milligrams of sodium pentothal. Do you approve, Dr. Sten?"

"Go ahead."

Delavigne cradled the syringe in the palm of his left hand and slowly depressed the handle. Once he had emptied its contents into the tubing, his fingers pried open Karamanov's lids to observe the movements of his pupils. "Lash reflex present," he announced.

"All right, the Anectine," said Nick. "And get him tubed as fast as you can."

Delavigne lifted the anesthetic mask from Karamanov's face. He attached a second syringe to the stopcock and injected the curare-like, muscle-paralyzing agent into his blood stream. Karamanov's jaw fell slack and his breathing stopped. Swiftly, Delavigne pushed back his chin, grabbed the right-angled laryngoscope off his tray and slid it over Karamanov's tongue, hooking it upward over the ledge-like epiglottis so that he could visualize the opening into his windpipe. Then he guided a hard rubber tube along the curvature of the blade until it slipped past the lax vocal cords and lodged in the trachea. Withdrawing the laryngoscope, he twisted a small metal bridge onto the end of the tube and attached it to the twin, pleated hoses of his gas machine.

Nick's eyes darted between Delavigne and the oscilloscope. He tensed as static burst from the monitor; Karamanov's heart fluttered rapidly. "Straight oxygen," he ordered. "And bag him hard!"

Delavigne adjusted the dials and began squeezing a bladderlike bag on a limb of the machine. Within seconds, the alarming run of extra beats stopped and Karamanov's heart reverted to a regular rhythm.

"Good. Good job," Nick said, as his own pulse slowed. "Now raise the head of the table and turn him slightly to the left so we can get him draped."

Nick eased past the instrument table to the nurse holding out a surgical gown for him. He slipped into it, turned so she could lace it in back, and changed gloves. Marandat and Lenhov covered Karamanov's chest with a thin plastic sheet; Nick stepped forward and clipped four sterile towels in a diamond-shaped pattern across the base of his neck. A cover sheet with an oval window in the middle was then drawn over him and fastened to the two intravenous poles at the head of the table, sealing off the anesthetists' area from the operative site.

Nick arranged his team: the instrument nurses and himself on the right, Lenhov and Marandat across the table, Chaikoff

watching the monitor. He looked at the
clock: eight forty, then at a forlorn-
appearing Galina, her hands clasped
behind her, and felt a momentary kinship
for her. "Stand here, Mrs. Gessler," he
said, nodding at a space in back of him, "if
you want to see the procedure better."
Silently, she circled the table and stood
behind and to the left of him.

Finally Nick turned to the trio in the
corner: Doumer and Gauthier, aliases for
the two cardiac surgeons who must have
been flown in from Moscow on very short
notice, and a third man, their pump tech-
nician, whose name he didn't know. "In
case we run into trouble, how long will it
take you to prime the pump?"

Doumer answered, "No more than a few
minutes, Dr. Sten."

Nick nodded. He reached to adjust the
prismatic overhead light so that its beam
focused sharply on Karamanov's neck. He
limbered up his fingers, quelled a rising
tremor of apprehension in his stomach,
and feeling the start of a certain detachment, an almost self-hypnotic calm that
regulated the flow of nerve impulses
through his system, picked up a scalpel
and, holding it blunt edge down, traced
the course of his intended incision. The
pale pressure mark ran diagonally from
the angle of Karamanov's jaw to the
sternal notch. Nick inspected it, reversed

the scalpel, and with one long slash cut deeply into the flesh of his neck. The taut tissues parted in the swath of the blade, yellowish at first with beaded borders of subcutaneous fat, then welling up with blood.

"Hemostat!" Nick reached out blindly and felt the nurse slap the instrument into his hand. He waited for Marandat to sponge the wound before clamping a bleeder. Simultaneously, Delavigne said: "Blood pressure falling. Ninety over sixty," to the sound of increasing static from the monitor.

"What gas mixture are you using?"

"Half nitrous oxide, half oxygen, with one percent Fluothane."

"What's his rate?" asked Nick.

"After a brief acceleration it has now slowed to eighty beats per minute," said Chaikoff.

"Must be the Fluothane. Try to get his pressure back up with a little methoxamine, and if that doesn't work cut down on the Fluothane."

"At once, Dr. Sten," replied Delavigne.

Nick looked across the table. "Nurse, sponge the sweat from Dr. Marandat's brow. . . . Are you all right, Marcel?"

"Yes, fine. But this drop in pressure worries me. It may drop even more when you reach the carotid sinus."

"I know. I plan to desensitize it with an

injection of procaine, if we get that far. . . .
What's his pressure now?''

"One hundred ten over eighty."

"Good. Let's get these bleeders tied
off."

As Marandat lifted his sponge, he
clipped several hemostats to the edges of
the wound. Working in concert, Nick lifted
the clamps while Lenhov slipped silk
sutures around their base and triple-tied
them dexterously.

Satisfied with the bloodless field
achieved, Nick cut deeper until the
reddish-brown belly of the major neck
muscle appeared. He put down his scalpel
and continued the dissection with the
spreading jaws of a hemostat and a long-
handled curved-blade scissors, tearing
through gristle and teasing away
gossamer connective tissue from the
muscle; finally mobilizing it with his finger
and anchoring it laterally with the tongs
of a self-holding retractor. Deeper and
medially, there lay the object of his search:
the ropy, grayish-white sheath of the
carotid artery.

Nick cleaned away the filamentous,
clinging fascia from its wall and he
reached the bifurcation where the trunk of
the common carotid arising from the aorta
divided into external and internal
branches. Putting his forceps down, he
palpated the bulbous part of the vessel.

"Feels damned near pulseless to me. I can maybe detect a faint thrill at the base but not much more." He withdrew his finger to let Marandat and Lenhov feel.

"Do you think it's worth doing, Dr. Sten?" asked the Russian surgeon.

Nick shrugged. "There's a good chance it might have closed off completely since those X rays were taken. I don't know. . . . Still, the wall feels soft and free of clot above the bifurcation, and even if he has a complete block we have nothing much to lose."

"But it adds time and risk to the procedure, does it not?" Lenhov said.

"That's right. But if we're lucky we might get some back-bleeding, which means we'll have an added margin of safety when we do the other side. Frankly, with his right carotid already blocked, I don't think he'll tolerate clamping his left for a minute, let alone the usual three."

"A valid point," said Lenhov. "Proceed as you think best."

"I concur," Marandat said.

"All right, we're agreed then. We'll risk gassing the right first."

Nick spent several minutes painstakingly stripping fat and connective tissue away from a four-inch segment of the Y-shaped bifurcation. Inserting a right-angle clamp under the artery, he attached a thin cotton tape in its teeth and pulled it

through. He repeated the procedure twice
more, slinging all three limbs of the artery
with tape prior to clamping them.

He straightened up and turned to Chaikoff. "All right, Valentin, we're ready to
gas. Let's test out the system."

Chaikoff wheeled a cart containing a
cylinder of carbon dioxide gas close to the
table. The instrument nurse lowered a
plastic connecting tube to him and he
attached it to the outlet on the pressure
gauge. Nick fit the hub of a narrowbore
needle to the tapered, sterile end. At his
command, the nurse poured distilled water
into a basin and passed it to him. "Set the
pressure at twenty pounds, flow rate
fifteen liters, then open it up, Valentin."

Chaikoff turned the reduction valve and
a jet of gas whistled out the barrel of the
needle. Nick immersed its tip in the basin
and watched it bubble, satisfying himself
there were no leaks in the line.

Pausing a moment, he looked down at
his blood-streaked gloves, the matted
hairs showing through the back, and concentrated on the rising bubbles until the
slight vibrations of his fingertips ceased,
his hands felt as steady as counterpoised
derricks. He removed the needle from the
basin and readjusted his hold on its hub.
He gazed at the clock, waited for the
second hand to straddle twelve, and cried:
"Now, Marcel! Clamp! Begin the timing."

Quickly, Marandat applied fine-toothed vascular clamps to the three limbs of the artery and locked them in place, isolating the segment to be gassed. Nick poised the needle parallel to the vessel, tipped it slightly, and in one swift, fluid motion jabbed the beveled end a few millimeters into the wall. Its sheath swelled immediately like an elongated balloon as the advancing gas wave dissected the porus outer layer of the artery from its diseased inner core. He withdrew the needle and inserted it twice more at different sites until he was satisfied the entire length of the segment had been gassed.

"Thirty seconds, Dr. Sten," the nurse announced.

"All right, scalpel. Quickly now," Nick said, acutely aware that Karamanov's brain might suffer irreparable damage if the clamps were not removed in three minutes, four at the outside. He grasped the blade and made an inch-and-a-half long incision down the internal carotid to the bifurcation, then removed the needle from the tubing, replaced it with a long, thin-barreled spatula with several gas holes in its flared tip, and inserted this into the vessel to complete the separation of the obstructing thrombus from its wall.

"One minute, Dr. Sten."

Nick blinked sweat from his eyes. He thrust the ends of a long forceps inside the artery, grasped hold of the core, and gingerly tried to extract it through his incision. The waxy, wormlike plug jack-knifed and he had it out. He dropped the five-inch segment on the instrument table: a grisly reminder to all present of the disease they as mortals suffered; nature's favorite way of aging and ending them.

"One and one half minutes, Dr. Sten."

Nick spread open the edges of the artery and observed the white, smoothly glistening apperance of its inner lining. "Looks pretty, but it doesn't do us a damn bit of good unless we get some back-bleeding from above."

"Two minutes, Dr. Sten."

"Vascular suture." Nick anchored a stitch above the apex of his incision and ran it half its length before he heard the nurse signal the two-and-one-half minute mark. "All right, Marcel. Let's see what we've done. Open up the top."

Marandat released the two upper clamps and reached for the suction tube. Nick held the stitches he had taken lax as he squinted at the rent. At first it remained dry, pulseless, but gradually a trickle of blood began overflowing its edges.

"Fogarty catheter!" Nick seized the long, slender catheter with the inflatable rubber balloon on its tip, uncoiled it, and threaded it up the internal carotid artery until he reached bone. Lenhov grasped the syringe attached to the other end and inflated the balloon by injecting water into it. Nick then withdrew the catheter, pushing out a soft, wine-red clot with it. The bleeding picked up immediately.

"Ah, *bien*. *Merveilleux!*" exclaimed Marandat. He applied the nozzle of the suction pipette to the bleeding site.

"Three minutes, Dr. Sten."

Deftly, Nick completed the closure of the artery with a running stitch, tied it, and ordered the bottom clamp removed. The restored conduit began to pulsate with the unimpeded flow of blood. A *vital dance*, Nick thought, gratified, but also knowing that the extra margin of safety it provided for tackling the other side was slim. It was the left carotid that supplied the dominant hemisphere of Karamanov's brain; the left, where the unusual location of the clot made the risks forbiddingly high.

That's where I would have killed him, he reflected almost surprisingly. He could have accomplished it swiftly and secretly by misdirecting the needle and blowing out the wall of the vessel, creating a deadly fistulous tract between artery and vein in a portion of the skull that couldn't be observed. He might still do it, Nick realized, only not intentionally.

He sponged the wound and watched for

bleeders. "Look dry to you, Marcel?"

"Ah, *oui*, If only we can be so fortunate with what remains."

"What's his pressure?" Nick asked Delavigne.

"One hundred ten over seventy."

"Good. I want it maintained at that level or higher from now on. Any sudden drop and he'll clot the whole left side."

"I understand."

"All right. Skin sutures, nurse. Let's move on."

The almost intolerable tension Bogdanov had felt since the start of the operation, began receding now. His eyes had stretched their restraining muscles to the limit when Nick had gassed the artery. He had watched the wall of the vessel blister out like the skin of a boiled sausage. It made him shudder. The last time he had seen blisters like that was on the frostbitten corpses of German soldiers thawing in the Crimean sun. Even so, he marveled at this Nicholas Sten's poise and quickness. He held his scalpel with the same deft touch Bogdanov had learned to hold a revolver—as if the instrument shared the same nerves and tendons as the fingers of his hand.

Ignoring the *Defense de Fumer* sign posted in the gallery, Bogdanov had lit a cigarette as the clamps were applied to

Karamanov's artery and the count-down begun toward the three-minute safety mark. His temples pounded like forging hammers. He wanted Karmanov to live, not only to safeguard his career, but for Galina's sake and the genuine esteem he felt for the man.

His breathing came easier once the clamps were removed. "The American is amazing," he said to Federov. "He has the fingers of a Paderewski."

Federov mopped his face with a handkerchief. "But can we trust him? The critical part is still to come."

"Trust him? What difference does it make when we are up here and he is down there? Still, the rules of the match are clearly drawn. He must know that if he kills Karamanov we, in turn, intend to kill him. . . . I hope not. He's a talented man and I would regret taking his life."

"But what happens if, in spite if his best efforts, Nikolai Pavlevitch dies anyway? What happens to the American then?"

"A difficult choice. If I were convinced from what I saw and from the autopsy report he did all he could, I would be in favor of sparing him. But I suspect that when Moscow learned the outcome, their orders wouldn't be so lenient."

Federov nodded. "It's only right. If one dies, both should die."

"Yes," Bogdanov replied, "an ancient

practice. The Code of the Hammurabi.
When an Assyrian ruler died, his physician was put to death with him."

The left side, the last barrier to cross in
this nightmarish episode, loomed large as
Nick rushed to it. He listened for the
rhythmic signal of Karamanov's stressed
heart. . . . If he should lose this one, if
despite his most skillful effort Karamanov
should die, he would lose far more than his
patient, Nick realized; it would make all
the torment he had suffered meaningless.
He would emerge a false hero—if his
Russian keepers permitted him to emerge
at all. But it had taken him years to
perfect his gas gun technique, and
provided he kept a tight rein over his
nerves, the abstract separation into robot
and master took place, he knew he could
do it again.

The three surgeons changed sides. Once
more, the operative site was painted with
disinfectant and draped. Nick felt another
flutter of apprehension as he picked up his
scalpel. To calm him, he thought of Noelle:
her serene, sleeping face beside him, the
special way her lips first evaded before
opening to his kiss. They had spent most
of yesterday together, making love before
fully wakening in the morning and again
before dinner. Despite his vigorous
protest, Noelle had insisted he sleep

soundly and alone the night before
surgery. . . . Once again, Karamanov's
skin parted under his knife, the wrinkled
layer of epidermis yielding to white fascia
and pale yellow fat. The bleeding from the
wound was profuse. "Hemostats—and
keep passing them," Nick ordered. The
harvest of torn venules was clamped,
ligated, and the dissection moved on.

. . . Noelle had changed with the passage
of the years. She seemed moodier, less
talkative, unperturbed by long silences between them. In unguarded moments, a
sadness emanated from her eyes. Except
during sex, he sensed a barrier, an
emotional armor, that prevented her from
accepting his love. Perhaps because he
had failed her once before—or, more dis-
turbingly, because she had assessed his
predicament with a cold Gallic eye and
never expected to see him alive again?

If only he could . . . the thought hung
incomplete as his probing finger tore
through veils of connective tissue and exposed the carotid sheath. He cut through
the more fibrous strands adherent to its
wall with his scissors, then dissected
bluntly with finger and forceps until he
reached the bifurcation. He continued
trimming and cleaning until he had
separated the artery fully, from the base
of the neck to just below the angle of the
jaw. A few inches above the superior pole

of his incision lay the inaccessible carotid
canal where the internal branch of the
artery entered the skull.

Nick palpated the cordlike vessel; felt
the hardness in its wall which began a
fingerbreadth above the bifurcation and
extended upward. He shook his head and
told Marandat and Lenhov to feel for
themselves. "If the clot has spread more
than a few millimeters beyond the canal,"
Nick warned, "he hasn't a prayer."

Marandat withdrew his finger and
sighed. "I agree, of course. The dangers
are great—perhaps insurmountable—but I
urge you to try."

"I, too, Dr. Sten," said Lenhov. "Otherwise, he has no hope at all."

Nick nodded. After slipping a sling
under the artery, he called for Chaikoff to
reopen the valve on the carbon dioxide
tank. Again, he tested the flow through
the tubing by immersing the needle in the
basin of water, and with barely a pause,
said: "All right, Marcel. Now!"

Marandat locked the vascular clamps in
place and Nick thrust the needle into the
artery. He watched the wave of gas propa-
gating up its wall disappear from sight,
removed the needle, and inserted it thrice
more. The blind assault on the lifeline had
been made; whether it succeeded, or
whether a tiny piece of the clot had broken
off and even now floated upward to lodge

fatally in the vital control centers of his
brain, they would soon know.

"Thirty seconds, Dr. Sten."

"Scalpel." He held the blade between
thumb and forefinger and slit a one-inch
gash in the hard, cartilaginous wall of the
vessel. Tossing the scalpel aside, he
inserted the hissing gas spatula into the
artery and ran it up until he could feel its
tip impinge on bone. Bleed, damn you, he
thought. Bleed! He rotated the spatula
and threaded it up once more; a rivulet of
blood   followed   its   removal.   With
trembling hand, Marandat applied the
nozzle of the suction pipette to the wound
while Lenhov sponged.

Nick steeled himself for the next step.
The easily fragmented clot must be
removed intact. He wedged a Kelly clamp
into the incision, spread its serrated jaws
and locked on the core. He tugged gently,
buckling it, and delivering its short,
proximal end; then, exerting slow, even,
backward   pressure,   extracted   the
remainder of the serpentine clot from the
artery.

"*Mon Dieu!* The size of it!" Marandat
gasped as Nick dropped the pencil-length
thrombus   on   the   drape   covering
Karamanov's chest.

"One minute, Dr. Sten."

"Blood pressure? Pulse?"

"Holding steady," answered Delavigne.

After an initial spurt, the back-bleeding from the artery slowed to a trickle. "Fogarty!" Nick inched the catheter up the vessel until he felt it slip past the lip of the canal, inflated the tip and withdrew it, expelling copious amounts of soft, mushy clot. The blood gushed out, overflowing the bed of the wound and seeping into the drapes. "Start a unit of blood," he said, holding his finger to the hole in the artery.

"Praise God, you've done it," cried Marandat. "You've saved him!"

Nick ignored him. "Suction! . . . Time, nurse?"

"Two minutes, Dr. Sten."

"Vascular suture, 5-0." Nick inserted his anchoring stitch and began running them up the wound. With each bite of the needle, the realization grew that his nightmare was drawing to a close. He felt relief but no exultation; a blighted victory. What if Avila had been right and Karamanov and the Russians had tricked him? But it made no difference; in the sterile realm of the operating room, he could not kill.

He finished the stitch and ordered the clamp released. The artery pulsated vigorously. Now, if Karamanov woke from the anesthetic, his work was done. "Blood pressure?" he asked.

Delavigne cleared his throat. "The same."

"Skin sutures." Nick had half closed the wound when a subtle change in the signal issuing from the monitor alerted him. Though Karamanov's heart beat steadily, the rate seemed slowed. He paused and timed it for a fifteen-second interval with the clock: sixty beats per minute. Previously, it had been running in the range of eighty to ninety.

Subconsciously, something else began to perturb him. Though unaware of its nature as yet, he felt as it as a prickly sensation on his neck. "What did you say his pressure was again?" he asked Delavigne.

"Good, Dr. Sten," the anesthesiologist answered hoarsely.

"Yes, but what?"

"One twenty over eighty."

Preoccupied by his sense of unease, Nick pulled the two ends of the suture he held taut and felt the point of the attached needle prick his thumb. Suddenly, he had it: the blood oozing from Karamanov's capillaires looked a shade too dark. He dropped the suture and put his finger inside the wound. The repaired pulse felt weak and thready. "Is he off the Fluothane?" he asked over his shoulder.

"*Comment?*"

Nick straightened and turned. He saw sweat globules croppng out on Delavigne's forehead, his pupils expanding with fear. He took a step forward to observe the settings on his gas machine, but Delavigne blocked his way. "You murdering son of a bitch!" Nick roared.

"The Fluothane! He has the Fluothane valve wide open!" Galina shrieked.

Fists clenched, Nick shifted his weight and was about to lunge forward when he heard the shrill, rising whine of the monitor. His blood chilled. Cardiac arrest! he thought and shouted simultaneously, and before his eyes the scene dissolved into chaos.

As he whirled around and threw the drapes off Karamanov's chest, he vaguely saw Chaikoff hurtle past him. He dug the heel of his right hand into the base of his patient's beastbone, reinforced it with his left, and began cardiac massage. "He must have oxygen!" he shouted at Marandat, but the dazed, trembling Frenchman stared back vacantly. Lenhov, trapped between him and the instrument table, tried to push past, but Marandat remained rooted. While Nick's pistonlike hands compressed Karamanov's sternum to propel stagnant blood from his heart, he looked up to witness an incredible sight: Federov, one foot raised, poised to crash through the glass partition onto the operating room and Bogdanov restraining him.

As Nick's brain reeled from the tumultuous sights and sounds, one thought prevailed. He was out of it now, safe from the wrath of the Russians as well as CIA. He had served them both. All he had to do was let Karamanov die and he was free. All he had to do was stop pumping and he could go home again, if he chose. All he had to do . . . He felt Karamanov's rib cage buckle under the renewed thrust of his powerful surgeon's hands. The IV poles supporting the bottles of blood and fluid wobbled as Chaikoff, a slender man of fifty, struggled with the younger, stronger Delavigne. The cardiac surgeons in the rear of the room finally came forward, weaving their way between the tables and equipment. "The defibrillator!" Nick shouted at them. "Get the defibrillator!"

Delavigne's chopping blow to the face knocked Chaikoff to his knees. Regaining his feet, he again lunged for the dials on the gas machine. Delavigne grabbed his arm and whirled him against the wall. His hands locked at Chaikoff's throat and he was about to press his thumbs into his windpipe when, in one blurred motion, Nick saw Galina grab a scalpel off the instrument table and plunge it deep into the side of his neck. Delavigne groaned and staggered sideways. The next instant, Federov had his arms around him and cracked his spine.

Bogdanov followed, gun drawn.

"Get out! Get the hell out!" raged Nick. "This is an operating room, not a shooting gallery!"

Bogdanov took a step back and stood at the door. "I must enter, Dr. Sten. I must question Marandat as to the full extent of the danger we're in."

The mention of his name woke Marandat from his trance. His face quivered convulsively. "I swear, General, I swear I had no part in this. None! None!"

Nick ignored them momentarily. "Doumer, look at the monitor. Is it fibrillation or standstill?"

"Standstill, I believe. A straight line."

"All right. Inject three tenths cc. of Adrenalin through the IV tubing, then come over here and replace me. My arms are tiring."

He turned back to Bogdanov. "Put on a mask and gown, General, if you're going to stay. I need Marandat here."

Their authorities clashed; they exchanged stared until Bogdanov bowed. "What's the chance of saving him, Dr. Sten?"

"Lousy. And keep the hell out of my way." He stepped back for Doumer to relieve him and moved to the head of the table. "What about his pupils?" he asked Chaikoff.

"I haven't looked."

"Keep bagging him." Nick pried open

Karamanov's lids and observed the large pupils going glassy: an infallible sign of a dying brain.

Gauthier stood by the portable defibrillator cart, greasing the attached paddles with lubricant. With the alarm switched off, the audio portion of the monitor stayed silent.

"An ampul of bicarbonate and five tenths more of Adrenalin," Nick ordered. He watched the unwavering straight line on the oscilloscope intently. Chaikoff continued to compress the black bladder on the anesthetic machine and Doumer Karamanov's chest.

An eternity seemed to pass in the space of the next minute. Suddenly, all eyes turned to the monitor. A crackle of noise followed by a blip on the screen. Another. A volley of ten. A silence. Then, another volley, gradually, accelerating until it ended in a burst of statis. "Now he's fibrillating!" cried Nick. "Quick, hand me the paddles!" He snatched the two Ping-Pong sized paddles from Gauthier and applied one to Karamanov's left rib cage, the other below his neck. Once he had them positioned, he shouted. "Everybody back. . . . Now!"

Karamanov's chest jerked as the fifty-volt charge passed through it. Nick withdrew the paddles and Daumer began to compress his sternum again. The monitor continued to register the chaotic heart-beat. "What's his blood pressure?" he asked Chaikoff.

"Eighty over sixty. Pupils still dilated."

"Inject one hundred milligrams of lido-caine direct IV." Nick's body was drenched with sweat. He said to Gauthier, "If this doesn't work, we'll have to put him on cardiac bypass."

The Russian appeared puzzled. "Bypass? What for?"

"To keep him alive."

"But by then his brain might be dead, might it not?"

Nick glared. His vision of an all-out attempt to save his patient's life, to open his chest and do a coronary endarter-ectomy if necessary, ended there. Kara-manov wasn't a man in their view, only a brain! He might still survive, but if so much as one hundredth of his precious brain cells were damaged he'd be of no further use to them. The two cardiac surgeons had merely humored him by their presence.

He searched the room for Galina and found her sitting on a stool in the center, quietly sobbing. Bogdanov, his implacable eyes showing above his mask, stood beside her. Nick picked up the paddles; a final try. "Turn up the voltage all the way," he told Gauthier; placed them front and side on Karamanov's thorax, drew in a deep breath, and pressed the trigger.

Karamanov's spine arched and his chest leaped. A smell of burst flesh wafted up. Nick looked at the monitor; an electric silence, an erratic run of beats, and in the last moment of his dying hope, the steady *kik kik kik* of a restored heart rhythm.

"He's back," he said softly. "We've brought him back."

24

They rolled Karamanov out of the operating room at eleven forty-five, a phalanx of security guards clearing a passage down the corridor for his stretcher and pairs of Russian doctors marching on either side. Wearily, Nick stripped off his blood-splotched gloves and gown and followed the small procession to the intensive care unit where they lifted Karamanov onto a bed and attached the rubber tube protruding from his throat to a mechanical respirator. At once, the bellowslike machine began a sibilant swishing as it forced compressed air into his lungs, and a fluorescent white dot depicted his heartbeat sweeping across the green monitor screen.

Nick bent over Karamanov and pried

open his eyelids. The pupils, though still
dilated, seemed a fraction smaller. He
pressed his thumb down hard on the bony
ridge under his left eyebrow, hoping for a
response to pain, but Karamanov's face
never twitched.

"Is there anything more we can do for
him, Dr. Sten?" asked Lenhov.

Nick shrugged. "Wait . . . . Keep him
alive and wait."

"Yes, of course. I speak for my
colleagues when I say that we will remain
under your command. We're all experienced surgeons, but it is better, I believe,
that one man takes charge. You don't
object, do you?"

Nick studied the Russian surgeon. A
good man, he thought. Good hands. They
were all good men—a fraternity whose
noble aims had been corrupted by political
expediency. "No, I don't object. The next
twelve, twenty-four hours should be
decisive. No nurses. We'll keep constant
watch ourselves. . . . Where's Marandat?"

"He's still in the operating room.
General Bogdanov is questioning him."

"I hope Bogdanov has sense enough to
leave him in one piece. He's the only one
who knows how to get things done around
here."

"Have no fear, Dr. Sten. For a KGB
officer, General Bogdanov is an eminently
sensible man."

"And Delavigne? What about him?"

"Dead, I'm told."

Nick grimaced. "What in God's name possessed him to do it? Does anyone know?"

"No, no one. It remains a mystery."

"Bogdanov's mystery, not mine. . . . Tell him I need Marandat here. I want him released soon."

"I will, Dr. Sten," Lenhov said, and left.

The four Russian surgeons conferred outside the door. Left alone, Nick stared down at Karamanov's cadaverously pale face, the mouth distorted by the endotracheal tube, a white rim of sclera showing under the slitted eyes, and felt a sickening sense of futility. This man had wanted to die: *It is not death I fear,* he had said, *only the uncertainly of its coming.* Now, a part of him was already dead. His cardiac arrest had lasted four, five minutes—more than enough time to destroy a major part of his brain. Perhaps the merciful thing to do now would be to let the rest of him die, too. Let God's will be done. Or would God choose to keep him on, a mindless, incontinent, infant-helpless shell? In the most callous of medical slang, a vegetable.

With nothing to answer his unspoken question except the rattle of mucus in Karamanov's throat, Nick paced the narrow room. Intermittently, he stopped to put his stethoscope to Karamanov's chest, to lift limbs and tap reflexes, if only to assure himself that this tube-sprouting, tube-nourished patient he tended lived on. . . .

Hours passed; Nick and his Russian colleagues maintained their beside watch. The dim, rain-filtered light outside the window darkened into night. The results of laboratory tests of lung and kidney function were reported to them at frequent intervals and changes made in Karamanov's medication. At 11:00 P.M., he was weaned off the respirator. Though he breathed spontaneously, he remained in deep coma. The silence in the room seemed accentuated without the deep, rhythmic sighs of the airbellows; the humidity oppressive.

At one in the morning, Bogdanov opened the door and beckoned. Nick went out.

"How is he, Dr. Sten?"

"Alive—at least part of him."

"I know you are doing all that you can."

"Do you?" said Nick irritably. "Is that the report your stooges are giving you?"

Bogdanov gestured mollifyingly. "I realize how exhausted you must be. And your hostility is understandable. But we are both working toward the same goal now, and I think the time has come for us to be friends."

"Friends? For what purpose? What do you want?"

"For us to talk."

"All right, General. Talk."

"No, not here. Can you be spared for a while? There's a small cafe open across the street. If you'll permit me, I'll buy you a coffee."

Nick hesitated. Ever since he had first seen Bogdanov's photograph, he had known a battle was inevitable between them. The iron will, the ruthless ego of the man, had been revealed in the Russian's face. Still, if we must clash, Nick thought, better with words than with weapons. "Very well," he said. "Wait for me here. I'll go and change."

Minutes later, Nick returned in his street clothes and he and Bogdanov strode in silence out the door. Outside the hospital gate, the storefronts on the Rue Didot were shuttered and the street dark except for the lights of the *brasserie* on the opposite side. The cautious silence between them continued until they had taken seats at a sidewalk table and ordered coffees.

"Would you like something to eat with it? A pastry, perhaps?" Bogdanov offered.

Nick smiled at his civility, suspecting it was merely a prelude to a more aggressive approach. "No thanks. I've no appetite.

I'd like one of your cigarettes, though, and after that let's hear what's on your mind."

Bogdanov gave him a Pimar Filter and lit it. "We have Avila," he said casually.

"You have what?"

"A-vil-a."

"Oh, Avila! You mean that journalist from *L'Express.*"

"I mean the CIA agent. I warn you, we have interrogated him thoroughly. There is no use your playing innocent any longer."

Nick glared. "Innocent I may be, General, but no fool! Whether Avila is a CIA agent or not, I don't know. He merely interviewed me for his newspaper. But what I damned well do know is you'd never have let me touch Karamanov if you thought I might be in with the CIA. So forget the little tricks you learned in spy school and let's talk sense."

Bogdanov smiled ruefully. "You're very quick, Dr. Sten. Yet I still believe you knew the true identity of the man you were operating on beforehand."

"If that's so, why'd you let me go through with it?"

"I had no choice. No proof. It was merely a strong suspicion on my part. And without the operation, Karamanov was doomed. Perhaps it was foolhardy of me, but I trusted you. I had to believe that a deliberate act of killing would be as abhor-

rent to a member of your profession as it is
natural to mine. You proved me right."

"What's happened to Avila?"

Bogdanov shrugged. "A certain eti-
quette exists in our trade, especially
between us and the Americans. Our jobs
are perilous enough, so we don't make a
habit of abducting members of the
opposing camp, except in the direst emergency. Once an enemy agent has been
fished up, however, it makes no sense to
return him to his pond. He's learned too
much about faces, locations, methods.
This Avila, for example, now knows about
a new truth serum, a powerful hallucin-
ogen, we're using."

"You used it on him?"

"We tried to. But he proved unusually
resistant and the dose was approaching
the toxic level. One more injection
would've either made him talk or killed
him. I chose to be lenient."

"Why?"

"For a practical reason. You see, it was I
who, through Yevgeni Lenhov, first
learned about your novel technique. It was
I who convinced the Special Committee of
the Council of Ministers to risk transporting Karamanov to Paris for you to operate
on. So there you have it. It was my career,
my future, my neck even, that was also at
stake. What could I have done if Avila
admitted you were a CIA-assassin? Called

the entire underaking off? Let Marandat
operate in your place and add another
casualty to his list? No, either was a
dismal alternative. I realized as much as I
was preparing Avila's final injection. Now,
he will probably be taken back to Moscow
with us. . . . Still, I'm curious to know the
truth."

"How curious?"

"Oh, enough to bargain for it. What
might tempt you?"

"Avila. His release for the truth. Is it a
deal?"

"An interesting proposal. Your concern
for him is almost an admission in itself."

"It could be that, General. Or it could be
my concern for any human being. After
all, I went all out today to save
Karamanov's life. Why should I feel any
less concern for one of my own countrymen?"

"You realize, of course, that even for me
his release now would present difficulties.
I could arrange it only at great personal
risk."

"Maybe so. But I'm too tired to haggle
over it right now. It's your curiosity that
needs satisfying, so it'll have to be at your
risk."

"Very well—a bargain," Bogdanov said
after a moment's deliberation. "Should
today's events prove my ruination, I feel I
have the right to know all I can about

them."

Nick called the waiter over and ordered more coffee, needing time to think. His adversary was a cunning man and he knew it was far more than curiosity that motivated him. "All right, General," he said, "I admit your hunch was correct. I've known about Karamanov—about all of you—for some time."

Bogdanov's mouth tightened. "I see. So the CIA knew, after all. My compliments to them. . . . Now, of course, we must expose their source. A thorough housecleaning must be made."

"I don't follow you."

"Follow me? Don't be naive. You've just revealed to me that your American CIA has an informant in the highest councils of my government."

"No, General. I merely said that I knew about Karamanov in advance. I didn't say the CIA told me."

"Not the CIA? Who then?"

"Karamanov himself. He told me."

"Karamanov!" Bogdanov's eyebrows leaped. "Impossible!"

"Is it? I'm sure you remember our chess match, don't you?"

"Yes, yes. Go on."

"He arranged that himself so he could tell me. This may be hard for you to swallow, General, but Karamanov wanted to die. Wanted me to kill him! That way

his antimissile system would never be
completed and no one, except possibly
yourself, would suffer for it."

"What you are saying is absurd. Utterly
incredible! Without proof, who could
possibly believe it?"

"Who'd believe it? You, for one. You
believe much of it now. And as for the
proof, it's in the form of Karamanov's own
handwriting. You see, General, when
Karamanov set up our rendezvous he
couldn't count on having much time alone
with me before your watchdogs showed
up. So he wrote down what he wanted to
say. It's all in his letter: the decisive
nature of his system, Kapitsa's sponsor-
ship of it before your committee, the last
remaining obstacle concerning the tangential force equation. And, most important,
his reasons for not wanting the project
completed; his distrust of your leaders,
General—the legacy left them by Stalin
that makes them corrupt and dangerous
men."

"Where is this traitorous letter now?"

"Quite safe, I assure you. Mailed back
to a bank in America."

"Why was it not destroyed at once? You
realize, of course, the virulence contained
in such a letter. If Karamanov survives, it
can disgrace not only him, Galina, me—
but countless others."

"I realize it quite well. I kept it for a

purpose. A personal bit of insurance against you."

"What do you mean?"

"It assures me that not only will I be allowed my freedom, but others, such as Avila, won't be harmed. Once I'm convinced of this, the letter will be burned."

Bogdanov sighed. "Checkmate. My hands are tied. But how can I trust you to do as you say?"

"You've already trusted me with Karamanov's life, why not his reputation?"

"Yes, why not? It's only logical." Bogdanov paused. "Will he live?"

"If he survives until morning, he has a fair chance. But his cardiac arrest lasted a long time. The probability is that his brain has been damaged."

Bogdanov's fist banged the table. "That swine Delavigne! Let the devil roast him! I shall take care of his treacherous master, Delouvrier, in due time."

"Delouvrier? What's he got to do with it?"

"We have established a link between the two. The other French anesthetist, de Musset, has admitted Delouvrier visited him last night and forced him to withdraw from the case."

"But how did this Delouvrier know about Karamanov?"

"As Minister of the Interior, he was our liaison with the French government. Zorin informed him a week ago of Karamanov's arrival in Paris and his forthcoming surgery."

"How much else did he know?"

"About Karamanov's work—presumably nothing. That part puzzled me for a time, but now I believe I know who told him."

"Who?"

Bogdanov lit another cigarette. "You, I'm afraid, Dr. Sten."

Nick blinked. "What?"

"Yes, you. Not wittingly, of course, but you were his likely source."

"I've never met the man."

"Not, but your woman friend, Noelle Cardin, has. She was a former student, as well as a former mistress of his at one time."

Nick reacted viscerally. His first instinct was to smash Bogdanov's face, but a sickening spasm in his stomach halted him. He calmed himself quickly. "All right, so she knew him. What does that prove?"

"Of itself, nothing. But the rest of what we've uncovered does. For example, did you know that Mademoiselle Cardin was in Algiers until Sunday, the eleventh? That a telephone call from Delouvrier summoned her to Paris? Did you also know that your chance encounter with her in the Place de l'Alma was hardly by chance? We have film to prove that you were followed not only by our agents that morning but by one of Delouvrier's men, who doubtless signaled her when to appear. It was admirable staging."

Nick tried desperately to recall how much he'd told Noelle of Karamanov's work. Not much, he felt sure, but quite possibly enough. And that had decided it. He had been used, after all—not by the CIA or the Russians but by a seemingly lesser player in the game, a French official. Even now, Delouvrier was only a shadowy presence to him, a few facts in a magazine. But obviously he was much more to Noelle.

Nick shook his head glumly. "So, if he dies, his death will be on my conscience after all."

"Mine as well. The information was in my hands. I simply pieced it together too late."

"Why did Delouvrier want Karamanov killed?"

"To serve his own ambitions. He sees himself as de Gaulle's rightful successor; first ruler of France, then all of Europe. With such grandiose plans, he could no more permit my country to emerge the dominant world power than your America. But he has dreamed his last—that I can assure you. His destination will quickly be the grave, not the Elysée Palace."

"And Noelle—what part did she play?"

"A crucial one. Since Delouvrier would've greatly preferred to have you, an American, kill Karamanov, it was essential he learn your intentions. That, doubtless, was her mission."

"And she succeeded grandly," said Nick bitterly. "She repaid me well for past mistakes. . . . Well, General, we both lose. At least, you did your job. What will happen to you now?"

"Happen? I am like a man who after devoting his entire life to scaling a mountain peak, suddenly finds the mountain sliding out from under him. . . . You see, I would have been promoted to chief of the KGB if this venture had succeeded. Now, of course, that dream has ended. My superiors are vindictive men. . . Still, if given the time, I may be able to salvage something. How much, depends on you."

"In what way?"

"By not letting Karamanov die; keeping him alive and with him the hope that he might someday recover. My country has invested vast sums in his project. The reputations of many others besides myself are at stake. And as long as the remotest chance exists that he can complete his work, they will persist. Naturally, from what you've told me of Karamanov's intentions, that can't occur. But they don't know that. I can only trust to you they never will."

"I plan to keep my part of the bargain."

"I too." Bogdanov paused. "Though in all fairness, I must admit I would've done anything to finally best you; to be able to bring back to my superiors the proof that a traitor sits in their midst. But you have protected yourself well and I'll try to abide by our agreement."

Bogdanov dropped a ten-franc note on the table and they rose. "How long will you be staying on?"

"Until I'm no longer needed," said Nick.

Bogdanov turned to face him and smiled ruefully. "Just think what we tried to do today. Had we succeeded, we might have made history. But now there will be nothing. We are merely failed, frustrated men."

Nick hesitated, then nodded. There was more he wanted to know, more he wanted to say to this Russian, but what good was commiserating? They had been adversaries for too long and now there was no common ground except their failure.

When Nick returned to the intensive care unit, Lenhov reported Karamanov's condition as stable. "He hasn't regained consciousness, but he's beginning to move his extremities a bit. Chaikoff and I will remain with him the rest of the night. Why don't you get a few hours sleep?"

"All right," said Nick. "I'll bunk in one of the rooms down the hall. Be sure to wake me if there's the slightest change."

"We will, Dr. Sten. Rest well."

But galling visions of Noelle barred his way to sleep. Though he still found the heartless excesses of her betrayal difficult to understand, he now remembered certain looks, certain strained moments between them, that lent credence to her treachery. He would deal with her in the morning, Nick thought, realizing that by morning she might well be gone. He was almost tempted to let her go. But borrowing from Bogdanov's ruthlessness, he vowed there would be no running this time —not by either of them.

He rose from bed and called her from the phone in the doctors' lounge. "Noelle? . . . This is Nick."

"Nicholas! Oh, thank God. I've waited so long for your call."

"I'm coming over."

"Yes, come, come. Did everything go all right with your patient?"

"No, all wrong," he answered flatly. "I'll be there in a few minutes."

Noelle, in a satiny robe, met him at the door. The look on his face stopped her from embracing him. "Nicholas, what is it? What's happened?"

"Karamanov's in a coma. Cardiac

arrest. The anesthesiologist tried to murder him."

"Murder him!" Noelle gasped. "Who?"

"A Frenchman named Delavigne. Know him?"

"Delavigne? No, of course not. But how could that be? How could a Frenchman—"

"A political assassination. He was acting under orders—as you were. You were his accomplice."

She winced. "What are you saying?"

"Delouvrier," Nick said with contempt. "Edgar Etienne Delouvrier, the new French messiah! Does the name sound familiar? It should. He was your former lover, I'm told."

"Edgar and I—lovers?"

"True or not?"

Noelle took a step back and steadied herself on the arm of a chair. She tightened the belt to her robe. "When I was a student at the Sorbonne and he was my teacher, well—yes—for a short while, an affair. It meant nothing to him. To me, either." Her voice hardened. "But since you're suddenly so well informed, let me spare you the rest of this ugly interrogation. Yes, Delouvrier asked me to come to Paris. Yes, he arranged our street encounter. And yes, I agreed to the deception. But not for the reason you might think. Not for petty revenge, to even an old score—" She shook her head

vehemently. "No, I've had enough of spite
and hatred in my life for that."

"Why, then?"

"Why? Because a man I had known for
most of my life, now a high official in the
government, told me it was my duty. Yes,
my duty! He swore to me he had been
informed by one of his agents in America
that your sole purpose for coming here
was to kill this Russian physicist. That
you were acting under orders of your
CIA."

"And you believed him?"

"Why not? The Nicholas Sten I knew in
Korea was capable of such an act. Didn't
you even admit that for a time you had
yourself convinced you could do it?" She
stared defiantly. "Do you think I relished
such a Judas assignment? Do you think I
was so low, so deceitful, I went to bed with
you merely to win your confidence?"

"I don't know. . . ."

"No, you don't, do you? You never will.
That should be punishment enough for
you. You'll never know whether the one
woman in all the world you profess to love
betrayed you."

Nick's anger ebbed, leaving him
benumbed and inexpressibly weary.
Noelle was right: he never would know her
true feelings. And the beginning burden of
that spurred him into asking her more.
"You met Delouvrier last night, didn't

you?"

"No, we didn't meet. I phoned him."

"How much did you tell him?"

"I told him only that you would not kill."

"Nothing about Karamanov? His anti-missile system?"

Noelle shrugged. "I might have. If I did, it was very little."

"No, not little. Enough to convince Delouvrier that Karamanov stood in his way. Enough to get him killed."

As if suddenly vulnerable, Noelle shut her eyes. "All right! Say I did it. I'm the cause of Delouvrier knowing. So much the better. You should be grateful."

"Grateful?" Nick said incredulously. "Are you mad?"

"Yes, grateful that because of me, another man was sent to do what you yourself could not—to murder in your place. You can go back home now. You've been exonerated for your momentary aberration."

"Is that all you think it was—an aberration? Not a man's life? . . . I was willing to forego everything for this man, because I believed his life was extraordinary, that it deserved saving. And I thought the decision was mine. But it wasn't mine, was it? I was only a lure to bring Karamanov out in the open." He gestured futilely. "You   could   have   told   me   about

Delouvrier. Not at first, but after you
knew my intentions."

"You, perhaps so," Noelle answered
softly. "I thought about it constantly.
There were times, fleeting moments . . .
but I couldn't."

"Why, for God's sake?"

"Because I was afraid that if I told you
it might change things, deter you from
operating, and they would blame me. . . .
Because I am what I am: a barren, cynical
woman who cannot bear to face any more
turmoil in her life. Yes, that's the petty
truth. . . . And to think I almost walked
away from you on the Avenue Georges
Cinq. That was no pretense, Nicholas. But
you looked so haggard, so beat down. I
hadn't the heart . . ." She retreated to the
couch and sat with her knees drawn up,
her head bowed. "Go now, Nicholas.
Please go. There can be no trust between
us, so there's nothing more."

Nick hesitated. He felt a stabbing compassion for her forlornness. Twice in his life
he had loved this woman, found the
courage he needed in her. But they had
each come to Paris for the wrong reasons
and so they had lost.

He dropped her door key quietly on the
table in the floyer and left.

In the days that followed, Karamanov
gradually woke from his coma. He could

move his limbs and swallow, but could not speak or respond to those around him. His doctors grimly accepted that fact that he had suffered severe brain damage and that prospects for his recovery were remote. Only Nick, when he squeezed his hand to say good-bye and saw the gleam of recognition in his eye, the faint smile, suspected that some of his incapacity might be pretended. The thought comforted him as he rode through the Sunday-still streets of Paris for the last time on his way to Orly Airport.

He checked in at the TWA counter, then sent a cable to Ann asking her to meet him in New York. The letter he had sent by surface mail probably hadn't arrived as yet, and he hoped she would come. If not, he was determined to go to her, do everything possible to win her back, keep his family together. Even with his doubts, a part of him still loved Noelle and always would. But he'd had enough of love and honor and conflict for one lifetime. He no longer cared if he had a passionate wife or became chief of surgery or created great drama in the operating room. He thought that never again could he feel such raw, anguished emotion; that his capacity for it had been burned out. But he was wrong.

The next instant, he heard his name over the loudspeaker system. "Dr. Sten, please report to the TWA office on the mezzanine floor."

The girl at the reception desk directed him to the inner office. He opened the door and found Canter inside.

"Come in, Doctor. Come in."

Nick's fingers tightened hard around the door knob before closing it. Canter sat perched on the edge of a desk, arms folded, as if posing for a picture. He must have stagemanaged this farewell scene carefully, Nick thought. And suddenly he knew. He had suspected it before, but now as he stared at the complacent smile on the agent's face the truth revealed itself with stunning clarity. Of all who had tried to use him, Canter had been the ultimate manipulator. Noelle was innocent, after all. Not she, but Canter had been Delouvrier's source of information. His Iago. The clever agent had somehow convinced him of the danger Karamanov's project presented to his own country, his personal ambitions, and made him responsible for the murder attempt. He should have known that Canter was too obsessed with Karamanov's genius to simply sit back and wait for something to happen.

"You never did expect me to kill him, did you?" said Nick.

"No, not really. We left the killing for someone else; someone we had a better hold on. From the very outset, I didn't figure you'd be able to do it. I told the French as much—only they went ahead and found it out their own way. But don't feel bad, Nick. You were invaluable to us all the same. Without you, we'd never have gotten Karamanov out of Russia or had the remotest shot at him . . . . Anyway, it's all over now."

"Is it?"

"Just about. We lost Avila, but overall, I'd say we came out of it pretty well."

"Avila will be released. I have Bogdanov's word on that."

Canter frowned. "Bogdanov? Why should he do that? I don't get it."

"That's right—you don't. There's a lot you don't get," Nick said coldly, "and you never will."

"How much does Bogdanov know about us?"

"That bother you, too? Want all the winner's medals for yourself? Well, don't give it a second thought. Bogdanov tried to get me to admit that I knew Avila was CIA, but the trick didn't work so he dropped it. Also, he owed me something for keeping Karamanov alive. Avila was it. But I wouldn't worry yourself about Bogdanov anymore. He's finished. Your little coup washed him up."

"So what if he is? Had the situation been reversed, he would've done the same thing."

"Maybe so. But he's a worldly man. He might have felt a few pangs of conscience about it. . . . Doesn't it bother you just a little, Canter, that you're responsible for destroying the greatest brain of our time?"

"Bother me? Hell, no, it doesn't bother me. I sort of think the world might've been better off without the Einsteins or the Karamanovs. And I'll tell you one more thing. This may be my last time in the field, my last mission, and I'm pretty damned pleased at how it came out. So are the people back home."

Nick stared back stonily. Though the fervid look on the agent's face discomfited him, his words left him unmoved. He realized Canter was not bragging so much as trying to justify himself; he had that much humanity left in him. But Nick had covered the same arguments before and found them fallible. There was no collective conscience nor collective guilt. Ultimately it was what people did, not nations, that mattered. Remembering Karamanov, the man of great strength and wisdom he once was, Nick felt only disgust for the agent of his destruction. Wordlessly, he turned to leave.

"Wait! I'm not through yet." Canter followed after him and put a restraining arm on his shoulder.

Pivoting sharply, Nick brushed it off.

He almost hit him. Canter's hand flew up to defend himself, but he lowered them quickly. "Easy, Nick. I know you've had a tough time and I can't exactly blame you for wanting to take a poke at me. But I have a tender enough nose already. Also, a lung operation to look forward to when I get back. I wasn't bluffing about that. It may not be as serious as I first made out, but you never know about these things, do you? The pathology report can go either way. Wish me luck."

Nick squinted: Canter's insensitivity amazed him. "I'll tell you what I wish you—" The word "cancer" was on his tongue but he couldn't say it. "The same luck as Karamanov's. That's right, Canter. I never talked, never told Bogdanov what a clever fellow you are, but Delouvrier might. If I were you, I'd ask to have that operation in a vault at Fort Knox. And I'd take a good, hard look at your anesthesiologist before he puts you under. You can never tell about the Russians, huh, friend?"

Nick reached for the door, paused to give Canter a chance to reply, and then walked out.

Spellbinding Medical Thrillers
From Leisure Books

THE ANATOMY LESSON   2344-x
Marshall Goldberg, M.D. $3.95 US, $4.50 CAN

NATURAL KILLERS   2339-3
Marshall Goldberg, M.D. $3.95 US, $4.50 CAN

INOCULATE   2333-4
Neil F. Bayne $3.50 US, $3.95 CAN

DISPOSABLE PEOPLE   2278-8
Marshall Goldberg, M.D. and Kenneth Kay $3.50 US
                                           $3.95 CAN

PAN   2238-9
J. Birney Dibble, M.D. $2.95

MORE ACTION AND ADVENTURE FROM LEISURE BOOKS